The Porosity of Souls

and Other Dark Tales of Anguish
Terry Campbell

This is a work of fiction. Names, characters, places, and incidents either are the product of the author's imagination or are used fictitiously, and any resemblance to actual persons living or dead, business establishments, events, or locales, is entirely coincidental.

© COPYRIGHT 2026 by Terry Campbell

All rights reserved. No part of this book may be used or reproduced in any manner whatsoever without written permission of the publisher except in the case of brief quotations embodied in critical articles or reviews.

AI was not used to write this book, to create the cover art, or in formatting.

NO AI TRAINING: Without in any way limiting the author's and publisher's exclusive rights under copyright, any use of this publication to "train" generative artificial intelligence (AI) technologies to generate text is expressly prohibited. The author reserves all rights to license uses of this work for genAI training and development of machine learning language models.

Warning: Not intended for persons under the age of 18. May contain coarse language and mature content that may disturb some readers. Reader discretion advised.

Cover Art Design by: Kelly Moran/Rowan Prose Publishing
Photo Credit: Adobe Images/Deposit Photos
First Edition
ISBN: 978-1-961967-77-9
Rowan Prose Publishing, LLC
www.RowanProsePublishing.com
Published in the United States of America

Table of Contents:

Stained Glass
Water This Cold
Lycanthrophobia
The Eternal Drifter
Armadillo Village
Retrocurses
Genocide For One
Options
The Eyes of the Gypsy
The Weak and the Weary
Anatomy of a Haunting
The Porosity of Souls
The Chill of an Early Fall
Tears on a Pillow of Down
Harvest Moon
Second Chances
Friday Night in the Gun Cabinet
Monkeyspeak

This collection is dedicated to all the great small press magazines of the 1990s/early 2000s, and their resilient, determined editors whose sheer love for what they did persevered against all odds. Without them, these tales would've never seen the dark of night. Names such as Ken Abner at "Terminal Fright," Dennis J. Kirk at "Outer Darkness," Pat Nielsen at "Crossroads," Kathleen Jergens at "Thin Ice," the late, great David G. Barnett at "Into the Darkness," and William G. Raley at "After Hours," to name just a few. These guys and gals gave a young writer his biggest thrills and inspired him to keep on pushing. Many thanks and admiration to you all. I truly miss those days.

Stained Glass

The young paramedic slowly made his way down the center aisle of the old church, holding his right hand over the thin dust mask that covered his nose and mouth, hoping to block out some of the horrendous smell. The mask offered little olfactory protection, since stuffed inside the tiny country church were the bodies of twenty-two parishioners and their pastor, and they had been there for nearly two weeks, locked inside the building with minimal air flow and temperatures outside soaring well over ninety degrees. It was the rookie's first call. Doubtful there would be a second.

The paramedic reached the aisle nearest the pulpit and passed the first row of benches. There was noise coming from his colleagues and local law enforcement officials near the entrance of the church. He paused for a moment to collect his thoughts before making the mistake of looking into the first row.

A little girl of about four, leaned stiffly against the wooden backrest, her hands locked in a clawing motion at her neck. The skin on her face was gray and taut, pulling her upper lip over her baby teeth in an eternal sneer. Flies buzzed around her head, crawled in and out of her nostrils. The young man's stomach undulated rapidly, and he collapsed onto the floor, the digestive organ's contents spewing forth before he had a chance to remove the respirator. The paramedic gagged and coughed, removing the mask and spilling the accident onto the church's worn hardwood flooring. Trying to regain his composure, he stared at his own vomit for a moment, mesmerized by the bubbles forming and bursting, the chunks of his Big Mac, and the colors that danced in the vile liquid.

The colors?

Vivid reds, yellows, blues, and greens danced across the floor, seemingly making the grain patterns in the wood come alive. The young man looked up, way up, at the small stained-glass window that loomed high above the pulpit. Shadows flitted behind the colored glass, apparently the effect of tree limbs swaying in the wind outside.

The stained-glass window was absolutely the most beautiful piece of work the young paramedic had ever seen. He stared up at the window, his mind oblivious to the smell of vomit and decomposing flesh all around him and tried to figure out what the colored shapes in the glass suggested. Then a cloud moved in front of the sun, casting a shadow across the window, rippling the light shining through the stained glass, and for a moment, just a split second, he saw something entirely different from what he expected.

◆

Tad Conlin meandered down the narrow aisles of East Fork Antique Mall, inhaling the pleasant, musty aroma of things old and almost forgotten. For once, he was relaxed and thoroughly enjoying himself. He loved visiting the antique stores, and this one was his favorite. Since he had recently purchased an old farmhouse just a few miles down Highway 71, he would be visiting East Fork more frequently than ever.

Tad paused at a booth displaying dozens of old, rusted farm tools. The implements looked as if they could have been taken from any of the old barns that lined the east Texas countryside. It was ambience like that, that gave the rural area its charm. Tad thought of his new home and smiled. There was a lot of work to be done on the old place, and he had already knocked himself out attempting to repair it. In fact, that was what had brought him to East Fork today. Window shopping was just an effort to get away from the headache of a new home.

The old farmhouse was a unique fixer-upper opportunity, but it wasn't far from the community college where Tad taught art classes, and the huge attic with the giant windows was going to make one kick-ass studio. Tad looked up at the sunlight filtering through the high windows of the warehouse, dust bunnies chased each other in the subtle breezes of the ventilator fans, and he thought of the attic.

Tad stopped in front of a booth containing dozens of old stained-glass windows leaning haphazardly against each other.

Curious, Tad began sorting through the windows that displayed a myriad of shapes and colors, when a particular piece caught his eye.

This window was smaller than most of the others. Perhaps its unimposing size was the reason he had passed over it the first time. It was hanging on the lower part of the wall at the back of the booth, with several larger windows leaning against it, partially blocking it from his view. Tad began stacking the larger windows off to the side so he could get a better look at the piece. Finally, he was able to get to the window.

Tad stooped to grab the piece, lifting it gingerly from the nail holding it to the wall. The window was surprisingly heavy for its size. It was surely an older piece, made of much heavier glass and possibly lead beading.

Tad managed to free the window from the confines of the booth and leaned it against the outer wall. He stepped back so he could fully drink in the spectacle of the stained glass. There was a green diamond shape in the center with a smaller red diamond in it. Two long triangles of yellow protruded to the right and left of the diamond, and green shafts of stained glass spread out from the bottom with a piece of blue between them. Tad wasn't sure what the work depicted, and since there was little light coming from the back side of the window, it wasn't done proper justice. He studied the window a few more moments, moving to the left and the right.

Then, there it was.

It was the Crucifixion. It was Jesus Christ. The style was very modern and abstract in design, which seemed to clash with the obvious age of the window. It was the Savior. The anguished face, the angular features in the diamonds and the splayed, spread-eagle pattern—as of a person hanging on a cross—was obvious in the long shapes protruding from the diamond. And the still, red diamond heart in the center.

It was quite a unique piece.

Then Tad thought of the attic in his new home. Three large openings graced dormers that looked out from the attic, offering plenty of natural light for his paintings. Then to the rear of the house, looking out across the pastures and the east Texas woods beyond, was a single, small window. Tad just remembered the window was cracked, and a draft seeped in around the edges. In short, it needed replacing.

Why not? Tad thought. He spied a small piece of masking tape stuck across the face of the window. Tad knelt closer. The window's dimensions—18 x 24—were written on it. A little too big for the opening.

What the hell. He would make it fit.

"Can I help you, sir?"

Tad turned, and one of the nondescript employees was facing him.

"I'd like to buy this window, please. How much?"

"It's a very unique piece," the man said. "Very old."

"Yes, I know. How much?" Tad said, almost impatiently.

"We're asking two-hundred twenty dollars."

"Done," Tad said.

"It's a very interesting piece," the man said. "Came from a church in deep east Texas, about thirty miles south of Tyler. The church was being torn down. The man dozing it down brought it to us."

"Yes, interesting." Tad reached for his checkbook.

"It's no different than many stained-glass windows, really. No definite shape. Just a bunch of unusual cuts of glass."

"What do you mean?" Tad asked. "It's the Crucifixion."

The man lifted his eyebrows. "The Crucifixion, you say?" Tad nodded. The man looked at the window for a moment longer, then shrugged. "Well, if that's what you see, but it is an interesting piece."

"Yes," Tad agreed, giving the man a wary look. "Very interesting."

He just hoped the window would fit.

◆

"I like the new studio, Tad," Linda said, slowly walking across the plywood pieces nailed across the length of the attic. Her heavy-heeled boots clicked loudly in the large open space, and Tad thought she looked so sexy, so graceful. He had a sudden urge to paint her. Either that or throw her down on the attic floor right then and there. "But why are you set up over here where it's dark? I would think you'd want your easel over here by the big windows."

Tad walked up behind her and slipped his hands around her waist. "I did have everything over there, but I decided I liked this end better. I don't know why."

Tad scooted Linda over in front of the new 36 x 52 canvas that balanced atop his easel. Linda, his lover and fellow teacher at the college, would be the first to view the latest addition to Tad's own personal home improvement. He gently kissed her on the neck and tilted her head up, directing her vision upward. Three dormers looked out from the roof on the front of the house, but only one such feature graced the rear. Linda looked down the short narrow section. At the end was a small stained-glass window.

"Do you see it?" Tad was as excited as a young boy showing his mother what he had drawn for her in school.

"What, the window?"

"Of course, the window. Isn't it the most beautiful thing you've ever seen?"

"Yeah, it's pretty."

"Pretty? Is that all you can say?"

Linda laughed. "Where did you get it?"

"Antique place up the road. Don't ask what I paid for it," Tad said.

"How much?"

"I said don't ask."

"How old is it?" Linda asked instead.

"You know, I didn't even ask. The owner said it came from a church somewhere around Tyler."

"I wonder if it came from England. I mean, originally. A lot of older stained-glass does. I have a student in one of my classes named Joanie. She's into a lot of new age stuff. One of her big kicks is psychometry. I could bring her out here and let her look at it. Might be fun."

"Okay," Tad agreed. He stared down the narrow opening at the beautiful piece of work. The excitement of the window still had not worn off for him. It was as if he had just installed it yesterday. It was the first home repair he'd done that had gone off without a hitch, and he'd been expecting the worst. He must've measured the old window wrong. Tad could've sworn the stained-glass window was going to be at least an inch, too wide and tall, but it had slipped into the space perfectly, as if Tad had special ordered it just for the opening.

"What's that sound?" Linda asked. "That high-pitched sound? Do you hear it?"

Tad cocked his head and listened. "Oh, yeah, that's the wind whipping around the corner of the house."

"The wind isn't blowing very hard today."

"You'd be surprised how little wind it takes to make an old house creak and moan," Tad said.

Linda nodded. "Can we go downstairs now? All this dust is getting to me."

"Not yet," Tad said, looking at his watch. "You haven't seen the best part."

"What?"

Tad shushed her and looked back at the window. "Just a few more minutes."

Slowly, the dying sun began to slip behind the tree line to the west, and as it did, the bright yellow rays caressed and fondled the slopes and valleys of the venerable old farmhouse. Inevitably, the shafts of light slid down the shingles, across the dormer and through the stained-glass window. Tad pulled Linda back a few steps. Finally, the full strength of the rays came through the stained glass, setting off the colors in a fiery display of beauty and reflecting down the length of the dormer and onto the canvas. The image cut into the window now blazed across Tad's latest painting.

"That's why I moved the easel over here. The lighting's not as good, but how can you go wrong with Jesus looking over your shoulder?" He stared at the canvas, at the warped colored image that rippled across the painting.

"Jesus?"

"Yeah, the Crucifixion. Don't you see it?"

Linda stepped forward and looked around the corner at the window, shielding her eyes from the intense sun. "I see a jumbled mass of colors, but then again, I'm not an artist." She shrugged. "Now? Can we go?"

Tad grinned. "Okay, but don't you think it's cool?"

"Sure, it's cool. I just don't get any divine inspiration out of it."

Tad took Linda's hand as they made their way down the attic stairway. Outside, the sun disappeared behind the distant tree line, but a hint of the vivid colors that had splashed across the canvas only moments earlier stayed behind.

◆

He didn't remember painting that.

Linda had left right after Letterman the night before, and Tad had gone into the studio-attic to continue working on his latest painting. It was an abstract rendition of a man's head with long, exaggerated features and bold, dark outlines. He remembered painting into the night and going to bed when the eastern horizon was just beginning to glow purple. Tad sometimes worked on his art during the night hours, and there were times when he couldn't remember certain parts of a painting, couldn't recall the exact moment when he created some aspect of it.

Tad would've remembered painting flies on the man's face.

Yet there they were, staring back at him from the painting. There were several flies on the subject's forehead and one big black one, complete with exaggerated, multi-faceted green eyes, resting on the man's nose.

Tad stepped back from the painting to look at it from a distance. It was entirely possible that he could've painted the flies (and obviously he had) and simply forgotten them.

The strange thing was, he had never planned on having flies in the painting. Whatever had inspired him to place them there, it had been a spur-of-the-moment decision. There were several blocked-in areas of dark paint in the background, just to the right of the man's head. Tad could only assume that his weary mind had begun something else unusual on the painting just before he had gone to bed.

There seemed to be something else. Just a faint image, barely registrable, hovering in the background of the painting.

Whatever the flies represented, Tad decided he liked them. Taking his palette in hand, he began to improve upon them. As the sun began to dip behind the tree line, the vivid colors from the stained-glass window stretched toward Tad's work area, the sun's dying rays warming his back as he worked.

◆

"That's weird, Tad." Linda studied the painting. "And you say you don't remember working on it?"

"I remember working on it, I remember getting out my paints and brushes and looking at the canvas...but the rest of it...how this stuff gets on it, I don't know."

Tad stared at his latest painting. He had called the painting "Despondent" when he first started it, but now he wasn't so sure. The title didn't seem to fit anymore. The man's face had changed. It was now haggard and pale, approaching emaciation. The flies were still there, and now, the dark shapes in the background had been fleshed out more. They were beginning to resemble seats, or maybe benches.

"I just wish I could remember what inspired me to paint this," Tad said, more to himself than to Linda.

"You don't remember any of it?"

"No," Tad answered, more harshly than he had intended. "No, it's a blank." Calmer.

"You know what it looks like to me? It looks like a church."

"A church?"

"Yeah, the man is at church. See the pews in the background? And up here," she said, her finger circling an area above the subject's head. "It looks like you've started a window."

"You may be right," Tad said, then turned away, frustrated. "I just wish I knew why I was doing it. It's like I'm blacking out while I'm painting."

"Tad, wasn't one of the main reasons you chose this house because of this attic? Weren't you turned on by these big windows and all the natural light that you could paint in?"

Tad had approached the stained-glass window. He peered out into the backyard, the image distorted by the pebbled effect of the glass. "Yeah, why?"

"It's just that, since you've started painting here, you're not taking advantage of the light. You moved your work area away from the light. Now, you're painting at night."

Tad turned to face Linda. "What are you getting at?"

"Doesn't it all seem a bit strange to you?"

"I don't know."

"And now you're painting a church-"

"You say I'm painting a church," Tad interrupted.

"Didn't you say that window came from a church?"

"Yeah, but big deal. Most stained-glass windows come from churches. What does that have to do with anything?"

"You're putting this window in the painting."

"No, I'm not," Tad argued.

"Yes, you are. Look. In the dark spot where you're putting the window. See?" Tad approached the canvas and looked to where Linda's finger pointed. "See the image? It's the same shape in the window. The shape you say is the Crucifixion."

Tad shrugged. He had to admit the dark shape blocked in above the man's head in the painting had the same basic angles as the image depicted on the stained glass.

"Remember when I told you about Joanie, the girl in my class? I want her to come look at the window."

"What good would that do?"

"I want to know more about the window. I want to know how old it is, where it came from."

"And this girl can do all that just by looking at my window?"

"I don't know," Linda answered, then grinned. "Keep an open mind."

❖

Tad didn't like Joanie the minute she walked into his house. She looked like some new age goddess-bitch you might find wandering the streets of Deep Ellum in downtown Dallas. Purple hair. Purple eye shadow. Fishnet stockings. Short black leather skirt. She just breezed into his house with Linda and started picking up things. She grabbed a little figurine of the Christ of the Ozarks he had bought in Eureka Springs, Arkansas and started talking to it. She sat that down and grabbed a candle holder he'd found at DeRidder's Antiques, frowned and sat it back down. She just kept grabbing Tad's things without even asking. Then she had the nerve to tell him she liked his house, that it was a happy house, that everyone who'd lived in it had been happy. What a flake.

"What do you think?" Linda whispered, while Joanie explored Tad's studio. They had moved on to the attic.

"I think she's a nut."

"Open mind, remember? I think this is fascinating."

"Wow, this is a perfect place for an artist." Joanie stood in front of the three large windows. "Lots of light."

"Joanie, the window I want you to look at is over here."

Joanie turned and moved past Tad's easel, stopping at the beginning of the narrow passage that led to the stained-glass window. Her gaze traveled from the floor up to the window. She stopped. "It's Jesus," Joanie whispered.

"What?" Linda asked.

"You see it, too?" Tad asked.

"It's Jesus," Joanie repeated.

"See, I told you it looked like the Crucifixion," Tad said to Linda.

Joanie slowly walked the length of the corridor and stopped at the window. She reached out and began to caress the frame. Tad had not touched up any part of the window. As far as he knew, that was the original paint. "It's very old," Joanie said, almost in a trance. "Hundreds of years old."

Joanie's fingers traced around the frame and then slowly slid over, contacting the clear, textured glass surrounding the colorful image. With her eyes closed, her fingers spread across the glass, caressing the Jesus image as if it were her lover. Tears began to well up in her eyes, finally spilling over and running down her pale cheeks in purple streams. "There are people in here. Thousands and thousands of people."

"What?" Linda asked, not sure she heard Joanie correctly.

"They can't get out," Joanie cried. Her head lolled. Her eyes remained closed. "Their souls are trapped."

"Is she for real?" Tad asked, leaning closer to Linda.

"I can't," Joanie said. "I can't help you."

"You put her up to this, didn't you?" Tad said. Linda shushed him. "You had this planned all along."

At that moment, a cloud passed in front of the sun, momentarily blocking the light from striking the window. Joanie's eyes snapped open, and she fell backwards, as if being physically pushed. She landed on her bottom and stared back up at the window.

She screamed.

"Joanie!" Linda shouted, running to her fallen student. "What is it? What happened?"

Tad looked up at the window just as the sun returned. The Savior stared down at him as always.

Linda knelt, taking Joanie's head in her hands. "What's wrong, Joanie? What did you see?"

"They're damned," was all she would say. "Those poor people. They're all damned."

Tad stood over the women, impervious to Joanie's feelings. As far as he was concerned, it was a charade, a hoax induced by some crystal-hogging, meditating Generation X-er. Besides, it was getting late, and he would be painting again soon.

The man in the painting was almost skeletal now. His eyes were sunken, his skin pulled taut over his hollowed cheekbones, and now, there were others just like him, lying across the pews, sitting up, some collapsed across others, a few sprawled on the floor in front of the benches. There were also more flies. The frame of the window in the painting had been more defined, but he had yet to complete the glass. Still, a dark, familiar shape hovered in the center.

And, as with all the other times, Tad could not remember painting any of it.

He knew one thing though, he liked what he saw.

"There is some truth to what Joanie was saying," Linda said.

"Oh, don't be ridiculous."

"Tad, she cried all the way home that night," Linda argued. "She was obviously terribly upset."

"She made all that up. Grandstanding. Acting like a big shot. Probably bucking for an A in your class."

"That's not fair," Linda said sternly. Tad merely shrugged. "Do you want to know why I think she was telling the truth?"

"Do I have a choice?"

"I did some reading about middle-ages religion," Linda said. "There was a group of monks living in Ireland in the sixteenth century. Their members regularly committed suicide."

"A medieval suicide cult?" Tad asked. "That's a good one, Linda."

"You agreed that the window likely came from England, and that it's probably very old."

"Are you suggesting that there are lost souls trapped in an antique window I bought in an east Texas antique shop, and that they're screaming to get out?" Tad asked. "That's ludicrous."

"Is it?" She nodded her head toward the painting. "Pretty disturbing stuff, wouldn't you say? And you don't remember doing any of it."

◆

Tad picked up the phone on the second ring. It was Linda.

"Joanie's dead," she said. "They found her in her apartment this morning."

"Are you serious?" Tad asked, showing, but not really feeling, remorse.

"She took a bottle of sleeping pills. Tad, it was suicide."

"Jesus, she's really taking this shit seriously."

There was a pause on the other end of the line. "Who the hell are you?" Linda asked, then hung up.

Tad set the receiver back in its cradle and glanced out the window. The sun was setting. Tad headed upstairs to his studio.

◆

"I just wanted to show you something," Linda said.

Tad squinted in the bright sunlight and took the piece of paper from Linda's hand. The glaring brightness of the paper almost blinded him.

"I went to Tyler today," Linda said. "Did some research at the library. I found that. Thought it might interest you."

The paper was photocopied from the front page of the Tyler Gazette. The headline read: *Mass Suicide at Rural Church*.

"What is this?" Tad asked.

"Twenty-three people, Tad. Twenty-three. Men, women. Children. They killed themselves."

"What does this have to do with anything?"

"The last paragraph says local authorities were planning to bulldoze the building, to forget it ever happened."

"Ahh, I see. And you're saying somehow a window survived. It wound up at an antique store, and I bought it. And originally, it came from some evil monastery in Ireland."

"Tad," Linda tried to explain.

"What about the rest of the windows? Ooh, could they still be out there somewhere, wreaking havoc on innocent people? Wait, let me guess, there was one of these windows at Jonestown, maybe one at the Waco compound. Koresh had one in his office. Am I getting warm?"

"God, I hope Joanie was wrong," Linda said.

"Look, what happened to Joanie is terribly sad, a tragedy, but face it, she was a little left of center."

"She saw something that terrified her, Tad. Bad enough to take her own life."

Tad sighed and ran his fingers through his hair. It was mid-morning, and he had worked on the painting all night. He was exhausted.

"Can't you see it, Tad? Can't you see what's happening? Ever since you got that damned window, things have been different. You paint at night. Your memory's for shit. You're belligerent."

"Linda, nothing's wrong."

"And look at what you're painting. It would scare the shit out of Clive Barker. And, Jesus, you don't even remember doing it. Doesn't that set off a warning siren in your head, Tad?"

"I'm fine," Tad said. "A crazy little cunt kills herself, and you're worried about me? You're the only one around here who's having any messed-up delusions. I'm fine."

"There's another piece of paper there," Linda said.

Tad rustled the papers, letting the copy of the headline fall to the ground.

"That's Joanie's suicide note, Tad. The police let me have a copy of it. I thought you might like to see it."

The note merely read: *the truth is not in the light.*

"Call me when you're Tad Conlin again," Linda said. "If you ever are."

Tad crumpled up the paper and let it join the other, allowing the warm east Texas breeze to take them wherever it saw fit. He didn't even watch Linda walk away.

◆

Tad grabbed the string hanging from the overhead light in the attic and pulled it, casting the attic into total darkness. Allowing a few seconds for his eyes to adjust, Tad approached his canvas. Moonlight filtered in, then turned crimson and yellow and blue by the colors of the stained-glass window.

And there, in the center of the window painted onto the canvas' background, was the image of the Crucifixion.

Tad had not painted it. He *knew* that. It wasn't there this afternoon when he had inspected his previous night's work, and he hadn't touched the canvas yet this evening.

Yet, there it was. The yellow outstretched arms. The green legs, dangling limp. The green diamond shape of the body, the red heart in the center.

Tad lifted a shaking finger to the canvas and touched the image of the stained glass. It was dry. There was no paint.

He had not painted it.

It had been burned into the painting.

It was then that Tad noticed how well the moon lit the attic, how favorable the condition was to his craft.

The moon was full tonight.

Tad turned to the window. In the distance, distorted through the textured glass, the moon shone through the darkness.

Then he remembered Joanie's suicide note: *the truth is not in the light.*

The truth was in the dark.

He painted in the dark. He remembered nothing in the dark.

The moon became obscured through the window. Tad thought something moved. *Must be the wind blowing the tree limbs around,* he thought. There was an almost constant screeching sound of the wind blowing around the corners of the house.

That's when he saw them.

The faces. Hundreds of faces. Thousands. They wavered in and out of focus, pulled themselves apart like a television set in need of horizontal tuning. They grew larger, then receded, then grew again, and there was the absolute anguish buried forever in their eyes. Then they screamed again and he realized that was the noise he had been hearing all along. The unnerving wails rattled the glass the way a window shakes when a tractor trailer drives by. The faces pressed against the glass, their features flattening out, the blood racing from their skin, but they could not budge the glass.

Tad forced his vision to focus on the image, past the tormented souls, to the Jesus image.

In the dark, it just didn't look the same.

The diamonds had separated, aiming at each of the window's upper corners. The yellow arms had shifted as well, pointing skyward. The green legs split to the sides like a great, forked tongue, and the blue diamond between them resembled a gigantic penis.

In the light . . .

—and the truth is not in the light—

. . . the stained-glass window appeared to bear the image of Jesus Christ.

In the dark . . .

—but in the dark—

. . . it looked like Satan.

The faces continued to wail and flit about the colored panels of the stain glass, and the Satan image bore down on Tad. Visions filled Tad's head—visions of ancient priests, of disillusioned parishioners following fruitless visions of eternal paradise.

Tad turned back toward the canvas, retrieved his palette from the floor. He squirted generous amounts of alizarin crimson, bright red, cadmium yellow, and orange onto his palette. His fingers steady, he held his brush. Behind him, the screams of the tortured souls begging for mercy continued. The green and red eyes of Satan warmed his back like a late afternoon sun.

But there is no truth in the light.

Bold strokes across the painting. Streaks of red. Swatches of yellow. Thick smears of orange.

The image of flames quickly obliterated the tortured soul depicted in Tad's painting.

The Elmo Volunteer Fire Department sifted through the rubble of the farmhouse, trying to find what caused the old building to burn to the ground. The smell of smoke was heavy in the air, despite the gusty afternoon breeze.

Elmer Finley skirted the pile of debris along what had been the rear of the house. His eyes scanning the ground, he caught a glimpse of something shining in the bright sunlight. Elmer kicked a charred two-by-six and revealed the edge of a window. He knelt and cleared away the remaining debris, unearthing the prize.

It was a beautiful, stained-glass window. Elmer Finley didn't know much about art, or history, but he knew something this pretty would more than likely fetch an equally attractive prize at any antique store in the area.

Elmer looked back across the pile of rubble. His boss was leaning against his pickup talking to the sheriff. Their backs were turned to him. Elmer's truck was no more than fifteen paces away. He could have the window stashed under the old, mildewed tarp he carried in the back before anyone could notice. Hell, he wasn't paid shit for being on the force, so why not take advantage of a little gift from God?

Elmer rose, checked his boss's whereabouts one last time, then held the stained-glass window up to the sun. It was a lot heavier than he thought it would be. Bright cuts of red, green, and yellow glared back at him. Elmer tried to understand what kind of a likeness was depicted in the colored glass, but the constant movement of shadows and the twinkling of sunlight off the glass chased any image away before it had a chance to form.

Water This Cold

The porcelain was smooth and unblemished. The flowing lines of the facial structure—the soft curve of the cheeks, the subtle valley of the eye sockets, the gentle kiss of the pursed lips—were exquisite. The color was shocking white, even after years and years of wear.

Who had played with it? How often had it been played with? Who could tell? How could anyone tell?

These were questions Collin Hayworth asked himself every time he viewed a new doll, and this was the most immaculate doll he had ever had the fortune of laying his eyes upon, and he had laid his eyes upon many. His collection numbered into the thousands, and it was insured for one million dollars. It was truly the envy of doll collectors all over the world, and here was one more, nothing overtly spectacular, just one simple little turn-of-the-century depiction, and Collin made up his mind that he must have it, he *would* have it.

However, this doll was in no elegant antique shop, no clearly marked price tag hanging from one dainty toe. It was not sitting atop a velvet table in a booth, in some collector show waiting for her price to be haggled over. This doll was two-and-a-half miles below the surface of the Atlantic Ocean, partially buried amid the sunken ruins of the White Star liner *Titanic*, and Collin refused to believe that peering at the beauty through binoculars and a nine-inch-thick glass window was the closest he was going to get to it.

He knew that several groups had been retrieving relics from the doomed ship for some time now. Hats, watches, eyeglasses, that sort of thing. Dr. Robert Ballard had placed a plaque on the stern of *Titanic* in 1986 when he had first discovered the tragic remains, imploring future explorers to look, but not touch. It now seemed that his wish was going unheeded. The overwhelming success of the James Cameron movie had seared dollar signs into the eyes of many, and anything *Titanic*-related was sure to fetch an equally titanic price, especially if it was the genuine article.

The small submarine slowly moved away from the doll, casting a veil of ocean floor silt over it, and Collin stepped back from the small crowd of folks pushing its way to the small windows. He shivered. It was so frightfully cold in the tiny craft.

Collin Hayworth was a man who knew how to get what he wanted, and he had the means to accomplish it. He smiled, with the face of the doll etched into his memory. It wouldn't take much—the right individual, the right price—and he would hold her, the first to claim ownership in eighty-six years.

His vacation with friends of equally sound financial status on the French Riviera had been extremely monotonous up until the morning Sophia mentioned that a Swiss submarine company was offering underwater tours of the *Titanic* for five-thousand dollars a head. Even then, there was really nothing of interest as far as Collin was concerned. He knew of the marine disaster, how the ship had struck an iceberg on the night of April 14th, 1912, had gone down in two hours, how she had been deemed "unsinkable", but he had only a passing interest in the history at best.

Yet, Sophia Renfield and her fifteen-year-old daughter, Amy, had become addicted to the movie, and the entire group had decided to take a break from their vacation on the Riviera and head for cooler climes. Collin had reluctantly agreed, more so for the fact of not wanting to be left out of the group's adventures than anything else.

Collin smiled the smile of a man who had achieved his goal. The trip was worth it. Well worth it. It had cost him roughly one million dollars, but now, looking at his bounty, he knew he would've paid twice that amount.

The doll was complete, and in surprisingly good condition. The clothing had long since succumbed to the harsh salt water of the Atlantic, but the porcelain was immaculate. It seemed that years of lying on the ocean floor had polished the surface of the porcelain, rather than deteriorated it, if that was possible. The paint on the eyes and lips was gone, if there ever was any. The overall visage of the stark white face was no less eerie to Collin than the moment the ghostly pale peered at him from the murky depths of the Atlantic. Here was the crowning glory to his already spectacular collection. Who else anywhere at all, in the entire world, could claim to have a doll salvaged from the wreckage of the greatest ship disaster in all of history?

"No one," Collin chuckled, caressing his prize. "No one at all."

◈

"We should have a seance," Stella Lloyd said.

"A seance?" her husband Leonard asked. "Are you mad, woman?"

Collin's group of friends had all been impressed with his acquisition, even if they thought the price tag was a little steep. Collin now kept the doll locked up in his safe, nestled cozily inside an ornate wooden box, its interior lined with red velvet, he had built specifically to house the doll. Sophia and her daughter were not as impressed by the doll as Collin imagined. Perhaps seeing it separate from its grave lessened the emotional impact for them, or perhaps they were simply more infatuated with Hollywood's *Titanic* than the real one. The others were probably just not all that interested in the history of the ship. It was something to keep them occupied for the moment, something to coax them away from the everyday monotonous existence of the wealthy, and when it was over, forgotten. The fact that the doll came from where it did, meant little to Collin himself. It was a beautiful piece, and it was *unique*, and that meant it was valuable, extremely valuable. Therein lay the lure for Collin Hayworth.

"Yes," Stella said. "A seance. We could try to contact the spirits of the *Titanic*. After all, tonight is the anniversary of the sinking, is it not?"

"Yes," someone agreed. "Eleven-forty tonight. Eighty-six years ago."

"Wouldn't that be fun?"

"What do you know, what do any of us know, about conducting a seance?" Collin asked.

"I've read books," she replied. "I know a little."

Curious glances were exchanged, as if everyone mulled the thought over and sought to seek the approval of the others. Sophia's husband shrugged and puffed on his pipe. Sophia and her daughter seemed extremely intrigued by the idea. Thomas Wilford refilled his drink, a sign that he was content. With no words being spoken, it seemed the clique agreed.

"I don't know," Stephanie Ashley said. "I don't like the sound of this."

"What's wrong with it?"

Stephanie shook her head. "It just doesn't seem like a good idea." The crowd began to mill around the dissenting voice. Stephanie was the only one who had not tagged along on the two-week sail to the *Titanic*'s resting spot, and she seemed no more ready to partake in this invasion of the spirit world than she did the probing of the burial ground of over fifteen hundred souls. "You people seem to have lost touch with reality. That movie has destroyed your way of thinking. You've let Hollywood glamorize this whole event. You've fallen victim to the romanticism. You're forgetting what a tragedy *Titanic* was. People died. Fifteen hundred people died. It may seem wonderful and glorious to have gone down with it when you watch a movie, or read a book, but I'm sure if you asked any of the people who were there, you'd get a different story. A much different story indeed."

There was a heavy silence in the room for an uncomfortable period. Eyes met each other and then locked onto Stephanie. A moderate rain had begun to fall just outside the veranda of Collin's villa suite.

"Well," Mr. Lloyd said, finally breaking the silence. "We'll find that out tonight when we ask them, I suppose."

Stephanie sighed, making it clear she would have no part of this evening's festivities. The group broke off into sections, some heading for the liquor cabinet, some to the lobby of the magnificent hotel.

Collin glanced over at the safe that housed his newest acquisition and walked out into the steady rain. It was the middle of spring in France, a pleasant seventy-two degrees, but the rain falling from the monotone sky seemed ice cold.

The scent of the candle—some kind of apple and cinnamon mix—was assaulting Collin's senses. He found himself wishing this nonsense would soon be over. He looked about the dark room, studying the curious highlights and shadows the flickering candle created across the faces of his friends. He started to reach for his brandy when Stella shot him a warning stare. She was obviously striving for the proper theatrics in this childish game, and any disruption would spoil the effect.

"The night is April 14th, 1912," she whispered, sounding for all the world like some gypsy fortune-teller in a black-and-white monster movie. "We feel your sadness, we can feel your fear."

Nervous eyes glanced about the room. Collin knew that no one believed, but there was that faint degree of uncertainty, that gnawing possibility that this could actually work, that Stephanie could be right about her anxieties at contacting the spirit world.

"Come to us," Stella continued. "Come through the murky depths, come up through the cold waters—"

—water this cold—

"—and join us here tonight." She paused for effect. "Speak to us. Share what you're feeling with us."

Collin closed his eyes, not to partake in the ritual, but merely to rest them. He was beginning to think that this extended escapade was more draining than it was relaxing, but then major acquisitions usually left him feeling this way. And his latest acquisition was the grandest of all. Collin smiled, his eyes still closed, and pictured the lovely doll, resting snugly in her velvet bed, safe from all prying eyes and hands inside the sturdy metal safe. Collin let himself relax, Stella's voice becoming merely a hum of background noise to his ears. The candle scent drifted into his nostrils. A tinge of brandy followed. Soothing. Collin breathed deeply and let the white noise of utter relaxation fill his mind. The rain was returning to splash along the cobblestone drive that led to the hotel. It had a pleasant effect, but underneath the aromas of candles and liquor was another scent, a faint underlying odor that Collin could not quite place, a cold, chilling smell he couldn't begin to describe. Somewhere in the distance . . .

—water—

waves crashed gently
—this—
upon the shore.
—cold—
Running water. He was listening to running water.
"Give us a sign." Stella's voice broke through the lull.
Not running water.
Collin opened his eyes.
Cascading water.
"Give us a sign."

There were terrifying screams in Collin's head, and the sound of crashing waves, of roaring water, was deafening. The others were staring at the candle, or at Stella in her faux trance, but there wasn't a sound. Stella's lips moved, but filling his ears was the sound of many people, crying and screaming in a fit of mass hysteria, and an ear-splitting wrenching sound he could not place.

"Come to us."
—could stop a man's heart in a matter of minutes—
"Speak to us. Come up from your watery grave."
—would feel like thousands of knives jabbing into your skin—
"Share with us."
—as cold as porcelain—

Collin opened his eyes and looked at Stella. He wanted to scream, but he could force no sound to escape from his throat. Stella's face had changed. It was no longer the subtle face of a wealthy middle-aged woman fighting the effects of aging with plastic surgery. There was nothing plastic about her face. It was porcelain.

Stella bore the same smooth untainted face of the doll that had stared at Collin through the submarine window. Startled and frightened, Collin fell back in his chair and landed hard on the floor.

There was laughter. "Are you all right, Collin?"

Collin looked up from his prone position. Thomas was standing over him, offering his hand. The scent of the candle was fading from the room, replaced by several flavors of pipe tobacco and various liqueurs, but that other unexplained odor from his dream still lingered.

"I think I may have fallen asleep," Collin said, embarrassed. It was the only explanation he could come up with for the strange sequence of events he had just experienced. "I'm sorry, Stella."

"And just when we were about to make contact," she said, and gave Collin a pert pout.

Collin took her hand and kissed it as a proper gentleman should. He had fallen asleep and had a short, terrifying nightmare, that was all it was. He took a deep breath and crossed into his bedroom, anxious to check on his prize.

Collin knelt to work the combination on the safe's lock when there was a cold dampness on his knee. He looked down at the dark spot on his slacks and then to the top of the safe.

Perturbed, Collin called out to the others, "Who sat their drink on my safe?" But the party was rapidly returning to full swing, and no one answered him.

Grumbling to himself, swearing to put a lock on his private bedroom door, Collin pulled out his handkerchief and wiped away the icy water that had puddled on the surface of the safe.

◆

That night, Collin had strange dreams.

It was as if he was floating in gelatin, and that he was trying to fight his way out of the cold, thick substance. It was dark all around him, but there was a light above him, a light that seemed to get farther away the more he struggled. He tried to call out to the light. Why wouldn't it answer him? There were dark objects surrounding him, and Collin was reminded of banana slices suspended in lime green gelatin, a concoction he'd often endured in grade school. Yet each time he reached for one of these dark objects, they would disappear.

Collin sat up in his bed, the bizarre nocturnal adventure rapidly fading from his mind. He swung his legs over, slipped into his night slippers and robe, and shuffled down the hall toward the bathroom.

Collin flicked the switch and turned the faucet on. The water was ice cold. He turned the hot water on all the way, but it seemed to only get colder. *The water heater must be malfunctioning,* he thought, and made a mental note to call the desk in the morning.

He turned the faucet off—

—water this cold—

and stopped.

What was that noise? It sounded like running water in the distance. Was it raining again? So much for the sunny Riviera. There was that sound again. No, not rain. It was a wet sound, as of someone walking around in drenched slippers.

Collin wiped his hands—they were numb from the cold—on a towel and flicked the switch when suddenly, there was a different noise.

It was impossible.

Outside maybe, but unlikely at this hour.

Impossible inside his suite.

—water this cold—

It was the carefree laughter of a child. Collin opened the bathroom door just in time for the appearance of the silhouette of a small girl running around the corner toward the front of his suite. He started to give chase when he slipped on the tiled floor. Collin caught himself and turned on the lights.

—water this cold—

Puddles of water lined the hallway, extending around the corner where the child had disappeared. There was no indication of a door opening, or closing. There was no means of escape.

There was no child anywhere inside Collin's suite.

Collin rubbed his eyes. A migraine was coming on.

The strange weather must be getting to him. The rain was making him think he was freezing to death. It was springtime on the French Riviera, and he was always cold. Maybe Stella's performance had unnerved him more than he cared to admit.

Collin made his way back into the bedroom and stopped suddenly at the foot of his bed. Small dark footprints wound their way from the door to the foot of the safe. When Collin removed a slipper and touched the spots on the carpet with his bare toe, a cold chill shot up his spine.

This is preposterous, Collin thought. *I refuse to even consider this possibility. I own many antique dolls, and I have not once had their past come back to haunt me.*

Collin could only stare numbly at the strongbox, his mind scrambling frantically for a way to comprehend the thin sheet of ice that had completely enveloped the safe.

Collin found himself trapped in the gelatinous sea again, wildly flaying his arms to either side in a mad attempt to reach one of the dark objects trapped beside him. Finally, as the last of the objects disappeared, his hand bumped against something else. It was a life belt.

—*water this cold*—

Collin quickly slipped into the flotation device. He seemed to be able to breathe, but he felt the need to don the equipment. Somewhere in his hazy state, he thought he recognized the gentle, bittersweet strings of "Nearer My God to Thee" floating somewhere above him.

At that precise moment, a tremendous roar of screeching steel and shattering glass drowned out the beautiful melody, and it was as if he was now floating in freezing water. He looked up to find a gigantic ship looming above him, its bow sticking straight into the air. As the unnerving roar increased in decibels, the great steamer broke in half with a heart-wrenching grind of twisting metal, and screams filled the air as dozens of people fell from the decks into the frigid water.

—could stop a man's heart in a matter of seconds—

Collin looked around himself to find that he was floating in water, the buoyancy of the life jacket holding him above the ocean's surface. A bright light exploded from overhead, and Collin looked up to the rocket's sparks dissipating in the night air. Screams and chaos continued to fill the air. Collin panicked as a man attempted to use Collin to hold himself up. Collin pushed the man away and stared with indifference as the man went under.

Collin returned his attention to the doomed ship. Its bow bobbed up and down a few moments before it began to sink into the black, frigid water.

—would feel like a thousand knives—

Collin turned to look about. Hundreds of others floated in the water around him, ice clinging to their faces and hair. In the distance, he could make out the shapes of the lifeboats, but they were out of reach, and none tried to come his way.

Collin looked back up at the stricken *Titanic* when the little girl appeared.

Her mother was holding onto her even as the ship slanted to an almost illogical degree. The little girl held onto the ship's railing with one hand, and in her other tiny hand, she held a small porcelain doll.

Collin's eyes met the girl's, and it seemed as if she were right in front of him, instead of hundreds of feet above him in the cold, starlit night.

Collin stared in horror as the ship continued to slide farther into the water...

—*water this cold*—

until it was gone.

A great suction created by the sinking ship swirled in a wide arc for many long moments. When it finally subsided, Collin was left floating in the freezing water, the cries and pleas of hundreds drifting in the night air. The sky was moonless, but there were many stars out, millions of stars. Slowly, surely, the cries and screams began to subside as many succumbed to the frigid water. Collin let his head fall back. The strains of the orchestra were faint, as he stared up at the sky. There was a falling star. Then another. He suddenly remembered something he was told as a child. Every time a star falls, it means someone has died. The cries diminished still. *There would be many falling stars tonight*, Collin thought.

There was a gentle lapping of water to his right, and he turned toward the little girl he had spotted earlier on the deck of the sinking ship. She was no more than two feet away from him. Close enough to touch if he could move his arms. She did not shiver. She did not appear to be cold at all. The little girl brought her arms out of the water, and still held the doll in her hands. She extended the doll toward Collin as if to offer it to him, but he could not raise his arms. The little girl's cold blue eyes—

—*water this cold*—

stared into his, but she never made a sound. Finally, the little girl released the doll, and it began to sink into the black depths. Collin followed its path as it sank farther into the water, and pictured in his mind the slow, wafting journey it would take. Two-and-a-half miles into the Atlantic, where it would nestle amongst the remains of a once mighty ode to man's progress, among the mingled remains of hundreds and hundreds of souls (no separation by class—down here, everyone is equal), joining them in a somber graveyard, where it would remain for eighty-six years, until one man who thought only of himself, a man who believed that the all mighty dollar could save the world's problems—or at least his anyway—would choose to wrench it from its final resting spot.

Collin looked back up to find the girl, but she was gone, and he didn't have the strength to look around for her.

Collin could not feel his legs, nor could he any longer feel his heart.

The water was just too cold.

Jonathan Denny could scarcely contain his excitement. This was a dream come true. A lifelong fantasy fulfilled at last. He was nineteen years old, a high school graduate about to enter his first college semester. This was something he had envisioned since he was twelve, ever since the day he had picked up a book from the school library for a book report, a book by a man named Walter Lord entitled *A Night to Remember*.

Ever since then he had absorbed every book, every movie (including Cameron's, which he had seen eleven times, so many times that even his girlfriend had gotten tired of seeing it), every article, every documentary on the subject he could find.

Then when his father gave him the exciting news that he had booked his son on an underwater tour of the sunken liner as a graduation present (who needs a car?), it was the best news Jonathan had ever received.

And now, here he was, two-and-a-half miles beneath the surface of the Atlantic. It had taken over two hours to reach this depth, and that waiting had been the hardest part of the entire trip. Now, the tour guide had instructed them to watch closely, since they were nearing the stern of the great ship. Jonathan stared intently as the submarine neared the sad remains. It gave him chills he would never be able to explain to anyone, the dark outline of the stern slowly appearing out of the murky gloom.

Jonathan listened as the guide explained all the visible pieces of the ship, pointed out the great gash along the side that had doomed the ship. Jonathan had seen every picture ever taken of the wreck, or so he thought.

The submarine had just passed over the last part of the stern and was hovering just above the ocean floor where a great deal of the wreckage was strewn about. Jonathan had seen these pictures before in all the books he'd studied. Toilets, pieces of wooden stairs, benches and all types of debris littered some six hundred yards of ocean floor that separated *Titanic's* stern from her bow.

And Jonathan remembered the picture of the doll's face protruding from the silt on the ocean floor.

Yet, he'd never seen any of the others. Surely, they had been photographed. How had he missed them? Why had he never read anything of them?

He'd seen the one photograph of the doll face, but only one. Nothing of the rest of them, and there were so many.

Scattered across the ocean floor, mixed in with the debris from the great *Titanic*, and amid wreckage that had called the bottom of the Atlantic home for eighty-six years, were the shattered remains of hundreds and hundreds of broken dolls.

Lycanthrophobia

Caribou Ridge had always been a nice town. Nestled amid the beautiful virgin wilderness of Canada's Northern Territories, it was a town that never had much in the way of a tourist business. I should know. I've been the mayor here going on fifteen years now. We just don't get visitors. Folks that did live here had lived here all their lives. They'd been born here. They lived in the same houses their parents had lived in, worked the same jobs their parents had worked. No one ever bothered the good folk of Caribou Ridge, and that's just the way they liked it. There was never any change, and to them, change was bad. Eventually, change *did* come to Caribou Ridge, and it came in a big way. It all started the day the werewolf came to town.

John Bunting was his name. He first appeared in Caribou Ridge in the early weeks of winter in '91. He was a big man, heavy set, with a full beard that all but gave away his true nature. He had a sort of mysterious air about him that I just passed off as ignorance, on my part due to my lack of familiarity with stateside mannerisms. He carried a load of camping gear and photography equipment, but the most peculiar thing about him was his pet—a full-grown wolf. Like some people might curl up with a poodle for companionship, Bunting just came waltzing into town with a wild animal at his side. He said it was a hybrid, but it sure looked like a wolf to me. Most people will try to tell you that they knew right then, but we were all completely fooled. No one suspected anything. I mean, who would?

I guess I was the first to actually contact Bunting. He came into my office on that fateful day so long ago. Seems he was some sort of biologist from Vermont. He had planned on setting up camp some hundred miles out of town, far away from the city. In the dead of winter no less. Gets forty below out in the valley. God, but we should have spotted it earlier than we did.

Bunting had hired old Carney Blake to fly fresh supplies out to him weekly: food, matches, film, that sort of thing. Carney never suspected the man at all. He was a trusting soul, always quick to take up with anybody. Carney needed the money, that's for sure, and he was a damn good pilot, so he took Bunting's offer.

Two days after Bunting arrived, Carney took him and his wolf in his plane and dropped them off near a big caribou herd. Bunting said that wherever caribou were, the wolves would be. Everyone knows that, but I just couldn't figure why he would come so far just for wolves. Didn't they have wolves in the States?

Several people pestered Carney for a couple of days after he returned. No one really suspected Bunting of being a monster, but we were all damn sure curious. We'd never had a visitor from the States before and to finally get one, and an extremely peculiar one at that, certainly sent us scratching for clues. Elmer Johnson, owner of the general store, was the first to corner Carney.

"What's that Bunting guy doing out there?" Elmer had asked.

Carney shrugged, leaned back in his chair like he always does 'til his head looks like it doesn't have a neck, and took a wad of chewing tobacco from his pouch. "Studying wolves, he says."

"Why?" Elmer asked.

"Don't know," Carney answered. "Says he wants to study the social behavior of the wolf pack in the wild. Study, take notes, take pictures." Carney spit in the dented Folger's can at the foot of his chair.

"Where'd he get that wolf?"

"Says he raised it from a pup," Carney said.

"Whoever heard of someone raising a wolf puppy? Don't that beat all, Carney? Don't that beat all you ever heard in all your put-togethers?"

"Carney doesn't care what Bunting does out there, just so long as he pays him. Right, Carney?" I asked.

I was just trying to make light of the situation. I'd been hearing rumors floating around town, and I expected the strange man, and his wolf was on everybody's thoughts.

Old Carney flew out to meet with Bunting and take him his supplies every Monday morning for six weeks. By this time, everyone in town had an opinion on the mysterious Mr. Bunting. Herb Weaver thought he was a Russian spy, digging some kind of pipeline to Alaska, so he could steal oil from the wells up there. Elmer had begun figuring he was building some kind of device to communicate with Martians. Something about the cold increasing the sensitivity of the fiber-optics in the cables. Clara Sinclair, bless her poor romantic soul, was convinced that Bunting was running away from a love that had gone sour. Of course, all these ideas were ridiculous. One man can't dig his way to Alaska, there ain't no such thing as Martians, and there're lots of better places than Northern Canada to make a man forget about a woman. No, it was Steven Grover and Todd Sinclair, Clara's grandson, who came up with the best theory.

They had approached me in my office on a Thursday afternoon, asking if we could hold a special meeting of the town council at Winky's Diner the following Friday night. Steven and Todd wouldn't tell me at the time what their thoughts were, but I could tell by the looks in their eyes that they thought they were on to something. So, I sent out word for the whole town to meet at Winky's at six-thirty Friday evening.

Everyone showed up promptly at six-thirty, except Elmer, whose arthritis had flared up again. He finally got there at around six forty-five, with predictions of another foot of snow by morning. Everyone ordered hot coffee, and Stella passed out pieces of chocolate pie, and at seven o'clock, I officially started the meeting.

"We think we know what John Bunting is here for," Steven said.

"And if we're right," Todd added, "there could be some big trouble."

Everyone in the room seemed to tense up. They all leaned forward, and it was as if we all knew the boys were right, even before they said anything.

"One thing's for sure. He sure as hell ain't just taking pictures of wolves. God knows, they've got plenty of pictures of wolves in the world." Gus Martin groaned.

"And there ain't no need to study up on wolves, to write books about wolves. They eat, they sleep, they shit, they howl at the moon, they make baby wolves. What else is there to know about a damn wolf?" Elmer whined.

"Elmer, everyone," I said. "I think that we are all in agreement that Mr. Bunting is here for more than just wolves. The question is 'What is he here for?' Steve and Todd have an idea." I motioned for Steve and Todd to take the floor.

The two boys walked up to me and turned to face the others. They had a lot of books and magazines in their hands, and I wondered what kind of wild story the boys had come up with.

"We think Bunting is a werewolf," Steve said bluntly.

Well needless to say, there was quite a commotion in the little diner. That theory was almost as ridiculous as Elmer's Martian theory (a theory he still stuck with). The room filled with the buzz of excitable conversation. I let it go on a few minutes before banging my gavel for attention.

"Think about it," Todd said. "How else can a man have a wolf as a pet? A wolf that doesn't attack, a wolf that obeys his every command."

"Yeah," said Steve. "And why else would anyone want to go out in the dead of winter, in forty below temperatures, to be with wolves?"

"Unless," Clarence Wilford said. "Unless he himself was a wolf."

"Precisely," Steve shouted excitedly.

I had to put a hand to my mouth to conceal my laughter, and there were more than a few chuckles, as well as some skeptical words, floating around in the diner. Most of us were still sticking to our own personal theories as to Bunting's true identity. We weren't about to believe the overactive imaginations of two teenage boys.

"But why would he come here to Caribou Ridge?" Stella asked from behind the counter. "Don't werewolves live in Transylvania, or somewhere?"

"No, you're thinking about that vampire guy. What was his name?" Clarence said.

I leaned against the bar quietly as the town came alive with the pros and cons of the existence of werewolves in our community.

"Where else would a werewolf want to live?" Russell Thomas asked, joining in with the boys. "Where else in the world are wolves as wild and free, as far from civilization, as they are up here?"

"Yeah," Clara Sinclair agreed, obviously rejecting her "jilted lover" idea and siding with her grandson, "and with all the caribou in these parts, he has all the food he needs."

"But why would he come here?" Sonny, Clara's son and Todd's father, asked. "What's the real reason, other than food and freedom?"

"That's what scares us, Dad," Todd said. "We think he may be starting a whole race of werewolves."

"What, you mean like turning all the wolves into werewolves?" Gus asked.

"That's exactly what we mean," Steve said.

"Then there'd be werewolves all over the countryside, terrorizing us, taking all the animals, our livestock, maybe even us," Todd added.

"Have you noticed the way the wolves have been acting lately? He's got them stirred up, like they know he's out there," said Elmer, his old eyes carefully scanning the ceiling, as if he expected to find wolves hanging from the light fixtures.

A crescendo of anxious voices began to swell, until it seemed the very windows of Winky's Diner would shatter in on us. Eyes showed concern, and voices betrayed base fears as the townspeople pondered the idea of a supernatural race of monsters invading our peaceful little town.

"And what if he doesn't stop at just the wolves?" Stella added, her voice near tears. "What if he plans to turn us all into werewolves?"

More panicked voices. In fifteen, or so years of mayoring the fine town of Caribou Ridge, I'd never dealt with a problem the likes of which we were beginning to realize. Deciding on the stop sign at Main and 1st had been the big decision of my career until that evening. I was still skeptical of the boys' story, but my rational side just couldn't come up with a logical reason for Bunting's appearance. The longer the meeting went on, the more involved I became.

"What are we going to do, Mayor Bradley?" my townsfolk asked me.

"We gotta stop him," Todd said. "We gotta stop him."

"But how," Clara asked. "How do you stop something that's straight from hell?"

That's when the boys brought out their tape. They had ordered it from a video store in MacKenzie City weeks earlier when they had first pondered the theory. The boys had brought their little television and VCR from home, and set them on the counter. Todd pushed the tape in the slot and turned on the TV. The tape was a movie called "The Wolfman," and according to Steve and Todd, was one of the first actual accounts of what they called lycanthropy. It was just a movie, a made-up movie, I knew that, but we all watched it as if it was a documentary, like something we could learn from. We sat, chewing our bottom lips, our faces twisted into frightened sneers, as a man named Lawrence Talbot wrestled with the demons in his body. I don't know about everyone else, but I kept thinking of John Bunting. He kind of looked like this Talbot fellow, and I just figured all werewolves looked alike. I weighed the possibility of Bunting being a monster, and if he was, I wondered if he felt bad the way Talbot did in the picture. I wondered if he wanted to take his own life to spare others. I wondered if, deep down, he wanted help. I wondered if I was going senile for even considering such things.

Finally, after Talbot was beaten to death with a silver-tipped cane in the shape of a wolf's head, the movie ended. There was an eerie silence, as if we were all afraid to speak.

"Silver," Elmer said, finally abandoning his Martian scheme. "I guess it takes silver to kill a werewolf."

"Oh," Stella cried. "We can't just up and kill John Bunting!"

"And what would you have us do? Just let him run wild? Let him make others like him, until an army of wolves comes into town and snatches us all up? Do you want them to take your baby, Stella?" Sonny shouted.

Stella backed away, tears welling up in her sunken eyes. Clara went to comfort her. "Damn you, Sonny! Do you have to be so rough? Can't you see she's scared? Hell, we all are."

"So where do we get the silver?" Gus asked.

"We can take some Hershey's Kisses to Bunting," Al Sherman suggested. Al was the town dimwit.

We all turned to look at Al, perplexity surely written across our faces. "Hershey's Kisses?" we asked, amused.

"Yeah," he continued. "Ain't they wrapped in silver? One little Kiss, and he falls over dead, sure as shit."

We all groaned. "You damn idiot!" Gus shouted. Gus wasn't much brighter than Al. "And how the hell you gonna get him to eat it? Ain't no damn werewolf in his right mind gonna eat something he knows is poison!"

"What if we get him to wear silver jewelry?" Edgar Kellums said. "That way he'd get so weak we could tie him up and throw him in jail. Just like Superman. I saw that happen to Superman once."

"Didn't you watch the movie, Ed?" Sonny shouted. "That Talbot guy carried that cane around with him the whole movie, and it didn't make him weak! Besides, we can't just toss him in jail. He could escape. We're gonna have to destroy him."

"It's going to have to be a silver bullet," Steve finally said. "That's what me and Todd planned on from the beginning."

Everyone seemed to accept the boys' idea. "We can melt down all our silver pieces and make bullets out of them."

Suddenly, the little diner was buzzing with excitement and anticipation. Wives began digging in their purses, pulling earrings from their lobes. Men began to remove their wristwatches and discuss the contents of their attics, as the boys' great plan gained momentum. Memory fails me now, but I think it was just about then that I decided things were going a little too far. As scared as we all were, there was still no hard evidence that could convict Bunting.

I was just about to call the meeting, when the diner door swung open, and a blast of arctic air shook the entire restaurant, chilling us all to the bone. We all turned madly about to try and understand what the matter was.

"This is insane!" Carney shouted.

"Carney! Where've you been?" everyone asked. Nobody had noticed Carney's absence.

"Have you people lost your friggin' *minds*? I can't believe what I'm hearing! You're actually planning to kill John Bunting, aren't you?!" Carney pressed.

"He's a werewolf, Carney," Elmer reasoned.

"He's a scientist!"

"He wants to live with the wolves! He wants to make a whole race of werewolves!" added Gus.

"He wants to write a book! He wants to study the behavior of wolves in the wild! I can't believe you people have let your imaginations run away with you like this! You were actually considering killing another human being!"

There was an eerie silence, and the air was so *thick*, you could almost hear everyone's thoughts. We all stared at Carney as he stood there, huffing and puffing like a...*like a wolf about to blow our house down.*

"John Bunting has been here over eight weeks. Don't you think he's had plenty of time to build his 'army of monsters?' Don't you think this town would be overrun with demons and spirits by now?"

No one said a word as Carney continued to peer down at us all. Everyone cast a wary eye to one another before staring back at the fuming pilot.

"Just one thing, Mayor," Carney said, looking me square in the eye. "You're the mayor of this town, and sometimes I think you're the only one here who has any sense. It's your responsibility to lead these poor people down the right path. You have to straighten this out, or I'll straighten it out for you."

I think it was that moment, when Carney's eyes locked onto mine, that all doubt left my mind. Hell, I was extremely skeptical through the whole meeting, but there was something in Carney's eyes then that I'd never seen before. It wasn't Carney I was talking to. I'd known him for years, and God help me, *that wasn't him.* I was staring into the eyes of some wild animal.

Carney stormed out the door, and that was pretty much it for that meeting. Everyone was tired, upset, and damned scared. Too much had happened. There were too many thoughts on our minds. Everyone went on home, except me and Elmer. We went back to my office. I brewed a pot of steaming black coffee, and we sat at the window for what seemed like hours, just staring out at the pitch night, thinking of John Bunting.

"You thinking what I'm thinking, Danny?" Elmer asked.

I nodded. I was pretty sure we were on the same wavelength. "Eight weeks. Eight weeks Carney's been flying out every Monday morning, taking supplies to Bunting."

"Surely, he's got Carney by now," Elmer said.

I nodded again and pulled open the middle drawer of my desk. That's where I kept the antique pocket watch my great grandfather had left me. The *silver* pocket watch.

"You thinking what else I'm thinking, Elmer?"

It was Elmer's turn to nod in agreement. "Yeah, part of what Carney said is true. Eight weeks is plenty of time to start an army. Good part of one anyway."

I sighed and took a sip of coffee, barely noticing the hot liquid was blistering my lips. "We're gonna need a lot more silver than this old watch will give us."

We held another meeting at Winky's the next Monday, when we knew Carney would be gone to find Bunting. We had to act fast. Old Arthur Corey had fought in World War II, and he had known how to melt the silver down to make bullets. There had been a lot more silver among the good folk of Caribou Ridge than I would've anticipated under normal circumstances. That was good. We would need quite a bit.

It had been decided that Todd, his father, and Elmer would be the ones who went after Carney. I had wanted to go, feeling it my duty as town leader, but the others had thought it best that I stay in town.

One thing was certain—we had to act fast. Once Carney let Bunting know that we knew about him, his army would be together quicker than we could react. The army was still a terrifying threat, but it would perhaps be easier to deal with if the leader were out of the way. Elmer and the others had taken Carney's other plane (Elmer being a fine pilot himself) and went off in search of our quarry.

The rest of us stayed huddled together for comfort at the diner. After what seemed like days, Elmer, Todd, and Sonny returned. Carney, Bunting, and the wolf were all dead. The silver had done the job. We mourned for old Carney, but we all breathed a little easier knowing that the beasts could be killed. Now we had to prepare for the retaliation from the other werewolves.

But nothing happened. A month passed with no sign of werewolves. We would listen to them sometimes at night, way off in the distance, but they never came to us. That's when I had a terrifying thought. *These* werewolves were multiplying. They were spreading the disease, spreading it on to other wolves and not just wolves. Foxes, wolverines, weasels, even the caribou were being turned into vicious, blood-thirsty monsters. The great army of supernatural beasts was growing nightly, just waiting for the moment to attack, plotting, scheming . . . waiting.

We set out traps. A good number of our townsfolk are trappers. The traps got some of the were-animals. They weren't silver, but they held the bastards long enough that exposure and starvation got them. We shot some others, but we had to conserve our silver bullets for the approaching great battle. But the longer we waited, then surely, the more powerful the army grew.

Elmer's dog tried to bite one of Stella's kids, and we could only assume the worst. The werewolves were slipping into town at night, unknown to us, and afflicting our pets. Shooting that old dog must've been the hardest thing Elmer ever had to do, but he had to do it. We had no choice but to use some of our silver to destroy all the pets. Chances are some hadn't been afflicted, but that's a chance we couldn't afford to take.

The days grew into weeks, the weeks into months, and still we waited. They howled from the distant mountains, but we never saw any of them. We just spent our days in the diner waiting. There's strength in numbers. At night, we all went home and slept behind tightly bolted doors. It got to where we were all as nervous as those little white mice you spot in pet stores wandering around the snake cages. Why weren't they coming after us? Why weren't they making their move? Why were they toying with us so? The waiting, the tension, was getting almost unbearable.

Then one day, a few months ago, the unthinkable happened. Al and Davey Webster got in a fight while playing poker. Davey Webster had never raised a finger in anger before. *Never* in all his years. We could only assume the worst. Somehow, someway, they had gotten to Davey. I hated to do it. We *all* hated to do it, but we had no choice. We couldn't have one of them living in our midst. Me and Elmer buried Davey along the outskirts of town at high noon one day. We *hated* to do it.

Of course, it didn't end there. The fears mounted, and the tension grew. No one knew how Davey had been infected, and that just scared us more. We were trapped. In all the years I've run this town, we all accepted the fact that there was nowhere to go from this town. It never bothered us, but now, in the face of adversity, everyone seemed to realize just how *isolated* we really were.

THE POROSITY OF SOULS

I said earlier that change was bad for the good folk of Caribou Ridge. Change is *very bad*. The change that John Bunting brought destroyed our town. It changed us all. It changed this town.

Al was the next one. He had seemed different ever since the ordeal with Davey. We could only guess that he had been infected during the scuffle with Davey. Me and Elmer buried him right next to Davey. Somehow, I think they would've both liked that.

It's amazing how fast a disease can spread. I never would've believed it if I hadn't lived through it myself. We took every precaution we could imagine, but the disease just kept on spreading. The germs, the bacteria, whatever evil it was that caused it must've been in the wind, floating in the very air we breathed. It just kept spreading. We could make it out in some. Others just up and admitted to it. They had lost their willpower. They were just drained. Fortunately, our silver supply never ran out.

It's lonely up here in the Northern Territories. This little town known as Caribou Ridge is even lonelier. I think back now, to the day when John Bunting first arrived here, and I can't help but wonder: *is there anything I could've done that would've made any difference? Was it all necessary? Could we have gotten outside help somehow? There are so many alternate outcomes that my grieving mind comes up with, but how can I know for sure?*

It's just me and Elmer now. *Just me and Elmer.* Out of a little over fifty people, it's just me and Elmer left. They won. The werewolves won. They're out late at night, shuffling through the deathly quiet streets, howling to the moon high in the mountains. They're still out there, and they probably always will be. The land belongs to them now. Bunting did what he set out to do.

◆

TERRY CAMPBELL

This disease is very strange indeed. Me and Elmer have been alone in my house for three weeks now. Alone, without any outside contact at all. Just the two of us. *It must be in the air.*

Late last night, Elmer started rolling over in his sleep, mumbling, sweating, crying out. I buried my face in my hands, shouted for him to stop, but he wouldn't. He just cried out in his sleep, screaming about wolves, silver, and Bunting. I couldn't wake him up. He couldn't stop screaming.

Lonely. It gets so terribly lonely out here. I buried Elmer next to his dog early this morning, all the while listening to the werewolves singing in the distance.

The Eternal Drifter

The little girl stared up at the colorless sky with lifeless eyes, several layers of hardened mud and grime spackling her innocent face. But she was just two-dimensional, and the dirt covering her face was merely hardened mud, caked onto the surface of a crushed milk carton. Biodegradable, both the milk carton and the little girl. Maybe somewhere out here, down one of these lonely, desolate roads, the little girl *did* stare up at this same monochrome sky with empty sockets as her poor little skull sat bleaching in the hot sun in a dry creek bed. Or maybe in a swift-running stream, where years of silt would bury her bones, beginning the delicate process of fossilization, and maybe millions of years into the future, after mankind is no more, a group of apes, or sponges, or whatever has taken man's place will find a rib sticking out of the hard rock, and they will excavate her bones and painstakingly piece them together again, and someone's missing little girl, a memory long gone and forgotten, will entertain the masses in a futuristic museum.

"Jesus, morbid bastard," Max mumbled to himself.

He nudged the milk carton with a worn boot. Several black beetles scattered from beneath it, frantically scurrying through the grass for the safety of darkness. Max turned his head to the sky—gray and menacing—and then looked back down the long stretch of empty rural highway. The boonies, the sticks, whatever you wanted to call them. As many times as he wandered aimlessly down these backroads of Texas, it was a wonder that Max didn't stumble across the remains of the missing. Yet, he never did, and why? Max pondered.

Because they were well-hidden? In crude hastily buried graves, under piles of branches and underbrush, at the bottoms of murky lakes and weed-choked ponds? Or was it because the statute of limitations on caring had been reached, and missing loved ones became nothing more than pieces of paper stuffed in a file in some law enforcement agency and forgotten?

Max looked back at the little girl. Somewhere, a mother and father struggled to fan the flames of a faintly lit glimmer of hope, but Max knew no one would ever see the little girl again.

Max headed down the road, continuing his way. He'd always been a drifter, and probably always would be. He wasn't one to stay in a particular place, too long. Itchy feet. Wandering was in his blood. He'd roam from town to town, taking odd jobs when money got tight. Now the rumbling in Max's stomach and the emptiness of his pockets told him it was one of those times. He'd have to look for something in the next town.

Yet the highway was like an old jalopy—running on empty. There hadn't been a billboard, a street sign, or even a speed limit posting, for miles. Just pine trees. Hundreds and hundreds of pine trees. Funny thing about east Texas—you can go for miles and miles and there wouldn't be one damned pine tree, then suddenly, there's a whole forest of them. Max kept on through the chilly, misty air, the soft crunch of wet pine needles under his feet. Something about his surroundings bothered him, but it wasn't until he strained his hearing, listening for any early morning noises, that he realized what it was. There was nothing but silence in the distance. No cars, no leaves rustling in the wind, no birds. Only a still silence. The thought sent chills up Max's neck as he continued down the eerie road. That's when he spotted the train station.

It was situated in a clearing among the pine trees, atop a slight, rolling hill. Excited by this sign of life, Max quickly climbed the hill that led to the tracks. The building itself was old and grayed. It looked as if it hadn't been painted in a long while. A thin metal sign reading *Train Station* hung from a pair of rusted chains, swaying gently in the cool breeze. The name struck Max as odd. He'd seen lots of train stations during his travels, and they always had a name of some kind. Either the town's name, or something stupid like one of the railroads on Monopoly. Not just "Train Station."

Max dismissed the thought and trotted across the tracks, the gravel crunching under his hiking boots. He walked up the creaky, wet steps and onto the waiting area. Except for a lone black man at the ticket window, there was no one there. Empty wooden benches lined the walkway, and every so often, a sheet of newspaper would blow across the platform. Other than that, the place was eerily quiet. Max couldn't quite place what was bothering him, but something didn't seem right.

He walked over to the ticket window. The attendant was sitting back in a big wicker rocking chair, puffing on a stinky cigar and reading *The National Enquirer*. He wore baggy gray slacks held up by a pair of dirty red suspenders, and there was a snot rag hanging from his back pocket.

The old man looked up at Max. "Oh," he said. "Just one, huh? I didn't hear the train. Card, please." He stretched to look beyond Max, toward the tracks.

"What?" Max asked.

Max noticed a faint look of surprise on the old man's face. "Oh, you ain't one of them. Sorry. Don't get many people through here no more. You surprised me. Can I help you with something?"

"I need work," Max said. "I need a job. Do you have anything?"

"A job?" the old man asked. He sounded shocked, as if he had just been asked to perform some sort of outlandish act. "What the hell kinda job you think you can git 'round here?"

"I don't know," Max said. "I could sweep, maybe clean up a little."

The old man laughed, then he coughed and gagged into the dirty snot rag. "Don't need no one to sweep, boy. Mother Nature do all my sweepin.' Wind just blows things right on outta here."

The old man continued to laugh at his own private joke. Finally, Max shrugged and turned to leave. "Well, thanks anyway."

"Wait a sec," the old man said, his laughter diminishing. He extended his hand. "Charles Henshaw. Friends call me Charlie."

"Max Greely."

Charlie's eyes met Max's, and Max suddenly made out the presence of years and years of experience and worldly wisdom in those bloodshot eyes. His skin was so black that the whites of his eyes seemed to reach out and grab Max.

"Alright, Max. I guess I could use a little help around here. Can't pay much, though. Don't get much myself. Hell, you'd be more company than anythin' else. It gets kinda lonely out this way sometimes. Spooky, ya know?"

Max thought back to the eerie feeling that had overcome him on the highway earlier, and he suddenly realized what else had seemed so out of place. For the last ten miles, or so, that he had wandered down the highway, there was no hint of a train. No whistle, no rumbling of the tracks, nothing.

"Charlie? Do trains ever come this way anymore?"

Charlie nodded, a glare from the overhead bulb flashing off his bald head. "Oh, yeah," he said solemnly.

"I've been hitching up this highway for a few days now, and I can't remember ever hearing a train. I mean, there's no town around here that I can see. Why a train station?"

Charlie picked up his paper and leaned back in the rocker, exhaling a foul-smelling cloud of smoke. "Ain't no town. Folks what comes around here don't come to sight-see. But as for the train, it'll come. It always comes."

◆

Nearly two weeks passed with no sign of a train. Max occupied his time by sweeping leaves and pine needles from the walkway and emptying trash cans that would've already been empty had it not been for the swept-up leaves, pine needles, and the occasional cigar butt. Max slept in a little room next to Charlie's, on a cot with a broken spring that poked him in the ass. But during the day, Max had little to do. Most of his hours were spent playing Checkers with Charlie. Max was beginning to wonder why the train station was even there. Two weeks and not one damned train.

"Charlie?" Max finally started to ask over one of the endless games of Checkers. "Is this railroad still active?"

"Sure, it is," he said, his eyes never leaving the game board.

"Then why don't any trains ever come along?"

"It'll come."

"You said that last time I asked. But where the hell is it?"

"It'll come, Max."

Charlie extended a gnarled hand, jumped two of Max's pieces, and went silent. Max didn't want to play Checkers.

◆

Three more days passed before the first train whistled, off in the distance, faint and indistinct. At first, it didn't even register in Max's mind that it *was* a train. He had just about given up on the idea. The train was getting nearer, and the whistle blew louder. At least, that's what Max *assumed* the sound was. The grating whine of the whistle sent chills running up and down his spine, like the sound of two cats fighting, or a woman's desperate screams.

Max turned the corner, and there was the train pulling to a stop in front of the station. It was an old type of train like the Cannonball on *Petticoat Junction*. Its sides were pitch black, and its red soot-stained smokestack belched a great cloud of steam high into the outstretched arms of the pine trees.

Max ran to the ticket window, sliding on the slick boards. Charlie just sat there, patiently awaiting his long-absent visitors.

"You were right, Charlie. The train finally did make it in."

Charlie gave Max a look as if to silence him and motioned for Max to step back.

There was another great spew of steam, and then a door opened on the passenger car. People began spilling out of the car, one after the other, in single file. They stepped in synch from the train, and moved to the ticket window like mute, wind-up toy soldiers. None of them spoke or made a sound. Max couldn't believe it. The people's faces were emotionless, lifeless. They stared straight ahead, moving sluggishly to the ticket window. After the train completely shut down, the station was as eerily silent as the morning Max had first stepped into it, except for the shuffling sound of the passengers' feet sliding on the wet boards.

Max stared in awe as the line of people moved to the ticket window. The people were all dressed differently, not in different styles, but as if from...different times. One man had on a long wool jacket and a round derby. There was a boy, no more than twelve, wearing a leather jacket and torn faded jeans.

That wasn't the worst of it. Some of the people wore ripped and tattered clothes, with dark splotches staining the fabric, and some were even *nude*. Completely naked, and it was only fifty degrees. Max sat on one of the benches, unsure of what to make of the ghostly procession. He continued to observe them, wondering why the people were going to the ticket window when they were getting *off* the train. They were handing cards to Charlie, and he was punching holes in them. Max could not look away as the people left the ticket window and continued their single file march out of the train station, where they disbanded and disappeared into the countryside. What are those little animals that dive into the ocean and commit suicide? Lemmings? Yeah, *lemmings.*

That's when Max recognized the little girl. She was the same one from the milk carton, he was sure of it. The poor little thing's eyes were as lifeless as the grainy black and white photograph, and she was naked. Standing in line between a tall, thin man in a black business suit and an overweight woman in a tattered terry cloth robe, she looked so miserably out of place. Just like the train station, just like the silent highway. Out of place and lifeless. Max stared in horror as her tiny feet shuffled onward in line. Dirt and mud smeared her pitiful naked body, and there was a lot of grime around her neck.

"Oh, darling," Max cried and ran to the girl. He knelt before her, throwing his jacket around her shoulders. She had to be freezing to death. The girl didn't seem to acknowledge Max's presence. Max licked his fingers and started to clean the dirt from the girl's face, when he noticed the marks on her neck were not dirt stains. They were bruises.

"Max!" Charlie shouted. "Git away from there!"

"But Charlie," Max said, tears streaming down his face.

"You're not supposed to mess with 'em at all! Now get away!"

Max sat at the bench, every muscle in his body tightened to the limit as the little girl walked out of the station. Soon, they were all gone. His eyes burning from the tears, Max glanced at Charlie, sorting and filing the hole-ravaged cards.

"Why did you stop me, Charlie? Why?"

"You got no business messin' with 'em."

"But she's just a little girl. Five years old, Charlie."

"I know," he said.

Max looked across the tracks into the misty woods, and there were still a few of the strange people, wandering aimlessly through the trees. He sat down on a bench and buried his face in his hands. Charlie's bloodshot eyes burned into his back, and he looked up.

"Who is she, Charlie? Who are any of them?"

Charlie shook his head. "They're just people. Just like you and me."

"But where did they come from? Why did they come to the ticket window? What were those cards?"

Charlie shook his head again. "I can't tell you that, Max."

"Why did they leave their cards here?"

"They be back." He paused. "Most of 'em, anyways."

"But where are they going?"

"Don't know," Charlie answered.

"When are they coming back?"

"Don't know."

"Why is the train still here?"

"Waitin' for 'em."

"Where will it go from here?"

Charlie shrugged and looked out across the misty landscape. "Next stop, I suppose."

A few hours later, the line of people began to flow back into the station, and Max sat anxiously as Charlie started punching cards again. He kept looking for the little girl, but she was nowhere to be found.

When the last person boarded the passenger car, Max walked up to Charlie.

"She didn't come back," he said. "The little girl."

"No," Charlie said. "No, she didn't."

"What happened to her?"

"I guess she found what she was lookin' for," Charlie said.

"What, Charlie?" Max asked, tears again forming in his eyes. "What was she looking for?"

Charlie's ancient eyes bore into Max as sounds crept into the train station from a distance. Not another train whistle.

Sirens.

Max stared out from the cover of the trees, watching as the emergency vehicles pulled alongside the narrow, rural dirt road. Policemen, medical examiners, and paramedics alike crowded around in a circle at the edge of the dry creek bed.

Max thought of the train, of the people, and of what Charlie had said, as the officials uncovered the little girl's skeletal remains. Stephanie Martin. Five years old. Three feet, five inches. Blonde hair. Brown eyes. The milk carton had all that information, too. She'd been missing for four years. That's a long time. A long time for a family to be torn apart, a long time for a mother to miss her little girl, a long time for a child to be alone.

A long time to ride the train.

Armadillo Village

Damned armadillos, Matthew Arnold thought.

The ugly little bastards were everywhere, especially since he crossed the Red River into Texas. The next town was even named after them, according to the state highway sign ahead. They waited from the bushes, their little red eyes glowing like demon spawn peering out from hell's gate. They played along the sides of the roads, oblivious to oncoming traffic. They danced their little "Texas Two-Step" trot practically in the middle of the roads. It was only a matter of time before he ran over one of the little bastards.

It was there in the road, appearing in a flash before Matt could react, as if it had purposely calculated the physics and timed its leap to bring it directly into the car's path. *Suicidal armadillos?* Matt thought as he swerved the car sharply to the left. For a moment, he thought he had missed it until there was the incriminating *thump!* under the car.

"Oh, Jesus, Matt," his wife, Kayla, said. "Did you hit it?"

"I don't know," he said, glancing in the rear-view mirror. "And I really don't care."

"Pull over," she said.

"Kayla."

"Pull *over*," she repeated, more forcefully.

Matt sighed and steered the little Isuzu over to the side of the road. Why she was so worried about the nasty, probably disease-ridden thing was beyond him. But she had that look in her eyes, *that look*, and he knew better than to challenge her.

Matt stepped out of the car and onto the gravel shoulder. The car's engine ticked and popped, and a cloud of dust stirred up by the tires drifted through the air. Shadows from the scraggly trees along the highway fell across the car. It was getting late, and Matt was tired. From the way things looked, they might very well be spending the night in Armadillo, Texas. *Whoopee.*

"It was back a ways," Kayla said from the car.

"I know where it was," Matt mumbled under his breath, careful to stay out of her earshot.

He shambled down the road, looking for the earthly, and more than likely squished remains, of one nameless nine-banded armadillo that had happened to be in the wrong place at the wrong time, and had lost a head-on confrontation with a small, foreign car. Japanese ingenuity wins out over American knowhow again.

But Matt couldn't find the armadillo. It wasn't there.

He turned back toward Kayla and the car. He had walked about a hundred yards and surely that was far enough. He looked back down the highway in the direction from which they had come, looking for any discrepancies in the road. There was only a blackened spot on the asphalt, evidently where the road had stripped a layer of rubber from the car's already balding tires. Matt couldn't recall hitting the brakes with enough force to leave a mark, and there was no streak of spent rubber, only the small circular pattern. Matt thought that the armadillo had possibly crawled into the bushes to die, but there was no blood on the asphalt, no guts, no tell-tale signs of the animal's sudden demise.

"Must've missed him," Matt said. He turned and headed back to the car.

"Well?" Kayla said as he climbed back in.

"It wasn't there."

"What do you mean, it wasn't there?" she questioned.

"What part of it wasn't there do you not understand?" he asked. "I told you. I didn't hit it."

"Then what was that bump?"

He shrugged. "Must've hit a pothole, or something when I swerved. We just thought we'd hit it."

"*You* hit it, not we," she said knowingly. "And you *did* hit it."

"Then I guess it already floated on up to armadillo heaven, or something," Matt snapped. Kayla could really get on his nerves sometimes, especially when he was tired.

"You sure are a grouch today," she said.

"I'm sorry. I'm tired."

Matt started the car and pulled back onto the highway. He had missed the armadillo, and that was that. Nonetheless, he couldn't stop himself from instinctively glancing in the rear-view mirror.

◈

The first building Matt came to in the small community of Armadillo, Texas, was a little curio shop called Armadillo Village. Matt pulled into the dirt and gravel parking lot, hoping to ask for directions to the nearest motel.

The shop was a medium-sized structure of weathered siding, with a full wrap-around porch. Wooden steps led to the porch, and handrails enclosed the entire length of the covered patio, all done in the same shade of drab gray indicative unattended wood. The store looked run down and touristy as hell. A painted, plywood cutout of a standing armadillo waving a ten-gallon cowboy hat stood to the right of the steps. A huge sign secured to the roof read *Souvenirs, Frankoma Pottery, Steer Horns, Knives*. Smaller signs graced the walls to either side of the front doors. One sign read *Snacks, Cold Drinks, Armadillo*

Enchiladas. The other declared *Live Armadillos*, so close in proximity to the previous notice that it made Matt chuckle.

"Oh, that's disgusting," Kayla said, having read the "menu" sign. She pushed back her hair and wiped her brow with a tissue. The evening air was hot and humid.

"I don't know. I've read that armadillo meat is a delicacy."

"Let me guess," Kayla said. "It tastes like chicken."

"Rattlesnake, actually," he corrected.

"Which tastes like chicken."

"All right, it tastes like chicken. You like chicken."

"I'm not eating anything with the word 'armadillo' in it," she warned.

They stepped up the creaking stairs, pushed the glass door open, and were immediately greeted with an odd buzzing noise from overhead. Matt and Kayla turned their heads upward. Attached to the door chime was a bevy of rattlesnake rattles, and whenever the door opened, the mechanism vibrated, causing the rattles to give off their distinctive sound. *That's a new one*, thought Matt.

At the sound of the rattles, a weathered-looking man glanced up from behind the counter. At first glance, he appeared to be about fifty, but then Matt thought he might be closer to thirty. His skin had just been dried by the sun, making him appear older. In a way, the man even *looked* like an armadillo. *He certainly has the same eyes*, Matt thought as the man glared at him and his wife.

Matt looked away from the man, who still hadn't spoken, and joined Kayla, who was already perusing the store's shelves. The entire perimeter of the store was lined with department store counters, flat surfaces with storage compartments underneath and strips of pegboard for hanging more merchandise above. The cabinets overflowed with touristy items. At the store's center were rows of banquet tables loaded with still more commodities. Decorative plates, money banks, backscratchers, bumper stickers and similar items made up most of the inventory, all of which were labeled with a picture of an armadillo, or had the words *Armadillo Village* stamped across the surface.

I'll be damned, Matt thought. The store is a shrine to the armored varmints.

"Welcome to Armadillo Village," the guy behind the counter finally said.

Kayla had moved to one of the banquet tables. It was well-stocked with armadillo baskets. Their hollowed-out shells made the pouch, while their stiffened tails curved from one side to the other, comprising the handles.

Behind the counter, the red-faced man was eyeing Kayla, giving her cut-off shorts and tie-front shirt a thorough visible once-ever.

"You certainly glorify the armadillos here," Matt said.

"Oh, we loves dillers here," the guy said. "Practically worships 'em, you might say." The man smiled. "Got some live ones out back. They be sleepin' in their holes now, though. Come back tonight, and you can sees 'em real good."

"They's night creatures," the man added. Even though he was talking to Matt, the man's eyes were fixed on Kayla.

"Look," Matt said, annoyed by the blatant voyeurism. "We just want a place to stay. How far to the next motel?"

"Just up the road," he said, pointing. "Armadillo Inn."

Of course, Matt thought.

"Thanks." Matt started to turn away, when some items hanging on a peg hook next to the cash register caught his eye. They looked like chicken feet attached to a ring with a thin chain.

"Key rings," the attendant said.

"They're armadillo feet," Matt said.

"Yeah."

Matt thought it was strange that the place would use the idea of the animals as a tourist attraction, then sell their dried remains for profit, even cook the flesh of the animals. "Why do you sell armadillo feet?"

"They're good luck," he answered.

"Not for the armadillo," Matt quipped.

"That's why they're good luck. They's pre-disastered."

"If you like these animals so much, if your entire business is built around them, then why do you hunt them and kill them for profit?"

The man blanched, as if Matt's question had offended him. "We don't never kill no dillers," he said.

"But how—"

"We takes 'em off the road," the man said, cutting Matt off. "You city folks is the one's what kills 'em."

"I'm *definitely not* eating the armadillo enchiladas now," Kayla whispered behind Matt's back.

Strange as it sounded to Matt, the man's answer made sense. He'd seen a lot of armadillos crossing the roads throughout Oklahoma and Texas. He'd even almost hit one himself, but didn't, he reassured himself. It was disgusting, but it somehow sounded logical, from a business point of view, especially considering the were-armadillo behind the counter. "How much?" Matt asked, pointing to the key rings.

"Matthew." Now it was Kayla's turn to sound shocked.

"Dollar fifty."

"That all?" Matt asked, removing two bills from his wallet.

"Matt, you can't be serious," Kayla whined. "That thing is nasty."

"Souvenir," he said.

The man handed Matt the key ring and his change. Turning to Kayla, Matt playfully clawed at her with the armadillo appendage. She was not amused.

"Well, thanks," Matt said to the storekeeper. "We're going to try to find that motel now."

"See ya, folks. Ya'll don't forget to come back tonight and see the dillers."

Matt gave the guy behind the counter an obligatory wave good-bye. *In your dreams, buddy.*

❖

Later, Matt decided to go check out the armadillos. Hell, what would a trip to Armadillo, Texas be without witnessing the backbone of the thriving metropolis? Matt glanced over at Kayla. She was asleep. He wouldn't wake her.

Matt locked the door behind himself on the way out.

The motel was just two buildings down from Armadillo Village. Matt trotted through the white gravel parking lot, stirring up tiny clouds of dust. His stomach growled. The tomato soup he'd had for dinner hadn't done much for him, but it was the only item on the menu at the hotel restaurant that didn't have the word "armadillo" in it. He tended to agree with Kayla on that particular subject.

Matt took the steps of the shop two at a time and tried the front door. It was locked, but there were voices coming from around the corner, so he followed the wrap-around porch to the rear of the establishment. A wooden fence encircled the back of the store, and there was a mingling of excited voices on the other side. He pulled the gate open and was amused by what was in front of him.

A square chain-link pen, roughly the size of several large dog kennels, sat in the center of the back yard. There was a crowd of people gathered around it, but Matt was able to sneak a look into the enclosure. Desert sandstones were piled haphazardly in the center of the pen. Yucca plants and various cacti dotted the sandy ground, along with a few bleached cow skulls. Matt started toward the pen.

There was a counter guy at the other end of the coop, but he made no effort to reach the strange local. Instead, he muscled his way through the crowd for a better look at the pen.

That's when he saw the armadillos for the first time.

They really weren't all that ugly up close, if you concentrated on thinking of them as cute. They scuttled around through the sand, darted in and out of the pile of rocks, their little heads poking out from the gaps intermittently. Nothing spectacular. Certainly nothing that would warrant a crowd of this size, and of such voracity.

Matt turned his attention to the people around him. The curious thing about them was that they didn't look like tourists, or travelers, but rather locals. They were all dressed in stained white T-shirts, overalls, or torn jeans, and most of them wore dirty baseball caps. They also looked to be as dim-witted, if not more-so, than the man who worked the store counter.

From the way the crowd was whooping and hollering, Matt thought they were racing the armadillos, or maybe fighting them. Maybe that was it. Matt had certainly heard enough about dog and cock fights. All the other eccentricities of this town indicated that it was capable of taking the game a step further.

Matt turned to the man next to him. "What's going on here?"

"With the dillers, you mean?"

Matt nodded. The man talked and acted exactly like the counter man.

"We's fixin' to have the ceremony," he said.

"Ceremony?" Matt asked, suddenly more interested in the goings-on than he cared to admit.

Just then, two tall, lanky men entered the cage. They wore dirty, ripped overalls and floppy, Jed Clampitt-looking hats, and they were carrying shotguns. The crowd noise began to grow.

The two men stepped to the rear of the pen. A large wooden box that he hadn't noticed earlier was nestled against the outside of the fenced pen. A man-sized chute led through the fence and into the enclosure. The opening was covered by a piece of plywood. One of the men shouted and banged the butt of his weapon against the plywood, and the other man slid the door open.

The crowd buzzed with anticipation.

There was nothing in Matt's view at first, but his heart pounded wildly. Although the hole leading into the wooden box was dark, there was what appeared to be a man's head inside. Matt cast a wary eye to the mound of rocks. The armadillos peered out from the rocks, their eyes glowing in the darkness. They had ceased all activity, turning to stare silently into the chute. Matt looked back at the box. A hand emerged, then another.

It was a man, crawling on his hands and knees from the wooden box. From what Matt could tell from his clothes, he looked like a business-type—dressed in a nice suit and tie, and definitely not a local. The rest of his attire, however, was very peculiar. Draped across his back was what seemed to be a gunnysack, or a heavy piece of burlap, the sides of which touched the ground. Strapped to the man's shoulders were several of the armadillo baskets Kayla had been looking at earlier. Two large, dried armadillo ears sprouted from the man's head, having been secured with twine. A series of tails, braided together, hung from the man's belt loops and dragged along behind him.

The crowd shouted and screamed. Matt could only stare, trying to comprehend what was going on.

"City slicker squashed a diller out on 75 earlier this evenin'," the local told Matt, shouting over the frenzied crowd. "That's its ears, its shell."

The man's earlier words rang in Matt's ears—*We's fixin' to have the ceremony.*

"He's got to replace what he took from the dillers," the man explained. "City man kilt a diller, now he's got to take its place."

The crowd pressed against the fence until it seemed the barrier would collapse with their weight.

"That's the way it is around here," he continued. "We has to do this to them city folk. They just don't watch out fer our dillers anymore."

Matt looked on in awe as the businessman continued to crawl around in the sand in the homemade armadillo outfit. The man was snorting and pawing at the ground. Armadillo noises, Matt assumed. The armadillos stared from their perches among the rocks and cacti as the businessman threw his head back and guffawed into the night.

Far as Matt could tell, the businessman didn't seem to be having any problems with the ritual. Then again, he also had a shotgun pointed up his ass.

The armadillos in the cage resumed their activities as the businessman crawled around before them. They ran around in circles and squealed, growing increasingly frantic by the second. Matt wanted to go check on Kayla, but something—morbid curiosity, he supposed—prevented him from leaving. A commotion in the crowd diverted Matt's attention from the crawling man. A new arrival was moving through the group toward the pen.

The man was a priest, or at least, he was dressed like one. He wore a black coat and slacks, a Roman collar, and he held a Bible in one hand. The crowd parted to allow him access to the cage. Matt looked on with a feeling that fell somewhere between amusement and dread as the priest began reading scriptures from the Good Book.

Only, it didn't sound like anything he'd ever read in the Bible.

"'And the Lord said unto His shepherds, send forth the beast and its nine bands, let it reclaim the night so that it may take what belongs to it once more.'" The priest bowed his head a moment, and the crowd grew silent.

Matt looked around the crowd, uncertain of how he should react to the sudden call for prayer. Bowing his head, he pretended to pray, studying the crowd around him with still-open eyes as he did. The priest finally said, "Amen." The gathering crowd repeated the blessing, and everyone looked up. Then a voice rang through the crowd.

"Kill the lights!" It shouted as the priest closed his Bible.

There was one light in the back yard, a single canister unit sitting atop a wooden pole high above the pen. Suddenly, it went out. Almost immediately, the patter of hundreds of little footsteps sounded in Matt's ears, and frenzied squealing split the still, humid air. Scores of flashlights lit up around Matt. Their beams danced and swirled along the rocks and sand, then settled on the costumed man.

"Give 'em back what's theys, city boy," the crowd screamed.

Matt turned to the man beside him, trying to find an answer in his eyes, but it was too dark. He was suddenly more afraid than he cared to admit.

"If you like this 'un, you might want to stick around," the man said. "They's gonna be more. They's always more."

Stumbling backward away from the man, Matt headed toward the gate through which he had entered. He had seen enough of this display. Tourist attraction, or not, it was growing too weird for his blood.

The wind picked up, its howling almost drowning out the drone of the throng. Empty wrappers and papers swirled above the heads of the crowd, looking like fireflies in the intermittent glare of the flashlight beams.

Matt had just reached the gate when the crowd suddenly grew silent. Against his better judgement, he glanced back toward the pen. As he did, a wicked bolt of lightning streaked down from the sky and struck the pile of sandstone. In the split second that the area was lit up, Matt caught a glimpse of the counter man, and his dark, beady armadillo eyes locked onto Matt's eyes.

Looking up, Matt noticed that there wasn't a cloud in the sky.

Having seen enough, Matt shoved the gate open and ran.

◆

Give 'em back what's theys.

The words haunted Matt's frantic brain as he sprinted back to the motel room and Kayla, his injured wrist throbbing with pain. He still wasn't sure he had hit the armadillo earlier, or not, but he didn't want to stick around to find out. They were getting the hell out of Armadillo, Texas—now.

Matt raced down the row of motel rooms, dug his room key from his pocket, and burst into the room. Kayla shot out of the bed with a wild look in her eyes.

"Jesus Christ, Matt!" she cried. "You scared the shit out of me!"

"Get dressed!" Matt shouted.

"What for?"

"Get dressed!" he insisted.

"Matthew Arnold, what's wrong? You look like you've seen a ghost," she said, reaching for her jeans.

"No, but we may be ghosts if we don't get the hell out of this fucked up town now! These people are insane! I think they just killed a man, Kayla, fed him to the goddamned armadillos!"

"Fed him to the armadillos?" Kayla asked. "What kind of talk is that? Matt, calm down and tell me what's going on!"

"There's no time for that now! I'll tell you later," he said. Matt fumbled through the items he'd earlier placed atop the dresser. "Where are my keys?"

"In my purse," Kayla told him. Fully dressed now, she was throwing their belongings into the suitcase.

Reaching into his wife's purse, Matt grabbed his keys and pulled them out. The dried armadillo foot swayed on the ring.

Matt turned and reached for his suitcase, and a searing jolt of pain shot through his arm just as a bright flash of lightning played across the window. Matt grabbed his arm, and the keys flew from his grip, landing behind the bed. "Dammit!" he shouted.

"Matt! What's wrong?" Kayla asked.

"It's okay!" he said. "Just get the keys!"

Matt grabbed the suitcase and turned as Kayla bent beside the bed to retrieve the keys. She stood, the key ring jingling in her shaking hands.

Matt reached for the keys when Kayla screamed.

A tiny human hand dangled from the key ring. Five shriveled, pink hairless fingers, not toes. Manicured nails and rough cuticles, not claws. A mark ran across the fingers. A zigzag mark. A tire track.

Matt attempted to swallow the scream that was rising in his throat. He hugged the suitcase, holding it tight against his body like a child holding a stuffed animal for security. There was a sudden crunching sound, as of something being ripped apart. Matt dropped the piece of luggage. The shredded cardboard lining spilled from the gaping hole in the suitcase.

Lightning flashed sporadically outside the motel room.

They's gonna be more. They's always more.

Matt finally found his voice, and he screamed. He looked down the length of his right arm to the large armadillo appendage attached to his wrist. The foot was leathery and sparsely covered with coarse hair. A faint musky odor drifted to Matt's nostrils. Matt flexed his muscles, and the four long toes wiggled and stretched. Bits of foam fell from the black claws.

Thunder rumbled outside. Lightning flashed against the windowpanes. The sound of voices, many of them, drifted through the open window. Matt turned, waiting for the residents of Armadillo Village to arrive.

Retrocurses

Amanda Collins peered through the rusted wrought-iron fence that surrounded the centuries-old Massachusetts cemetery, past the scraggly tree limbs that cut through the chilled October air, breaking up the crisp blue sky like cracks in an old oil painting. From her vantage point, Amanda could not see the six new graves, but she could detect the acrid odor of freshly turned soil over the clinging aroma of the moist, rotting leaves that covered the grounds. Amanda moved closer, toward the front gate, and when she spotted the large piles of upturned earth near the rear of the cemetery, she knew the rumors were true.

Amanda frowned. The cemetery had been a place of solitude for her at one time, but now it seemed only cold and forsaken, as cemeteries often are. Was it the encroaching winter, the bitter nip in the air that clawed at her clothing no matter how valiantly the sun fought? Was it the dark cloud of her recent problems that hovered over her and cast a pall over Amanda's presence?

Or was it the idea of the six soon-to-be new inhabitants that had turned her sanctuary from the cruel taunts of her classmates into a dismal setting with all the charm of a prison cell?

Amanda slid the bolt back and pushed the front gate open. She had always enjoyed the grating sound the hinges made, but now the noise seemed excessively loud, as if an alarm sounded at her intrusion. Amanda apprehensively entered the graveyard, trying with no success to soften the crunch of the dry, brittle leaves on the ground.

She moved deliberately past all the familiar old tombstones inscribed with the names of faceless people she had learned to call friends, until she stood before six sparkling white granite markers—new markers all bearing the same date of death: October 16, 1692.

These names were forever etched in the memories of the residents of Downers Grove, the names of six young women tried and convicted of witchcraft and hanged during a dark time in the town's history.

Amanda paused and reflected on each grave, wondering why the arrival of these poor, unfortunate girls was making her so uneasy. They were probably a lot like her, perhaps misunderstood by the adults who governed their world. But when Amanda reached the last stone, she stepped back, suddenly startled for reasons she could not understand.

Abigail Martin. Born October 16, 1676. Died October 16, 1692.

A noise erupted from somewhere behind Amanda, like the unison fluttering of many small birds. She turned with her eyes wide.

A horned owl sat solemnly atop one of the rusted spikes that adorned the fence. Its round, yellow eyes locked onto Amanda's. Tiny ear tufts rose slowly from above its eyes, making it look like a tiny, feathered demon.

Amanda's gaze drifted from the new arrival to Abigail Martin's grave, then back to the owl.

Do you know who I am?

Amanda turned in circles, trying to locate the owner of this voice.

Do you know who I am?

Until she realized the voice was in her head. "No, not again," Amanda moaned to herself. "Go away. Just leave me alone."

I'm the devil.

Amanda stood breathless, staring at the owl through watery eyes, her body shaking uncontrollably.

Sounding distant, yet very near, just behind her, yet all around her, encircling her, cloaking the cemetery with its pitiful mewling, a baby wailed.

Amanda turned and bolted for the entrance, oblivious to the noise the dry, brittle autumn leaves made under her feet.

◆

"Loyal denizens of Downers Grove, Massachusetts," Reverend Denny Brown said. "We have all gathered here today outside our humble church, a church that was built over three hundred years ago with the blood, tears and sweat of our forefathers, for a sort of spiritual healing."

Amanda stared through the crowd of people gathered at the back of Downers Grove Cemetery, catching momentary glimpses of the six black holes cut into the moist, cool earth, her attention focused on the crude, yellow pine boxes at the foot of each grave.

"We all know, even the relative newcomers to our tiny community, what happened on this day in the year of our Lord 1692. A gross atrocity was carried out that day. Six beautiful young women, Sarah Lawson, Rebecca Giles, Abigail Martin, Mary Elizabeth Hawthorne, Patricia Goode, and Susan Winthrop were sentenced to death by hanging. In a time of ignorance and uncertainty, when the well-meaning, yet gravely mistaken town elders were searching for solutions to problems they couldn't quite understand, these victims were singled out and accused of bringing about the troubled times through the devil's magic."

Amanda's mother noticed her daughter's distraction from the proceedings and nudged her. Amanda turned her thoughts back to Reverend Brown, but her attention was soon on what lay within the wooden boxes.

Bones, Amanda. Bones and insects and worms.

"These poor women have lain at the foot of the tree from which they were hanged for three hundred and two years, almost forgotten, their souls in turmoil and bitter unrest. Excommunicated from their church, this church of Downers Grove, they have waited these many, many years for retribution."

"What happened to these girls has been a dark cloud hanging over our community ever since. Today we correct that shameful wrong by readmitting their names into the church records and giving these poor souls a proper burial in our own Downers Grove Cemetery."

The congregation applauded the minister's words, and the appointed pallbearers moved to the foot of each makeshift coffin. The crowd fell silent as the first box was lifted to the edge of the waiting hole.

"Oh, look," Mrs. Spencer said, pointing to the bare tree limbs. "It's an owl."

"Oh, how beautiful," old Mrs. Syler said.

"You don't see many owls in daylight."

Do you know who I am?

Amanda began to shake, her teeth began to chatter, but not because of the chill in the air.

I'm the devil.

"I've heard that an owl appearing during the day is a sign of good fortune to come," someone said.

Reverend Brown stood before the six new graves. "Then it is truly a time of healing. Let us remember this blessed day."

The pine boxes were gently lowered into the ground. Inside, bones that had remained undisturbed for over three hundred years rolled restlessly with the motions.

Bones and insects and maggots.

As the last box, the one holding the remains of Abigail Martin, was returned to the earth, the owl screeched loudly once and flew away.

Amanda closed her eyes tightly and wished she was somewhere far, far away. There was a subtle thumping of clods of dirt hitting thin wood as the homemade coffins were covered.

Something bumped the tip of her nose.

It was a feather.

Don't worry, Amanda. I'll never go away.

◆

Amanda awoke from a restless sleep to the sound of tapping at her bedroom window. She sat up in bed, eyes heavy with sleep, trying to decide if she had dreamed the noise. Another soft rapping confirmed she had not. She pushed the bedspread back and slid from the bed.

The tapping continued as Amanda cautiously approached the window. Her heart beat rapid, and her nightgown stuck to her body from cold sweat. Amanda peered around the edges of the sheer curtain covering the window.

A girl stood outside motioning for Amanda to open the window. Her dark blonde hair floated on the cold, night breeze. An old, tattered dress, seemingly made from some heavy material hung loosely to her pale body, but the girl did not seem to be affected by the chill. Amanda did not know this girl, but something inside her commanded her to open the window.

"Who are you?" Amanda whispered.

"You must not let them keep Abigail Martin in the church," the girl finally said. Her speech was slow, monotonous. "She does not belong."

"She is a witch."

Amanda's heart began beating frantically in her chest. The cold air had dried her lips, and her tongue held no moisture with which to wet them.

"They...they were all witches," Amanda stammered. "According to legend."

"No," the girl said. "Only Abigail. It was she who cursed the town, she who brought the famine. Only she got caught up in her own little game, and she was convicted as well. The curse ended with her death. But she has been given new life now."

The girl looked back nervously over her shoulder. It was then that Amanda noticed she could see right through the girl.

"You must remove her. If she stays on church grounds, her curse will return."

Suddenly, the wind began to intensify. The girl's dress whipped against her thin, white legs as her hair slapped against her soiled face. The spectral visitor's eyes turned skyward, and as the owl descended, its gnarled, yellow talons ripped into the girl's face.

Amanda stepped quietly from the porch, pausing to listen at the front door for any indication that she had awakened her parents. When there was no indication of them waking, she started, flashlight in one hand and shovel in the other, toward the cemetery.

She could not go to the townspeople. She had told her parents earlier about the ghost's visit. They thought she was going crazy again, had probably even called Dr. Prescott already. If her parents didn't believe her, what made Amanda think anyone else would? The townspeople would tell her parents for sure, and then she would have to go back to that horrible place where she had spent six long agonizing months. It was up to her to correct what had been done.

She couldn't blame the townspeople. They had no reason to believe in witches, just as their forefathers had no reason not to believe in them, but the forefathers had been right. They had succeeded in removing the town's curse by disposing of the instigator of the curse, but now, the modern town officials were unwittingly bringing the curse back.

Amanda stopped. She had reached her destination. She placed the flashlight on the ground, aiming it toward Abigail Martin's tombstone. Cold dew clung to the neatly cropped graveyard grass, shining silver in the beam of the flashlight.

The first bite of the shovel dug into the ground, surprising Amanda with the ease at which it slid into the freshly turned earth. Amanda's heavily booted foot pushed it further into the black soil. The damp odor of soured earth wafted to her nose as the shovel repeatedly uncovered more earth. Soon, Amanda found herself at eye level with Abigail Martin's tombstone.

At long last, the shovel made a thumping sound as it struck something solid. Amanda laughed out loud.

She stopped when suddenly an owl cried.

Amanda looked around, but she could not locate the owl in the dark. Working frantically, attempting to ignore the hooting, she dropped to her knees, clawing at the remaining layer of dirt covering the casket until the tips of her fingers were raw and bloody.

They'll put you away forever this time.

Amanda looked up from the grave.

She had never seen a girl so beautiful. The ghostly arrival had pale smooth skin that seemed to glow, framed by long dark hair that almost disappeared in the surrounding blackness of the night. Her lovely white eighteenth-century gown floated in the brisk wind. The bottom hem kissed the pile of earth Amanda had removed.

Poor little Amanda. All that abuse and all those mental problems have finally taken their toll on her. You'll never come back this time.

Panic rose in her throat, and she looked over at the other fresh graves. Against each tombstone, curled in a fetal position and weeping uncontrollably, was a girl clad in a knee-length dress of dirty coarse fabric. Amanda recognized one of them as the girl who had visited her.

The girl looked up from the tombstone. "You can't fight her," she cried. "They won't listen to you, just as they wouldn't listen to us. She'll always win."

"What the hell's going on here?" a man's voice cried out in the darkness.

Amanda turned and was blinded by the high beam of a flashlight. The beam shifted momentarily, allowing Amanda to realize it was old Barney Wilson, the cemetery's caretaker.

"Amanda Collins?" he said, surprised. "Is that you?"

Wilson shined the light into the grave at Amanda.

"Lord a'mighty, girl. What've you done this time?"

They'll put you away forever. You'll never see the sun again.
Abigail Martin stood next to Barney Wilson, staring down at Amanda.

The staccato flapping of wings sounded from overhead, and an owl lit on Abigail's shoulders.

Do you know who I am?

"You crazy dumb girl," Wilson said. "Ain't no one ever gonna believe another word you say, you know that?"

Do you know who I am?

Amanda's eyes grew wide as Barney Wilson unhooked his belt, letting his oversized work trousers fall around his knees.

"Ain't nobody gonna believe nothin' you tell them, girl."

There was a loud thump as Wilson landed beside Amanda on top of Abigail Martin's grave. He smiled, revealing blackened nubs of teeth, and his breath stunk of alcohol.

THE POROSITY OF SOULS

I'm the devil.

◈

It was a sunny, but chilly, Sunday morning when the Downers Grove Church held its first Sunday service since reinstating the victims of the 1692 witch hunt and placing their remains on hallowed grounds.

Reverend Brown's sermon was sincere and passionate, calling for forgiveness and mercy on all lost souls. There were more than a few tears shed.

As the sermon ended and the congregation began to filter slowly from the church, some stopping to pay respects to the hapless victims, Mrs. Abercrombie approached Mrs. Collins.

"Becky, I'm so sorry about Amanda. How is she doing?"

"Well, they're going to keep her indefinitely. I suppose it will be a month-to-month thing from here on out."

"It's sad it had to come to this. She's been through so much. It's the way the world is today. Kids just have too much to deal with. My daughter Tammy has been acting strange lately. Staying out late, coming home smelling of alcohol. It's a troubling time."

"Well, I look at it this way. Amanda was at the end of the road, and we had to make a decision. Things can only get better from here."

Amanda's mother pulled her coat tighter around herself as they stepped outside. The sun was still low on the horizon, and the stiff cool breeze chased brittle, autumn leaves around the dozens of tombstones that dotted Downers Grove Cemetery.

"Oh, look," Mrs. Abercrombie said, pointing toward the back of the cemetery at the last tombstone. "There's our good luck symbol again."

The owl landed elegantly on the crest of Abigail Martin's white granite tombstone and spread its great wings, the long dark shadows thrown by the early morning sun stretching across the other tombstones, cloaking the church grounds in a shroud of darkness.

Genocide for One

The urge was getting to him again, the third night this week. He had to see her.

Raymond stopped at the foot of the stairs that led up to his run-down "efficiency" apartment (there wasn't a fucking thing efficient about it) in Sewell district, one of the more well-to-do shit holes in the inner city. He looked to the skies. He could remember a time when you could check the weather at night by looking for stars in the skies, but not anymore. A flash of lightning, muted by the layer of filth that hovered over the skyline, lit up the night and reflected back at him in the glistening city streets. It might rain, but Raymond didn't want to mess with the cumbersome deflector. So, he'd get stung a little. He'd had worse.

Raymond pulled the collar of his overcoat up over his ears and started down the street. A single, obstinate streetlamp remained burning, keeping a lonely vigil over the desolate scene. Raymond passed the rows of vacant, boarded structures that stared out perpetually from the sidewalks like empty skulls at the rare pedestrian. Somewhere to his right, down a dark narrow alley, an unseen sewer rat snarled, searching for victims of the disease. They used to be called dogs, back in the days before. Raymond had seen pictures, and these sewer rats didn't resemble them at all. They had been known to attack people, but most of the scavengers didn't bother humans unless they were rotting, worm-ridden, and lying on the city streets. Judging from the smell in the air, the sewer rats had plenty to keep their minds off Raymond on this night.

A mere half block later, Raymond found himself breathing with difficulty. The combination of the thin, hot air and the constant film in the sky had sucked the oxygen from his lungs.

A man lay in the shadows coughing, probably dying of the disease. Raymond stepped over him and continued on his way. If the latest rumors flying out of Disease Central had any truth to them, then Raymond was cutting a path right through a sea of the virus. Undoubtedly, this was not a good night to be out, but when was there a good one? The stench of carrion, the possibility of contact with the diseased, the boiling clouds threatening to drop their burning tears on the unprepared—these did little to quell Raymond's desires for her.

Raymond stumbled into Juan's Emporium just before the skies split apart, releasing a torrent of rain that hissed upon the slimy city sidewalks. Heads turned in unison to inspect the newest arrival. The place was crowded tonight. That surprised Raymond a little.

Everyone gets lonely, Raymond. Not just you.

"They sell deflectors here, you know," a stranger said. Raymond couldn't tell if he was being genuinely kind, or just being a smartass. He tried to read the man's eyes, found an empty page, and turned away.

Raymond paused at the knife cabinet and peered into the streets past the iron bars that protected the establishment's windows. The rain was really coming down, and the sky was taking on that sickly orange glow that was so indicative of a good evening storm. Raymond glanced casually at the many knives showcased in the glass cabinet, at the guns stockpiled behind the counter, the deflectors, and other various necessities. *Juan's Emporium—Everything That's Wrong with the World.* The owner kept the illegal stuff stored away in case any government people came snooping around. That wasn't likely, considering the neighborhood.

Raymond moved closer to the counter. Juan was behind the cabinet showing a man one of the government-issue laser-scoped Kilmont rifles he had managed to obtain. A new guy was working the counter, showing an eager youngster some of his choices on the monitor. The sound of computer-generated come-ons filtered through the speakers surrounding the system as the kid flicked through the files. The kid's lust-filled eyes studied the screen. He'd probably never even been with a real woman, and probably never would be. This is what you have to look forward to, kid.

"Yeah," the new guy said, looking in Raymond's direction.

Raymond pointed at the monitor and motioned toward the back of the store.

"Papers, please."

Raymond removed his wallet and pulled out his government card, and a copy of his latest update. The guy took the card and inserted it into a small unit behind the counter. The computer beeped once and ejected the card.

"You're about to expire."

"I know that," Raymond said gruffly. "Don't you think I know that? I still have a few days."

"There'll be a line," the guy said. "End of the check period."

"Just give me Lita," Raymond said, annoyed with the new help.

"I need a number," the guy said.

Raymond wanted to slap the shit out of the punk. "I don't know the fuckin' number," he snapped. "I just know Lita."

The guy gave Raymond an exasperated stare and turned the monitor away from the kid and toward Raymond. Raymond took the small computer unit in his hand and began searching the files. *If Juan was working the counter, I wouldn't have to go through this shit.* But Raymond knew where she was.

The screen stopped scrolling.

"There," Raymond said. "That's Lita."

The guy leaned forward to look at the monitor. His face brightened. "Oh, number 210-LT."

Raymond didn't know why the punk was so fucking happy all of a sudden.

"She's a popular stop tonight," the guy said, waving his hand toward the gathering crowd. He rested his elbows on the counter, and his head moved closer to Raymond. There was something stuck between his two front teeth. "Maybe not all of them, but I'd say most of them."

Raymond turned and looked at the waiting customers. Some sat in the few tattered chairs Juan managed to provide. Others stood at the windows watching the orange rain, and a few pretended to amuse themselves by shopping the shelves and counters. *A sorry looking lot,* Raymond thought. *I wonder how many of them are healthy. I wonder if they're all diseased.*

Of course, they're all healthy. They couldn't be here if they weren't.

Maybe they're healthy physically, Raymond thought, *but there are all kinds of diseases out there.*

"Care to wait?" the new guy asked.

Raymond snatched his card, papers, and pushed his way through the crowd to the store's entrance. The rain still fell heavily on the concrete, gathering in smoking puddles. He pulled on the handle and despised the stares of the vermin waiting to see *his* Lita. Raymond braced himself, gritted his teeth, and sprinted out the door into the rain.

◆

"Jesus, Ray!" the man at the bar shouted. "What are you doing out in this weather?"

Raymond stood just inside the bar's entrance, shaking the stinging droplets of water onto the worn varnished flooring. He looked at Floyd the bartender and gave him a sheepish grin. "It didn't look like rain when I left the house."

"It always looks like rain," Floyd said. "What'll you have?"

Raymond approached the bar, the warm rainwater seeping into his boots making his feet toasty. It was almost soothing. "Gimme a shot of Kloot-Kloot and make it a double."

"A double?" the bartender asked.

"I always order another one anyway, don't I?"

"Can't argue with that logic," Floyd said. He reached for a dark, amber-colored bottle with the shape of a squid etched into the surface and poured the magenta liquid into a small crystal tumbler. A froth formed around the lip of the glass, sneaking over the edge and collecting on the bar top.

Raymond reached for the glass and took a sip of the smooth poison.

"That stuff's gonna kill you, you know," Floyd said.

"If it doesn't, something else will," Raymond said. "I've always wanted to take all of my bad habits, indulge in them like there's no tomorrow until it totally saps my health, then have the doctors tell me which one did me in. Kind of a decadent suicidal race, if you will."

"But what if you died before the doctor could tell you?" Floyd asked, always the philosopher.

Raymond stared past the bartender for a moment, then held the glass up to him. "Then I could say I gave it a good ride." Raymond smiled at his friend. He knew that deep down, Floyd considered him pathetic, a depressing tragedy of the city, but Raymond didn't care. After all, he wasn't the only basket case that Floyd the bartender was forced to shoot the shit with.

"You seem troubled tonight, my friend."

Raymond stared out the grimy windows at the still-falling rain. "The rain," he said. "I hate the rain."

"That why you go out in it without your deflector?"

Raymond didn't answer him, didn't look at him. "You know, my grandfather used to tell me what life was like in the past, before everything got so bad. The kids used to run in the rain wearing nothing but these little swim trunks. They'd run and splash and build little grass and rock dams against the curb to block the water."

"I 'spect it was nice," Floyd said.

Raymond snorted. "It's ancient history now. Nothing's like it used to be. No more cats. Dogs are fucking rodents. Birds are all gone," Raymond said, his eyes glazing over with the memory. "They had nowhere to go, or they were too stupid to know. I read somewhere that scientists once believed that dinosaurs evolved into birds, that they didn't really go extinct. You've heard of dinosaurs?" Raymond asked, finally facing the bartender again. Floyd shook his head. "Well, doesn't matter. Looks like they finally did go extinct anyway. I guess everything dies out eventually, in its own way." Raymond downed the last of his drink and held the tumbler out for another.

"I went to see Lita again today," Raymond continued.

"Oh, how was that?" the bartender asked, refilling Raymond's glass with the squid juice.

"Didn't get to see her. Everyone was waiting for her. Line was long. New kid there's an asshole," Raymond mumbled. "None of those hard dicks care about her. Not a damned one of them. It's just a game to them. It's just sex. That's all."

"You know, Ray," Floyd said, "it's not real."

Raymond looked up from the glass suspiciously. "What do you mean?"

"Juan's Emporium. The virtual sex thing. Lita. She's not real, Ray. She's just an image. She's not real."

Raymond looked down the length of the bar, absorbing the bartender's statement for a moment. "But she's the closest thing there is anymore."

"That may be true, buddy. But you have to keep the whole thing in perspective."

"There isn't any perspective anymore, Floyd. It's gone. Went extinct with the birds and the cats. You can't tell one thing from another. Lines intersect, shadows melt into one another. Angles are all wrong. Nothing makes sense anymore. You can't tell what's real and what ain't. Except for the rain...and...other things." He smiled seemingly at nothing. "Yeah, some things you can."

Floyd poured himself a shot of a milder drink and leaned over the bar across from Raymond. He took a small swill of the liquid. "I went in last week for clamping."

"I'm due in a couple of days, but I don't know if I'm going, or not," Raymond said."You have to go, Ray. It's the law."

"I know it's the law, but when you get right down to it, it's genocide," Raymond argued. "Controlled genocide. Gradual, fucking controlled genocide."

"It's not genocide, Ray. It's the only thing the government could do. You know that. It was showing signs of mutating, of becoming airborne. If it does that, we're all dead."

"It ain't right," Raymond said. "That's what killed the cats off. A neutering here, a spaying there. Population control, they said. A few die here, a few die there. Next thing you know, there's none left. And that's what's going to happen to us, if the government has their way."

"I have to disagree with you there," the bartender said. "The only way to destroy the disease was to limit the ability for it to be spread. If sexual contact is made temporarily impossible, and those already afflicted die, then we have a chance."

Raymond slammed his fist down on the bartop. "No one has the right to control my fucking mind!" he shouted. "*No one!* No one can shoot a laser inside my brain and cut off a nerve to shut down any part of my body! It just ain't right!"

"But it's the only way, Raymond."

"What if it takes too long for the disease to die off? What then? We might miss an entire generation! We, as a society, might never recover from that!"

"It's a chance that has to be taken. You have to understand that."

Raymond stood up from the bar and lifted the tumbler to his mouth, downing the last of the drink. He laid his credit chip down on the bar top.

"Things might even get back to the way they used to be, Ray, like your grandfather told you about. Wouldn't that be something to see? You'd like that, wouldn't you, if things were like that?" Floyd asked, scanning the chip.

Raymond stopped in front of the closed door as a brilliant bolt of lightning flashed wickedly across the night sky, turning the boiling clouds a bright red orange. The rainwater that dripped from the protective roof and splashed against the windowpanes etched little concavities into the surface of the glass, distorting the view of the city streets.

Raymond reached for the door handle. "Not fuckin' likely," he said, without looking back.

It was a little past two in the morning. The rain had stopped. Only a few cooling puddles remained in the streets and on the sidewalks. Juan's Emporium had closed at one, but Juan was inside, moving around behind the counter under the few bulbs that remained burning. The new kid was nowhere to be seen. Raymond tapped sharply on the window. Juan looked up and mouthed the words, "We're closed." Raymond rapped harder on the pane, and Juan came around the counter toward the door.

Raymond waited impatiently as Juan unlocked the door and pulled it open to the tune of the door chimes overhead.

"Ray," the owner said, "I didn't know it was you."

Juan pulled the door open further and allowed Raymond to step inside before closing and locking it again.

"I didn't see you leave earlier," Juan said.

"Too many people in here. Too hot and crowded. And I don't like the new kid," Raymond explained.

"He's just a street kid," Juan said. "He's doing the best that he can."

"That's a cop-out," Raymond snapped. "He's just another liberal rat. Wanting the government to fix everything, to take care of everything, to hold their fucking hand all the time." Raymond followed Juan to the counter. "Well, they got what they wanted. Total government regulation. Only, it doesn't work the way they thought it would, and now they blame the government for all the problems."

"Maybe." Juan shrugged.

"You know, that's why we have the clamping. People bitched and moaned long enough so that the government finally came up with their own way to deal with the disease."

"Tommy said your papers are almost expired," Juan said.

"Almost," Raymond said, reaching for his wallet. "But not yet."

"What do you want at two in the morning, Ray?"

"I want Lita," he answered. "I want her alone, not with all those other jerks standing around."

"It's late, Ray."

"I've got credit," Raymond answered. "You know my chip is good."

Juan reached for the computer console behind the counter. "She's not real, you know. It's all in your head."

"Maybe this whole messed up world's just in my head, Juan. You ever think of that?"

Juan shook his head. "Go on back. I'll set it up."

"Thanks, Juan. You're a real friend. And Lita thanks you, too."

Juan smiled, and Raymond headed toward the back of the establishment.

"You know, Raymond," Juan called out. "If you don't get your papers renewed, you're not gonna be able to keep doing this. Nothing personal, but the law's the law."

"Why do you suppose they make you check papers, Juan? If this isn't *real*, then why does it all have to be so fucking monitored? What would it hurt?"

"I don't make the rules, Ray. I just play by them, just like you."

"Is Lita ready?" Raymond asked.

"Go on in and get ready. She will be."

Raymond sat in the console chair, the bulky visor-helmet strapped securely to his head, the earplugs placed firmly in his ears, annihilating all sounds and senses. Darkness surrounded him, and the smokey visor blocked out all remaining light. Raymond closed his eyes. He could not discern the difference.

He leaned back in the suspended lounger, and didn't acknowledge the leather squeaking beneath him. His arms rested on the sides, though he didn't notice the cool material of the armrests at his fingers.

The mark grew on his head, the tiny point of laser entry just above his right ear, nestled in the center of the small tell-tale bald spot.

That, he could feel. Always, that he could feel.

Raymond tried to discard the thought and concentrated on the relaxation. There were no sounds, saved for the white noise drone of silence.

Then, the touch on the shoulder. Soft, light, feminine. A touch he knew wasn't there.

The playful sensation of strands of hair, platinum and shiny, cascading over his ears, down his neck, across his shoulders, sliding down over his bare chest, farther to points beyond.

The warmth of her breath on his neck, the soft touch of her lips on his shoulder, the pleasurable experience of her wet tongue pressing against his chest, his belly, and beyond.

His hands gripped her head, his fingers wove in and out of the silky wisps of her hair like an erotic tapestry, his nostrils drank in the aroma of his excitement, his sweat, her femininity.

And all the while, Raymond longed to touch her.

◆

At four in the morning, Raymond was walking through the humid city streets, heading home at last. The streets were quiet. Not even a sewer rat stirred in the dark depths. There was an odd sensation between his legs as he walked and was aware of a feeling that he at one time considered uncomfortable, a feeling that had been, too long gone. A miniscule wet spot had formed on the inside of his briefs.

He welcomed the sensation.

◆

Raymond hid in the shadows of the alley across the street from Juan's Emporium. Juan stood alone in the darkness, locking up the establishment for the night. It had been only a few hours since Juan had denied Raymond entrance to his business. It had been a week since Raymond had been inside Juan's Emporium.

And a week since he had seen his Lita.

Raymond removed the papers from his deflector and crumpled them in his hand—the papers that he had tried to alter—and tore them, tossing them into the air and following them, as they scattered in the breeze. He wouldn't get them updated. *He couldn't.*

He was through with the governmental control of his life. He didn't need it. Though he longed for the days that his grandfather experienced, he knew they were over. They would not return. Dogs would not chase cats. Birds would not sing in the spring. Children would not frolic in April showers.

People would not reproduce.

That was the short end of it. That was at the bottom line of the facts, no matter how small the print. The longer the government kept intruding into people's minds, the longer mankind would be stunted.

He was through with it. He would play the game no longer.

Crowbar in hand, Raymond checked the streets in either direction and trotted across to Juan's storefront. Raymond slid the crowbar between the first rod of the burglar bars and the brick wall and then pulled. The bars pulled easily from the crumbling, acid-weakened mortar and fell crashing to the sidewalk, almost hitting his foot. The distant yelp of alarmed sewer rats was the only response to the noise. Raymond brought the crowbar over his head and shattered the first window, raking the bar across the bottom of the window to remove any jagged shards of glass. Raymond pulled himself inside Juan's Emporium.

The only light burning in the building was a single bulb hanging over the counter. Raymond swiftly smashed the bulb and pulled a small penlight from his pocket. The tiny beam of light settled on the computer console lying atop the counter.

Raymond hit the "power" button and waited. The computer whirred, beeped twice, and then the monitor flickered. A smiling female face appeared on the screen. *A whore's face.* Raymond slapped frantically at buttons on the keyboard, and finally, the whore faded away. Another took her place. Then another. And another.

Until *she* appeared. Number 210-LT.

"Her name is Lita," Raymond said under his breath. "She's not a fucking number."

Raymond entered the coding sequence necessary to activate the system. He knew the procedure. He had seen Juan do it enough times. The name of the last customer to use Lita was still entered in the file's databank. Raymond did not type his own name into the system. Lita knew him. She knew his name. Lita loved him.

It was dark again. Raymond's senses were nullified. He floated in the deep void.

And then, she spoke.

"Raymond," the sultry voice said in the darkness. "It's so nice to see you again." The voice was soft, inviting, not electronic, not contrived. *Not fake.*

"Lita, I'm sorry it's been so long since I saw you last. I'm sorry I left you to all those...others."

"They mean nothing to me. Absolutely nothing."

Then, she appeared in the light, not fuzzy and distorted as she was on the screen, but soft, glowing, and alive. Her round, tear-filled blue eyes pierced his senses, her luscious red lips invited. Her long, shining blonde hair draped across her shoulders and over her breasts, her dark round nipples peeking ever-so-slightly through the strands. Her flat belly followed a gentle sloping curve to the golden thatch of hair that nestled between her long, bronzed legs. She approached him gracefully, like a long-extinct cat.

Raymond was growing, his member pressing furiously against the material of his trousers, snagging his pubic hair and pulling at them painfully. He shifted his weight in the lounger.

"You're so different from all the others," she whispered as her face leaned toward Raymond's. "You're so real."

Her lips met Raymond's lips softly, and he reached for her, taking her satin-soft hair in his hands, accepting the full length of her darting, moist tongue, tasting appreciatively the delicate flavor of her mouth. She pulled away and stared into Raymond's eyes.

"Take me there," she said. "Take me where they used to play, when people were alive."

Raymond took her in his arms and kissed her, his hands running across her smooth, toned back, his arms squeezing her until he feared she would snap in his hands. He closed his eyes and inhaled her scents. Her soft hair, her warm breath, the musky aroma of her sex.

The first drops of the gentle rain, cool and invigorating, bounced across his bare back, a back free of weighty deflectors. He experienced the joyous laughter of the children playing in the distance. The birds flitted and chirped, chasing each other in a romantic, spring courtship. Cats chased butterflies and dogs chased frisbees in the flowing meadow.

She laughed, let her hair fall back, and Raymond absorbed the intoxicating feeling of her long mane brushing his arms as they encircled her waist. He took her mouth to his again, and laid her down in the soft grass, among the dandelions and sunflowers.

His hands moved along her sides, slipped up under her breasts, played momentarily, and drifted back down to her waist, subtly parting her legs. He closed his eyes as he entered her and embraced the warmth of her body. Warm, wet, but not burning. *Not like the rain.* The sun shone down from above, and the cool rain continued to splash down on his back.

She moaned and closed her eyes as the tall flowers swayed and danced above them. Nature's voyeurs. Her tiny hips undulated beneath him, grinding against him pleasurably as his gentle thrusts reciprocated the sensation. She threw her beautiful head from side to side in her mounting passion. Wet strands of her hair, darkened by the rain, slapped at his face. The intensity in his loins grew with a fire that he hadn't felt for a long time, but that he had experienced only weeks earlier. She cried out passionately, biting his shoulder. Raymond threw his head back as the intensity was reaching its peak. She screamed and squeezed his neck tightly, shuddering, her breath coming in sharp, orgasmic rasps. Raymond's fingers dug into her shoulders as he began to throb spastically. He pushed himself deeper inside of her and cried out as he spent himself. It felt as if it wouldn't, shouldn't, stop.

The rain continued to fall. The flowers looked away.

Raymond stood outside the shattered window of Juan's Emporium. The streets were empty and death quiet. Nothing unusual about that. No one had responded to the break-in at Juan's store.

Light splatters of rain smacked against the awning above his head and spilled over the sides, collecting in smoldering puddles on the sidewalk. Raymond started to don his deflector, decided not to, and tossed it into the gutter. The rain didn't bother him anymore.

He turned once more and looked into Juan's Emporium. He wouldn't see Lita, 210-LT anymore. After all, she was just an image. She would *always* be there, for everyone to know.

Raymond loved her, but she was everyone's favorite, and she could never love him and only him.

I've got your fucking genocide.

Raymond coughed and looked at his forearm. He squeezed his arm just below the elbow, as the veins bulged from under his skin. A tiny droplet of water bounced from the sidewalk and found his arm, sizzling slightly.

The virus wasn't airborne, not yet anyway, but it wasn't that difficult to contract the disease if you wanted to badly enough. After all, the streets were practically littered with its victims. You just had to get there before the sewer rats did.

Raymond started for home, his heart still pumping from the exertion of exiting through the shattered window. Beneath his coat, under his skin, through his veins, the disease roared at high speed, eating him alive, burning at his being more than the stinging rain could ever hope to. The same old disease, yet a new disease, an improved disease. One that the government could never hope to control.

I've got your fucking genocide.

A sewer rat peered out anxiously from the alley across the street. Their keen sense of smell could always locate death. They could always find the disease.

A virtual disease. A virtual hell.

And the line was long, indeed.

Options

April "Angel" Anderson leaned back in the bathtub in her dirty, modest apartment, her head just above the surface, letting the warm, calming waters soothe her tainted soul. She reached for the soap and began to scrub vigorously over her face and breasts. His sweat, his saliva, his semen was physically gone from her body, but the emotional scars that his body fluids left behind—scars that cut deeper and deeper with each passing trick—would never disappear. After a while, as it so often did, the mounting mental anguish surpassed the delicate façade her will displayed, and April cried, burying her face in a washcloth.

After a brief interlude of tears, April reached for the shower radio and flicked it on. The end of Bad Company's "Shooting Star" emanated from the tiny crackling speaker. April had always thought that was a sad song, but she preferred the sad songs. For reasons she could not explain or deny, the sad songs always made her feel better.

Aerosmith's "Angel" came on the radio next, followed by U2's "Angel of Harlem." *Why does every other goddamn rock 'n roll song have the word "angel" in the lyrics?* April pondered. Angel was April's "professional" name, and all those damn songs served as constant reminders. One of her first customers had started calling her "Angel," and the term had stuck, much to her chagrin.

April closed her eyes, hoping to prevent the tears from returning. *How had it all happened?* she mused. It wasn't supposed to be like this. She had run away from home at fifteen to be a dancer and to escape the abuse of her alcoholic stepfather. That was all she wanted. That's all she had ever wanted, but her decision had been disastrous. Now, several drug overdoses, a couple of abortions, and countless sin-filled evenings later, nothing had changed. How had it happened? April didn't know. The only thing she was certain of was that her former life was a thing of the past. What was that old saying, "you can never go back?"

If you can't go back, and it hurts too damn much to go forward, what's left?

Suicide.

Suicide, April's thoughts repeated. There it was again. That word was always finding its way into her thoughts, slipping into her head like an alley cat through a forbidden door. She tried so hard to keep it away, but it was always there in the back of her mind, just waiting for a moment of weakness to allow it to come forward.

And why not? It had worked for Sarah.

April thought of Sarah, her co-worker and lone true friend on the streets. She had confided in Sarah, trusted her, turned to her when she thought all was lost. Sarah had taken a nose-first dive from a twelve-story window a few days ago. Witnesses had said she screamed something about wanting to fly. She did for a while. Until the air gave out and the sidewalk began.

And now April was alone. Truly alone. Sarah was gone, and April would never see her again.

Unless you kill yourself.

April looked across the toilet to the pack of razor blades lying on the vanity.

Do it...do it...do it.

She had tried to throw them out many times before—*do it...do it*—but something deep in her soul would not allow it. *You might need them someday*, that something had whispered to her. *You might need to shave your legs—do it...do it—or you might need to open a tightly wrapped package, or...*

You might need them to slice open your wrists.

Oh, Sarah, how could you do this? Can't you see what it's done to me? April had considered suicide countless times in the past, but Sarah's friendship had always kept her from going through with it. And now, in that ironic kick in the groin that life so often is, Sarah had been the one. Sarah, who never seemed down. Sarah, who never talked of taking her life. Sarah, who never dreamed of flying.

April's eyes focused on the razor blades, intensified, sharp. The shampoo bottles, the make-up, the ceramic tile behind the small box blurred around the blades.

Do it...

She could see everything clearly, read the entire wording on the colorful package. Use only as directed. Please do not use contents to slash wrists. The publicity would be bad for our company.

It would be so easy, she thought. *It would be so easy to take one blade—it couldn't weigh more than an ounce—one tiny blade, place it horizontally across the soft skin of your wrist, press down ever so slightly, allowing the sharp edge to explore the depths of your epidermis, gently slide the blade from one side to the other, back and forth, as the layers part and spread to either side, and watch your life blood—ooh, the pretty colors—ebb from your ravaged veins.*

April looked away from the blades and leaned back further in the warm water. She was not Sarah. She was better than that. She reached out and turned up the volume of her melancholy, but sole, companion.

TERRY CAMPBELL

◈

April closed the door behind her and entered her apartment, pausing at the entrance to wipe the waning tears from her face. This past evening, her latest trick had turned violent. April had been slapped around by customers a few times before, but never with this severity. That's what happens when you worked without a pimp. Some bastard decides he doesn't want to pay, you demand your money, he beats the shit out of you, and there's nothing you can do about it.

April reached for a tissue to wipe the blood from her mouth, wincing as her ribs cried out in pain. She stared at her haggard reflection in the mirror, her face purple and black with bruises. April turned from the mirror, coughing and choking, and struggled to her bedroom, where she fell face down in tears.

There was no radio playing now. No sad songs, no ballads about angels. They wouldn't help her any way. Not anymore. A superficial stimulus can only provide hope for so long until you're forced to face reality. April had reached the end of her tolerance. She wanted to die.

She turned her head to the other side and stared at the sleeping pills sitting on the nightstand. The bottle appeared distorted through her watery eyes, and she wondered what it would feel like to just go to sleep and never wake up. She enjoyed sleeping. It was the only time when she wasn't thinking about her miserable life and wondering how things had gotten so crazy.

It would be nice to sleep forever. *It wouldn't be so bad if I took the pills,* she told herself. It would be like going to sleep, just taking a little nap. Nothing wrong with a little nap, is there? Of course, not. You like naps, April.

It's not so bad, April.

No, it wouldn't be bad at all. April knew she could never slice herself with a razor blade, or dive out of a hotel window, or put a bullet through her brain. Those things would be too painful, too messy.

It's not so bad, April. Really, it's not.

She might want to die, but she didn't like the idea of pain, even if it was to be only a brief encounter, but the sleeping pills wouldn't be so bad. No, not bad at all.

It's not so bad, April. Listen to me.

April sat up in bed, staring wide-eyed at the window. She slowly began to realize that she had been hearing voices outside her window. Voices? Outside the window? Nine floors up?

Then there was a fluttering noise, as of the flapping of great, feathered wings. An angel? And then the voice, soft, dreamy, the voice of a woman coming from outside the window. A rapping on the panes. Pigeons? Raindrops striking against the glass?

It's not so bad, April. Let me in. Let me show you.

April rose from the bed, mesmerized by the disembodied voice, a voice that sounded all too familiar. She moved slowly, quietly over to the window and pulled up the shade.

Sarah stood on the narrow ledge outside the window. April's initial reaction to the sight was not shock, or surprise at seeing her dead friend nine stories up. Instead, her first thoughts were of how beautiful Sarah looked. Her long golden hair shimmered in the cool breeze, framing her soft, pale face in a glowing aura of subdued light. The blue of her eyes was obvious even through the grimy glass of the window. She was dressed in a long flowing white gown, and her feet were bare. Sarah had never looked lovelier.

Instinctively, April opened the window and stepped back to allow Sarah to enter the room. Sarah's hair and gown continued to flutter in the breeze until April closed the window.

"Hello, April," Sarah said. "I came back to see you."

"Sarah, they told me you were dead."

"I was, but now I'm back."

"I don't understand," April said.

"You don't deserve to live like this, April. I didn't deserve to live like I did. We didn't choose these things for ourselves. But I changed it. And so can you."

"What do you mean?" April asked.

"You've been thinking certain thoughts, haven't you? I know that you have because you used to tell me."

"So, what if I have?" April stiffened, trying to put on an aloof, brave front. "What's it to you?"

"Oh, it's a lot to me."

"Well, if you came here to give me a speech about how wrong suicide is, you can just save it for someone else. You left me. I needed you, Sarah. You were my only friend, the only one I could trust. You're a fine one to be talking."

"Exactly. I'm the perfect one to be talking. I didn't come here to tell you how to run your life. I simply came to offer you an option."

"I can fly now, April," Sarah said. "I can fly."

April looked into Sarah's crystal-blue eyes. "Really? You can fly?"

"How do you think I got up here?"

April shrugged. "Are you an angel now?"

"I suppose you could call me an angel. I've come to show you something, April. I've come to offer an alternative to your life." She took April's hands in her own. "Close your eyes, dear. Close your eyes, turn off your mind, and relax."

April closed her eyes. At first, there was only darkness, but gradually a white mist began to swirl in front of her. Billowy clouds floated along an endless white road, followed by stars. So many beautiful stars. And colors. All the colors of the rainbow intertwined among the bright stars. "Is this Heaven?" April asked.

"Not really," Sarah answered. "I guess you could call it Heaven. Everyone interprets it in their own way."

"You *are* an angel," April said.

"No, I'm not really an angel, April. Angels are from Heaven, and I'm not really from Heaven. You see, I did the same thing you always contemplated. All those times I talked you out of it just made it harder for me. I was adding your burden on top of my own."

"I'm so sorry, Sarah. I was so selfish," April cried.

"No, no, April. You don't need to apologize because it's all better now. If it weren't for you, I wouldn't know this place, the wonderful, glorious place. And I couldn't show it to you."

"It's so pretty there, and so peaceful. I want to go there," April insisted.

"You can go there, April. You can go there with me. It's a much better place than this sad existence you're in now."

"But if it's not Heaven, then what? Surely not hell," April said.

Sarah paused. "No, not hell. I don't know what it is. It's just an alternative. Sometimes, people are dealt horrible cards in life. Is it fair that God allows His children to live the shameful lives they've lived? Is it fair to punish lost souls because they simply could not survive in their terrible worlds? Some people have no choice. If God can't understand that, and if He is so cruel as to allow these people to spend eternity in hell, then maybe there should be something better. This place, this better place, is an alternative to Heaven and hell. I don't know where it came from, or who controls it. All I know is that it works. Trust me, April. Believe me. I've been there, and tonight, I've shown you what it's like. I don't want to see you live like this anymore, April."

"It can be like this always?" April asked, not daring to open her eyes from the pleasant visions in her head.

"Always," Sarah said. "Always and forever."

"I'd like that," April whispered. "I'd like a better place."

When April opened her eyes again, Sarah was gone. She looked to the window. *Was she ever here? Did she dream the whole thing?* April stared at the pill bottle on the nightstand.

"I want to go there, Sarah," she said softly. "I want to see you again, in a better light. In a better place."

◆

April's eyes were closed, and her head was spinning. She thought she could see the same mists and clouds that Sarah had shown her, but everything was swirling so rapidly she couldn't be sure. Yet, the thought of the wonderful alternative, the better place, and of seeing her only friend again calmed her anxieties.

When her world stopped spinning, April opened her eyes and found herself sitting in a waiting room with several other people. She looked around at the others, but they all quickly looked away to avoid eye contact with her. The walls all around her were so stark white, the edges so seamless that she couldn't tell where the floor ended, and the walls began. Finally, a space opened on one wall, and a woman dressed in white called her name.

"Yes?" April answered nervously.

"You may go in now," the woman said.

April rose slowly, feeling very apprehensive, and followed the woman into the next room. This room looked exactly like the waiting room, except for the huge black desk in the center. A tall, thin man dressed in a sharp suit and tie, sat in a chair behind the desk.

"April Anderson?" he asked. His voice was like the rough bark of a tree. "Please, sit down."

"Where am I? What is this place?" she asked, her voice quivering.

"You don't know?" the man asked, sounding somewhat surprised. He ran a pen down the length of some paperwork. "Oh," the man said, obviously seeing something of interest in his papers. "Oh, now I understand. You're the first one. Congratulations. You're in the Option."

"The Option?" April asked.

"You really don't know, do you?" the man smiled. He looked like every trick she had ever performed all rolled into one. April didn't like this place. It didn't look anything like the place Sarah had shown her.

"The Option #8936. It's a new deal we're offering down here. It's kinda like making a swap, trading straight up for someone else." The man looked down at his paperwork again and pushed a button on the intercom. "Ms. Fields, have Sarah #125,345 brought up from Number Seven," he said into the box. He looked back at April. "I don't know what she told you, or how she got you here, but I must inform you of this, Ms. Anderson, you've been duped. That's what this new plan is all about. You see, Mr. Big Man Upstairs set down some laws long ago. One of them was that suicide is the ultimate no-no. You commit suicide, you screw up big time. When God gives you something, he gets pretty pissed if you try to give it back."

"What...what do you mean I've been duped?" April stammered.

The man looked at his paperwork again. "A woman named Sarah come to see you?" April nodded. "A good friend of yours, too, wasn't she?" The man chuckled. "Oh, I love this. The Option is something new we came up with down here. It's sort of a way of giving suicide victims a second chance when they get down here and find they don't like what we're all about. You ever read Dante? No? Didn't figure you did. Not many people do anymore. Anyway, we let suicides have a chance to reverse what they've done. But there's a catch."

"What are you talking about?" April demanded to know.

"Suicides can get their souls back and go home to good old Earth like nothing ever happened. The catch is, they must talk someone real close to them into taking their place." The sleazy man chuckled again. "Plays hell with their minds."

The intercom buzzed. "Yes?" the man asked, leaning over into the speaker.

"Sarah #125,345 is here," the box said.

"Send her in with her file," the man answered. "This is gonna be good. You see, she tricked you. Made you take your own life so she could have hers back."

"But that's not fair," April cried.

"Hey, sweetie. First rule of hell. We don't have to play fair. And being a suicide, you don't have much to say about it. If you were in the first, or second circle, maybe we could talk. But the seventh. Honey, you're in deep."

A door opened, and Sarah stood in the doorway, a file in one hand and a suitcase in the other. She realized April was sitting in the chair and looked quickly away to the man behind the desk.

"Congratulations, Sarah #125,345. As one of the first to complete your agreement in Option #8936, you have your soul back and are free to return to your former life. And as soon as you sign these papers, you're outta here."

"You didn't tell me she was going to be here," Sarah said sternly.

"Why, my dear," the man said, a wide toothy grin stretching across his pallid face. "That's all part of the fun. You didn't think we'd let you out of here without just a little bit of guilt, did you?"

April stood up and raced over to Sarah. "How could you? How could you do this to me? I trusted you! You were supposed to be my friend! I believed what you said! I believed in what you showed me! I believed in a better place!"

"April, I'm sorry," Sarah said. "I'm sorry it had to be like this, but I had no choice. If there was any other possible way, I would have done it. I had no choice. You don't know what it's like down there. You just have no idea."

The man in the suit was covering his mouth to stifle his laughter. He was enjoying himself.

"I just don't see how someone could be so selfish, so self-centered that they would talk a friend into taking their own life," April argued.

"I'm sorry, honey. I really am. But you don't have to stay here. You can do the same thing. You can do the same thing that I did."

"No, I can't do that," April said forcefully. "I could never do that to anyone. Never."

Sarah nodded. "You can say that now, but what will you say for the rest of eternity, down in that damned jungle?"

"*La mesta selva*—the sad wood," the man said. He looked at Sarah. "She hasn't read Dante. That's where you'll spend eternity, Ms. Anderson. With the rest of the suicides. Anyway, sign here Sarah #125,345 and you'll be on your way."

Sarah hastily scribbled her name across the dotted line and threw the pen back at the man. "You bastard. I hope you're having fun with your new plan."

"You can always kill yourself again and come back," the man laughed.

"Piss off," Sarah said, and turned for the door. She paused in front of April. "I'm sorry, April. I really am."

April did not look up. For some reason she could not quite explain, Sarah's eyes did not seem to be as pretty as they had before. The blue had faded. Sarah touched April's cheek, wiping away a tear before leaving the room.

The man spoke into the intercom as April stood in front of the desk, still staring at the white floor.

"You know, she's right," the man said. "You can sign up for the Option as well. All you have to do is find a friend, or a family member, anyone close to you." April did not answer. "Well, maybe this will help you make up your mind."

April looked up, and one wall of the stark white room became a gigantic television screen split into two halves. On one side was an image of herself, sitting on the bed moments before her spectral encounter with Sarah, staring at the bottle of sleeping pills. On the other half of the screen was Todd Wright, April's old boyfriend. They had dated right up to the time April ran away. He sat on the edge of the bed in his room, a small caliber handgun gripped tightly in his hands. April sat in horror as Todd placed a bullet slowly into each chamber, paused, his face dripping with sweat, then tilted the gun, letting the bullets slide freely to the floor. He repeated the motion again and again.

The man moved up behind April. "Wow, he's a real mess. He's been that way ever since you left. He blames himself. You know. Says he should've been there more for you. What a guy. Two years. Two whole years of thinking about it, putting it off, thinking about it some more." The man sighed and headed for the door. "What to do. What to do."

April winced as the door slammed behind him, once again turning the room into a seamless white cubicle. *The Option,* she thought. *Could she, do it? Could she do to someone else what Sarah had done to her? Could she withstand the tortures she was sure to endure now, or would she break and enter the Option?*

April looked back up at the huge split screen. Herself on one screen. Beaten, deflated, exhausted. Todd on the other screen. A day-to-day struggle to cope.

Two lives, lost in self-doubt, uncertainty, and pain, each just needing the heartfelt advice of a friend to push them over the edge.

The Eyes of the Gypsy

Robbie's eyes studied Josh's reflection in the rear-view mirror, observing the careful, tedious manner in which he cleaned his .357. Something in the way Josh treated that gun was unnerving, the way his hands seemed to caress the cold blue steel of the barrel, the way his fingers slid across the magazine, tracing every curve in the metal. That gun was a part of Josh, his own flesh and blood.

Sometimes, Josh frightened Robbie. He wondered if Josh had the capability to kill another human being. He had known Josh since high school, but he had never really known him. He was so moody, so strange, and a little on the unpredictable side. So far, they had been lucky. No one had been hurt in their little cross-country spree. Twelve hold-ups, twelve clean escapes. *What would happen if they were ever challenged? What if someone else had a gun, and knew how to use it?* Robbie turned his eyes away from Josh. He didn't want to think about that.

He looked across the seat at Cindy, and the sight of her made him smile. She was staring out the window, watching the beautiful mountain scenery roll by, oblivious to all. Robbie silently wondered what was going through her mind. Mexico, perhaps? That was the real reason for this little adventure, at least from their standpoint. They hoped to get enough money to run away to the border, maybe even get married. That wasn't important. There was plenty of time for that later. He just wanted to give her a good life, something he could never manage on an honest man's wages.

He looked once again at Josh, still tinkering with his .357. He opened and closed the magazine, back and forth, like a child amazed by the actions of a light switch. *He hasn't put the damn thing down since the last heist,* Robbie thought.

He tried once again to take his mind off Josh. He reached down and changed stations on the radio, catching the end of some Steely Dan song. Robbie looked ahead at the winding mountain road. They hadn't passed a gas station, or anything else for that matter, in quite some time. He glanced at the fuel gauge. They would need to stop for gas soon.

They drove on, each of them saying nothing, entertaining their own private thoughts.

It was Cindy who finally broke the silence. "How much did we get back there?" she asked, turning to face Josh.

Josh snapped the magazine shut and laid the gun gently between his legs. He pulled out a roll of bills from his pocket and began to count slowly, pausing to inhale the aroma of the money.

"Eight-five," he muttered. "Eighty-five fuckin' dollars."

"That's not much, is it honey?" she asked Robbie.

Robbie sighed. "No," he answered. "No, that won't last long."

"We'll just have to pull another job," Josh said in his low monotone voice.

Robbie looked back at Josh again, trying to get some clue to his feelings by the look on his face. Josh was holding a slug in his hand, rolling it around in his palm, caressing it the way you do a girl's tits for the first time. But his face was emotionless.

Robbie could hold his feelings back no longer. "Why do you have to carry such a heavy piece, man?"

Josh didn't look up, didn't take his eyes off the gun. He gingerly held the bullet in his fingertips, and carefully slid it slowly into a cartridge. Without missing a beat, he replied, "Why not?"

"We're not looking to kill anyone, man. If worse comes to worse, we hurt them. They can't stop us. We get away. You plug someone with that, even in the leg, they don't walk again."

Josh took out a cigarette and lit it. Snapping the cover shut on his lighter, Josh exhaled slowly and met Robbie's gaze in the mirror, the smoke masking his face. He smiled, but there was no humor in it.

"That why you carry that piddly-ass B.B. gun of yours?"

"It'll do the job," Robbie said sternly.

"Bullshit."

"Bullshit, it will."

"Supposin' you have to defend yourself, man. Lotta good a .22'll do you. You use that on someone, and they'll just laugh at ya."

"I doubt that," Robbie argued.

"What about cops, man?" Josh pressed, tapping ashes onto the floorboard. "Cops don't mess around. They carry some heavy shit. Put yer ass down in a heartbeat."

Robbie started to say something else, but Cindy grabbed his shoulder to restrain him. She hadn't said so, but she was frightened of Josh as well. He could see it in her eyes.

Josh laughed, a wave of coughs coming from his nicotine-stained lungs. "Yeah, I can see it now," he said through his hacking. "You'll be layin' on the ground with this big fuckin' hole in yer guts, squeezin' down on that goddamn .22, cryin' 'Shit, I shoulda listened to Josh.' Wouldn't that be somethin'?"

Josh stopped laughing and looked intently out the car window. "Besides," he said slowly, "I like my gun."

Robbie shook his head, but remained silent. Cindy took his hand and squeezed it, offering him comfort. Robbie flashed her a warm smile. She made him feel better. Maybe things would be okay. Maybe his nerves were just getting to him. Josh wasn't such a bad guy. Not really. Springsteen came on the radio wailing "Born to Run." That was them. The three of them, born to run. Troublemakers and hell-raisers since they were old enough to know better. He should have known they would end up like this. Running. Stealing. He glanced back at Josh, toying with his gun once again. Maybe even killing.

Robbie pulled the old Nova into the dirt parking lot, stopping next to a set of old rusted gas pumps. Dust surrounded the car, obscuring their vision. He put the car in park and killed the engine.

The store appeared to be some sort of roadside souvenir shop. The front of it was in an advanced stage of decay. The wood was stripped clean of any color, the exterior walls a dull, weathered gray. The windows were dirty and cracked, an antique Coca-Cola sign hanging in one. The sign above the torn, damp awning read *Antiques and Souvenirs*. An old Nehi machine, consumed by rust, sat on the creaky, wooden porch.

"So, what do you think?" Cindy asked.

"I don't know," said Robbie. "Hardly looks to be worth the trouble."

There was the click of a gun cocking from the backseat. Josh stuffed his .357 in his coat pocket and grinned.

"It's perfect," he said, taking a big gulp of Jack Daniels. "Now, here's the plan. Robbie, you go in and scope the place out. Me and Cin'll pump the gas. You signal us when it's cool. We'll come in and get some stuff, cigarettes and shit, then pull the job. Got it?"

Robbie nodded. The three of them stepped out of the car and into the brisk mountain air. A light mist had begun to fall. Josh pulled a nozzle from the pump and began to fill the tank. Robbie pulled his jacket tighter to his body, pausing to give Cindy a quick kiss. He looked over at Josh. Josh gave him a wink of encouragement, and Robbie turned for the store, a slight twinge of uneasiness gnawing at him.

Robbie opened the stiff old door and stepped into the store. It was cluttered and gloomy inside. The aroma of pipe tobacco hung in the air, along with a faint, underlying odor of mildew. The room was lit only by a single dim bulb hanging over the counter. An old man sat in a rocking chair behind the counter, a copy of *Reader's Digest* propped under his nose. Robbie greeted the old man.

To Robbie's left was a magazine rack, and beyond that was a shelf displaying bread, potato chips and other snacks. Along the back wall, to the left of a refrigerated storage box, was a set of faded cafe doors leading to another room. A sign reading *Antiques and Souvenirs* hung above the opening. Curious, Robbie walked through the swinging doors, slapping at a spider web that fell across his face.

The room was very dark. It was lit only by whatever sunlight managed to filter through the dust-laden windows. There were several aisles running the length of the room. Robbie moved slowly down the center aisle, the boards straining and creaking under his weight.

The walls were covered with antiques. An old clock hung majestically above one shelf. Its rich mahogany finish grayed by layers of dust. There were some nice paintings on the walls, but most of the antiques were just junk. Robbie turned his attention to the items on the shelf. He immediately spotted an old pair of ice skates, the blades thick with rust. Robbie picked them up and inspected them closely. They looked like a pair his grandmother wore in an old photo. He wondered what his departed old grandmother would think about what he was doing and set the skates back down. He picked up a stuffed bird and shook the dust from it. It was a crow or a raven. He wasn't sure which. He sat the bird back down.

Robbie looked back towards the door he had come through. It was even darker now. *Clouds must be getting thick,* he thought. He moved farther down the aisle. It was darker still towards the back wall. He couldn't tell what anything on the shelves was now. They were merely silhouettes in the blackness. Robbie reached the back wall and stopped. He considered turning around when a faint flicker of light from the corner of the room grabbed his attention. Robbie moved closer to investigate.

It was an old arcade game of some type. The sides were stained wood, most of the color long since faded away. Painted in red at the top of the game was *Madame Rosa Lee*. Inside, shrouded by purple curtains with yellow fringe, was a dummy of a gypsy. Although the puppet's face was worn and archaic, her brown marble eyes were clear and vibrant, a hint of light glimmering deep inside them. Her jewelry, probably glamorous at one time, no longer sparkled, and her dress and headband were faded and colorless. The puppet hovered over a dingy crystal ball.

Robbie bent to read the directions. "I am Madame Rosa Lee," he read quietly. "Ask me three questions and I shall give you three answers. Then I will look into my crystal ball and see your future."

Robbie looked back to the windows for a glimpse of Josh and Cindy, but he was too far back to see anything. He was supposed to signal them that it was all clear.

He shrugged. "They can wait," he said, digging in his pocket for a nickel.

He slipped the nickel into the slot. Nothing happened. He waited a moment. Getting impatient, Robbie shoved the machine.

"Piece of shit," he cursed, slapping the sides of the game.

Still nothing. He put his hands on his hips and sighed. His mind told him to leave it, that he would get his nickel back and more when they robbed the place, but his heart wanted to play the game. He started to kick it when he noticed the cord was unplugged.

"Well, hell. No wonder," he said, embarrassed.

As Robbie bent to plug the cord in, a whirring sound came from inside the machine. He jumped up, and stepped back, his eyes wide with amazement. A light was on in the machine, and the puppet was moving. The gypsy's head nodded up and down, and her hands waved mystically around the crystal ball. Robbie looked back at the plug, still lying on the ground. The gypsy's dark eyes stared into his.

"Fuckin' A," he muttered. Robbie assumed that the game was battery operated, though he didn't know how that could be in a game so old.

A plastic card popped up to the right of the crystal ball. It read, *Ask your first question*.

Robbie hesitated, still a little shaken. The gypsy continued to move her head, and her eyes seemed to follow his.

Not knowing what to say, he finally asked, "Will I be rich?"

The whirring sound of machinery began again, then it stopped. Silence. A card dropped into a slot under the coin slot. Hesitating slightly, why, he didn't know, Robbie picked it up and read it. It said *no*.

Josh and Cindy were in the store now. They must've gotten tired of waiting for his signal. His pulse began to quicken, anticipating the approaching moment of action. He looked at the gypsy.

"Shows what you know, stupid bitch."

Another card popped up, stating *Ask your second question*. Robbie considered going back up front, but he had another question he wanted to ask.

"Will Cindy love me forever?"

The whirring sound again, and a card dropped into the slot. Robbie picked it up. This one, too, said *no*.

This annoyed Robbie. *What did this old beat-up machine know about Cindy anyway? What did it know about love?*

"Fuck you. I know she loves me," Robbie said, tossing the card on the floor.

A third card appeared, and Robbie decided to have some fun with the game. He recalled a story his cousin had told him about a guy who supposedly had brought about his own death by asking a Ouija board about his mortality.

"Okay, if you're so smart," Robbie said smugly. "When will I die?"

The gaze of the gypsy puppet seemed to intensify. The light burned brighter. Robbie suddenly wished he hadn't asked that question. The card dropped into the slot. Sweating slightly, Robbie reached for the card. Feeling foolish for his nervousness, he turned the card over. It was blank.

"What the hell?" he muttered.

Robbie kicked at the machine, somehow feeling cheated. He scolded himself. *Like it was really going to tell you when you're going to die,* he thought.

Robbie turned to walk away when the gears inside the machine sprang to life again, and a final card dropped into the slot. Robbie took the card and turned it over. Before he could read it, the sound of gunfire, sounding like thunder in the small confines of the building, filled the air.

"Holy Jesus!" Robbie cried, stuffing the card in his coat pocket. He quickly pulled out his .22 and bolted for the front of the store. He dashed through the door near the counter to find Josh and Cindy standing over the body of the old man. A small caliber pistol lay on the ground near the body, a thick pool of blood moving precariously close to it. Smoke drifted from the barrel of Josh's .357.

"Jesus Christ, what the fuck did you do?!" Robbie screamed.

"He pulled a gun on me, man," Josh explained. He showed no sign of concern, or remorse.

Robbie ran his fingers through his hair and sighed deeply, telling himself not to panic. "Okay," he said, trying to contain himself. "Okay, we gotta get out of here."

He grabbed Cindy's hand and led her to the door. Josh headed for the counter.

"What are you doing, man?" Robbie asked nervously.

"I ain't leavin' without the cash!" Josh yelled.

"C'mon, man! We ain't got time for that!"

Josh slammed his fists on the counter. "I'm tired of you always tellin' me what to do, man! Now look, we're in the middle of nowhere! Ain't nobody coming here anytime soon, so don't worry about it!"

Josh forced open the cash register drawer and began stuffing money into his pockets. He worked quickly, deliberately, with all the intensity of a madman.

"Well, hurry up," Robbie said. "Jesus man, why did you have to shoot the old man?"

Josh hopped over the counter and moved to the front door, having claimed his bounty. He looked Robbie in the eyes.

"What's the matter, man? Can't handle it?"

Robbie said nothing as they fled the building. They sprinted across the parking lot, the rain falling a little harder now. Josh jumped into the front seat. Robbie dove into the back seat, trying frantically to catch his breath. Josh hit the ignition and pushed the gas pedal to the floor, sending dust and gravel shooting backwards. The Nova screeched around the gas pumps and onto the main road. They were running again.

Robbie sat in the back seat, watching the world go by his window. The rain was falling steadily now, making the roads hazardous. Josh didn't seem to worry. They were still moving fast, slowing down only slightly around the treacherous curves.

Robbie looked at Josh, his hands gripping the wheel tightly. Robbie was worried. He couldn't get the old man out of his mind. Josh had killed. He had taken another human life. Would he stop at nothing now? Robbie remembered shooting dogs on the farm for killing chickens when he was a kid. His father's words kept playing through his mind like a broken record. "Once they've gotten a taste of blood, they'll keep on killing," his father had said. *They'll keep on killing.*

Robbie stuck his hands in his coat pockets and his fingertips brushed against something. It was the last card. Hoping to take his mind off his troubles, he took the card out and read it. On one side it read, *Your fortune*. Robbie turned it over and read the other side. "Beware the ones you love, for they will betray you," he read to himself.

Robbie shook his head and squinted his eyes. He crumpled the card and tossed it on the floorboard. Suddenly, the car began to slow down. He looked out the window. They were pulling over.

"Why are we stopping?" he asked.

He looked up. Cindy turned around in her seat and looked at him. Her expression was very strange. He had never seen such a look on her face before. He started to say something to her, but his gaze drifted to Josh. Josh engaged the parking brake and turned off the engine.

"What's going on?" Robbie asked.

Josh was caressing his gun, slowly spinning the magazine, pushing it in and out, back and forth, back and forth.

The Weak and the Weary

The front doors of the Crossroads of the Pines Baptist Church blew open with a biting cold gust of wind and a frantic swirling of wet snowflakes. Everyone thought for a moment that the doors had merely been blown open, until the darkened shape of the stranger took form. The congregation fell silent as the man stood there alone in the doorway, in the biting cold, the backdrop of snowflakes and sleet looking like a swarm of winter moths attracted to the glow of the forty-watt bulb just outside the door. The entire building was totally quiet. Even the record of top forty dance music had stopped playing, and no one could tell if the album had just ended, or if someone had stopped it when the stranger entered. Not that it mattered. No one seemed to notice anyway.

The odd mixture of folks who made up the congregation of the Crossroads of the Pines exchanged wary glances, as if all were waiting for the next to make a move. Telma and Willy Blankenship and their chubby daughter Katie, who was deaf and dumb, stared at the wet stranger, then at each other. Katie said something that amounted to little more than "Ugh", but no one reacted. Elmo Higgins, the church janitor, looked at the stranger, then down at his feet before picking his nose and wiping the bounty on his already-crusted jeans. Lenny Watkins, the retard, looked at Elmo and squawked like a crow that had just discovered some especially ripe roadkill. Sadie Gooley, who was really a man who always dressed like a woman, took one look at the stranger standing in the doorway, then reached in his purse for some lipstick. Graney Hawkins, weighing close to four-hundred pounds looked up from half a blackberry pie, stains across his teeth and all three chins, belched, then dove back into the dessert.

That was about it for the small church's members. They had gathered at the church situated down the dirt road away from Cumby, Texas for their annual New Year's Eve celebration to watch Dick Clark count down the final seconds of the old year in Times Square. As always, a good time was sure to be had by all.

Then the doors opened, the wind and snow blew in, the stranger appeared, and life had changed for the members of the Crossroads of the Pines.

As the eyes of the congregation adjusted to the darkness surrounding the stranger, his visage became more evident. Tiny pieces of melting sleet and snow clung to the grubby fatigues jacket that clung to his almost skeletal frame. Water dripped from his greasy hair and into his sunken, forlorn eyes. He was obviously a homeless drifter passing through the area on his way to God knows where.

The clicking of Reverend Phelps' heels as the staunch leader approached his flock finally broke the silence. The man of God, dressed in his omnipresent black suit and thin, wire-framed glasses, turned to face his followers, the light shining off his bald head.

"I can sense your urgency," he said, surveying the others. "But what does the Bible tell us?"

The congregation said nothing. Katie ughed. Elmo scratched his balls. Graney farted, but none made any intelligent motions.

"Matthew 11:28," the reverend continued. "'Come unto me, all ye that labor and are heavy laden, and I will give you rest.'"

"But...ain't he...he...a stranger?" Willy finally said.

The reverend smiled. "Were we not all strangers at one time, Willy? Did you know me before you came to Crossroads of the Pines? Did you know God before you let Him into your life?"

Willy stared down at the floor. Telma placed a pasty, clammy arm around him. "No, Reverend," he said.

Reverend Phelps turned away and held his arms out to the stranger. "Bring unto Him the weak and the weary, and He shall give them rest. Please join us, my child."

The stranger poked his head a little farther into the fellowship hall, then cautiously entered. He paused to stamp slush from his hole-riddled boots. Water-logged socks squished and formed puddles on the tiled floor from the action. The stranger looked at the reverend with his sallow eyes, but did not speak. Reverend Phelps placed a gentle hand on the stranger's shoulder. The man flinched slightly, then accepted the gesture.

"Terrible weather out tonight," Reverend Phelps said. "An awful way to ring in the new year, wouldn't you say?"

The man pulled his dripping jacket closer to his body and looked around, spying the buffet table line well-stocked with potato chips, soft drinks and other snacks.

"When was the last time you had a good meal, son?" Reverend Phelps asked, handing the stranger a package of Snowballs.

The man stared at the pink confection for a moment, then snatched it, stuffing the cakes into his coat pocket.

"You're drenched to the bone, boy." Reverend Phelps turned back to his laity. "Elmo, bring our friend a dry coat from the closet. And some shoes and socks."

Elmo looked at the reverend, then back at the others.

"Does anyone know who he is?" asked Sadie, his lips shining Candy Apple Red.

"Ain't never seen him 'round here," Graney said around a mouthful of Wavy Lays.

"I think he might be homeless," Telma Blankenship said.

"So what? You're homeless," Elmo snapped.

"Well, we've been homeless in the same place for a while. It ain't like we're strangers. We belong here."

Telma, Willy, and their stupid daughter lived in an abandoned tar shack near Cash Creek. Gold miners had made the modest dwelling their temporary home at the turn of the century, but it had been the Blankenship home ever since they blew into town and joined the others at the Crossroads of the Pines a few years earlier.

"I don't like it," Elmo said. "I don't like it one bit. Who would just walk into a church, dripping wet and cold on New Year's Eve, like he ain't got no home or family? A person would have to be out of their mind to be out on a night like this. I don't like it."

"You ain't got no family," Telma said.

"Don't need no family," Elmo shot back.

"Elmo, hurry up with those clothes. Our friend is drenched to the bone," Reverend Phelps called out.

Elmo looked quickly at Willy again. "I don't like it," he repeated, and went for the clothing.

"What's your name, son?" Reverend Phelps asked the stranger.

The man looked down at the floor and lifted first his right foot, then his left. "I'm getting your floor all wet," were the first words he spoke.

"Oh, don't you worry about that, now. Elmo can mop that up later. You just worry about getting warmed up. It's a miracle of the Lord you haven't caught your death of cold out there.

"My name's Duke," the stranger said. "Just Duke."

"Duke," the reverend said, shaking the new arrival's hand. "I'm Reverend Phelps. Welcome to the Crossroads of the Pines Baptist Church. Come, let me introduce you to the others."

◆

"He might be one of them serial killers you read about," Graney said after introductions had been made. He held the scant remains of a pumpkin pie in his puffy hands.

"Do you think so?" Telma asked, fear in her eyes.

"You never know," Graney said. "You know how they just drift into town, kill some people, and then move on."

"I don't think he's any such thing," Sadie offered. "I think he's just a stranger who's down on his luck. And just as the Lord said, we should give him rest." His eyes traveled up and down the stranger's lank form.

"You just want to give him head," Graney said. "You just want to suck his nasty old pecker, you goddamned homo."

Telma covered her daughter's ears as Katie's eyes stared dully at Duke. "Graney Hawkins, you watch your mouth around the child."

"Shit, Telma, she can't hear a damned word I'm saying. Wouldn't understand it even if she could."

"You're a lowlife scum, Graney," Sadie said. "Why don't you just keep eatin' all that fried, fatty food. Clog up that black heart of yours just a little more."

Graney grunted and shoved a handful of crumbled chips from the bottom of the bag into his mouth.

"Maybe he's a...a...how do you say it? Sex offender," Lenny suggested.

"You oughtta know," Elmo said. "You come from a long line of 'em."

"What...whadduya mean?"

"Your daddy's also yer granddaddy, ya inbred retard. And what about the time I caught you whackin' your thing in the bathroom when I was cleanin' it."

"Reverend Phelps," Lenny started. "He said I could. On account of it's safer like that."

"Reverend Phelps just keeps you 'cause no one else'll have ya," Elmo said, taking his glass eye out and wiping the dust off it.

"Maybe he sells drugs," Willy said. "Maybe he has drugs in his pockets right now."

"People don't just show up in the middle of the night," Telma said. "Not right people, anyway."

"That's what I say. I don't like it," Elmo said again. "I think we should tell Reverend Phelps."

The congregation agreed, and Elmo motioned for the reverend to come over. The reverend approached the group slowly, almost as if he sensed what his followers had to say.

"My adoring flock," Reverend Phelps said. "What troubles you?"

"It's the stranger."

"Duke? Duke is no longer a stranger. He is one of us now."

"He's not one of us. We don't think he's right. He bothers us," Elmo said.

"He bothers you?"

"He looks different. He acts different."

Reverend Phelps put his arm around Elmo. "Elmo, dear boy, everyone one of us is different. Our entire congregation is different. Each and every one of you."

"But he frightens us," Telma said, gripping Katie's pudgy shoulder.

"He's just a man down on his luck," Reverend Phelps said. "I've talked to him."

"We think he might be dangerous," Graney said.

"We think you should ask him to leave."

"You mean, cast him out, as the Lord cast out Lucifer? Make him go back out into that freezing rain and snow?"

"He could keep the coat and the shoes," Elmo said. "Heck, we'll even let him take some food with him."

"He doesn't belong with the rest of us," Telma said. "Not tonight."

Reverend Phelps looked into the eyes of each member of his flock, then glanced across the room at the stranger who had entered their humble country church on a snowy New Year's Eve. Duke stood at a window, watching the world outside.

Reverend Phelps smiled. "Perhaps you are right. Perhaps he does not belong with the rest of us tonight." He paused as if looking inward. "Perhaps he is not one of you."

"You'll ask him to leave then?" Telma asked.

"If you all think it's best."

Everyone nodded.

"Very well then," the reverend said, and returned to his guest.

The congregation stared as Reverend Phelps escorted the frightening stranger back out into the cold dark night.

"Remember what you said about no one having Lenny?" Sadie asked. "Well, maybe that's why he keeps us all," Telma said.

"What?"

"That's why Reverend Phelps keeps us all. Because no one else will have us. Just like the stranger."

Graney shrugged. "Shut up, ya goddamned homo."

❖

"Be careful on your travels, son, and know that the Lord watches over you always," Reverend Phelps said, as he stood in the freezing rain outside the church. Tiny pellets of sleet bounced off his glasses, making tiny plinking sounds in the still of the dark night. "Follow the star of Bethlehem just as Mary and Joseph did. The Lord will show you the way."

"Thank you, Reverend," Duke said. "Thank you for the food and the warm clothes."

"You're welcome, Duke. And Duke. The Lord will forgive my congregation on Judgement Day. Won't you please forgive them as well? They're a troubled lot. They know not of which they speak."

Duke turned back to face the reverend. "Sure. Sure. They have no reason to trust me. I'm sure I look a sight."

"You have no reason to trust them. To trust any of them. Yet, I think you would've."

Duke shrugged. "I suppose. But do you know what I really trust, Reverend Phelps?"

"What's that, Duke?"

The stranger pointed upward at the cross adorning the church's steeple. Droplets of cold rain and sleet swept across it, barely visible in the dim light.

"He always provides rest for the weak and the weary."

"Amen, brother Duke."

Reverend Phelps eyed Duke as he walked away into the misty night, the tiny pellets of sleet stinging his face, until the stranger disappeared into the blackness of a new year. "Goodbye, son. You truly do not belong here tonight."

Reverend Phelps closed the door of his '75 Malibu, the sound muffled by the shallow accumulation of snow and ice on the ground.

He paused to dig for the key that opened the door to his office, which overlooked the fellowship hall. He unlocked the door, stepped inside, and closed the cold world and the New Year's Eve stranger behind him.

Reverend Phelps jangled the extra rounds in his jacket pocket as his other hand clutched the 30/30 deer rifle tightly and began to climb up the stairs. The rifle had grown cold, very cold, lying in the back seat, but the heat from his hands quickly warmed the steel.

Bring unto Me your weak and weary, and I shall give them rest.

Reverend Phelps opened his office door and closed it behind him. Through the window overlooking the party, he could see them. Sadie. How the Lord hated homosexuals. Lenny. The product of the devil's lusty works. Graney. The result of the sin called gluttony.

Reverend Phelps smiled inward as he thought of Duke, now several miles down the snow-dusted dirt road, on his way to God knows where.

As for the congregation of Crossroads of the Pines Baptist Church, God knew exactly where they were going.

They were weak. They were weary.

Reverend Phelps let the cross hairs of the rifle's scope play along each member of his church, stopping and resting on one before dancing to the next, thoughtfully mulling over which one he should send to their eternal rest first.

Anatomy of a Haunting

It always starts with the little things.

How many times had she heard that on countless episodes of *Unsolved Mysteries,* or *Sightings*? A family moves into an old home, gets settled in, and then the little things start to happen. The *strange* little things. The unexplained oddities. A light turns on by itself. A door closes mysteriously. A knock on the door and there's no one there. Funny at first, then annoying, then finally frightening.

Little things.

Judy sighed and pulled the cushions off the stained, foam-spewing sofa. She reached down behind the seat, feeling her way through months-old potato chips and the occasional scum-coated penny. She had already checked the sofa three times—checked the entire house—yet there was no sign of the twenty-dollar bill Bobby had given her for a case of whatever beer was on sale at Jim's Liquor. She looked worriedly at the clock. Two-thirty. She had two hours to find that damned money and make it to the liquor store before Bobby got home. She didn't want to think about not having any beer for him.

The little things.

Judy had already accepted the fact that the old farmhouse they moved into four months ago was haunted, and it didn't bother her. Not really. After all, the ghost had done nothing to harm her, not directly anyway. Just little things, but when you live with an abusive, drunken asshole, little things can very easily turn into big things. Such as a missing remote control that causes you to miss taping the first fifteen minutes of last week's *Walker, Texas Ranger*. Or the last cigarette from a package disappearing. Or the *TV Guide* winding up in the trash before the week is through, a wad of coffee grounds giving Jerry Seinfeld's face on the cover an impromptu beard.

What might look like a whimsical little prank to your average mischievous poltergeist could easily escalate into a black eye, or a bloody lip for the average battered housewife.

Judy turned away from the pile of magazines and newspapers on the kitchen table and glanced at the clock again. Almost three o'clock.

"C'mon, where is that money?" she pleaded nervously.

She had turned the house upside down repeatedly, and there was still no trace of the money. Judy dropped to her knees to look under the recliner again, when the sound of Bobby's beat-up Dodge Ram pulling into the gravel driveway sent waves of terror shooting up her spine.

He was home early.

"Oh, shit," Judy mumbled under her breath.

She grabbed her purse and hurriedly scrounged through it, hoping to find enough money for at least a six-pack. Her husband called out to her, followed by the sounds of his work boots crunching gravel as he made his way to the front door. She turned her purse upside down. A dollar bill and a handful of change fell out, but nothing more. Judy couldn't help but grin to herself. That reminded her of her life. *A dollar bill and a handful of change.*

There was nothing Judy could do, but take the brunt of Bobby's outrage. She stood up, took a deep breath, and opened the door.

There was no one there. The gravel driveway was empty.

How can that be? Judy wondered. She knew that earlier the truck had come up the drive. She *knew* it.

Her knees suddenly feeling too weak to support her, Judy collapsed into the recliner, where she stayed a few moments until the Dodge Ram pull into the driveway. This time, Bobby did walk into the house, and when there was no cold beer waiting for him, he was neither happy, nor merciful.

◆

"What was it this time?" Winnie asked, inspecting her sister's blackened eye. "Burn the toast? Coffee too cold?"

"I don't want to talk about it."

"You need to talk about it, Judy. He does this all the time," Winnie continued.

"I don't want to talk about it," Judy said. She touched her bruised eye and winced at the pain. "I just thought it would get better when we got out of that cramped apartment."

"Oh, yeah, you're living in a regular paradise now."

Judy glared at her sister. She hated her biting sarcasm, hated it even more because she knew Winnie was right.

"So, where's the Wonder Husband now?"

Judy shrugged. "Friday night. He's off drinking with the guys somewhere. It's my best night of the week, actually. He won't come home 'til three, and when he does, he just pukes and passes out. I'm good 'til Saturday afternoon."

"Such a charmer," Winnie said. "I don't know what you ever saw in him."

"Winnie, just drop it, okay?"

Winnie held up her hands in surrender and sat down at the kitchen table, stirring sugar into her iced tea. "So, have you heard anymore from your ghost?"

Winnie was the only person besides Judy who knew about the ghost. She had told no one else. They would think she was crazy. Quite honestly, Judy couldn't tell if Winnie was just humoring her, or if she really believed the ghost story.

"It took Bobby's beer money," Judy said.

Winnie chuckled, iced tea dribbling down her chin.

"It's not funny," Judy snapped. "That's how I got this black eye."

"Ghosts that cause domestic strife on the next *Geraldo*," Winnie joked. "I'm sorry, Judy, it's just that it's so ridiculous."

"I didn't think you believed me," Judy said, sounding hurt.

"That's not what I'm talking about, honey. I believe in spirits from another world just as much as the next person. But let's face it, Judy, you were being haunted long before you moved into this house."

Judy stirred her tea, listening to the ice cubes clink against the glass—glasses she got free from Diamond Shamrock with each fill-up. They were about the nicest thing she owned and, when it came down to it, they weren't really hers either because the gas was bought with Bobby's money.

"Hey," Winnie suddenly said. "I know what. Let's have a séance."

"A séance? Are you crazy?"

"Why not? Shit-for-brains won't be back until way in the morning. You said so yourself. What would it hurt? You might even get to meet your ghost."

"It wouldn't show," Judy said.

"Why not?"

"You're here," she answered. "It never does anything when someone is with me. You've never seen anything. Bobby's never seen anything."

"Bobby wouldn't know a ghost if it flew up his ass."

Judy stared out the patio door to the dark fields and the tree line beyond. "It's dark out."

"What better time to have a séance?" Winnie asked. "Got any candles?"

"In the junk drawer," Judy answered, then realizing she was adding fuel to her sister's insane idea, added, "I don't want to do this."

"C'mon, it'll be fun. You need some fun."

The golden glow of the candle sitting atop the overturned wooden box was the only light in the tiny farmhouse. Judy looked around the room, studied the way the flames reflected off the walls. At one time, the tiny farmhouse had really felt like home. She had let herself be absorbed by the history of the old home, but things had changed. Now, she was as alienated here as she had been in the tiny one-bedroom apartment. Everything belonged to someone else, either in the past, or the present. Nothing was hers. Judy sighed and returned her attention to Winnie's illuminated face. Her sister was humming, or chanting, or something.

"I'm calling on the spirits of anyone who's ever died in this house," Winnie said slowly.

Judy looked around the walls and ceilings. The wavering reflections of the flame danced and created shadows, but there was nothing else to be seen, or heard.

"If you can hear us now, give us a sign. Let us know you're here."

The room grew very still and quiet. The candle—cinnamon apple—began to overpower the musty odor of the old house. Judy looked across the table at Winnie. Her sister's eyes were scanning the ceiling as if she expected to see something at any moment.

"Is it male, or female?" Winnie whispered.

"I don't know," Judy answered. "Female, I think. Yeah, female."

"Ma'am?" Winnie called out. "If you're here, come to us. Speak to us. Are you here?"

"I'm here," Judy said.

"*Shh*. Shut up."

"I'm here," Judy repeated.

◆

"Hey," Winnie suddenly said. "I know what. Let's have a séance."

Judy looked up into the brightness of the small kitchen. Her eyes drifted to the imperfections in the kitchen that gave it its' personality. The cracked linoleum flooring at least forty years old, the faded cabinets badly in need of a fresh coat of varnish, the ancient two-inch Venetian blind above the sink. Judy stared at the glass of iced tea before her as condensation dripped down the surface of the Diamond Shamrock glass.

"I found the candles," Winnie said, holding a small red candle in her hand.

"They're in the drawer," Judy answered from a mental distance.

"I know. I found them."

"Huh?" Judy responded, looking up at her sister.

Winnie touched Judy's face. "Are you okay, Judy. You've gone pale. We haven't even had the séance yet, and you look like you've already seen a ghost."

◆

"Judy, you were just messing with me the other night, weren't you?" Winnie asked her sister over mid-morning coffee. "When you kept saying 'I'm here' during our séance."

"What séance?" Judy asked. "We had a séance?"

"Yes. Hello. Where were you?"

Judy's mind drifted back to Friday night, to the events in the kitchen and the living room. She rubbed her eyes briskly. A real good headache was coming on. "Oh, yeah, the séance."

"Yeah, the séance. You were just pulling my leg, right?"

Judy took a sip of coffee. The steaming liquid burned her lips, but she barely noticed. "Yeah, pulling your leg."

"Because this house can't be haunted."

"Why do you say that?" Judy asked. Her attention was only half on her sister.

"Because I did some research. I went down to city hall and investigated this house's history. It was built in 1892, gone through twelve different owners, but no one has ever died in this house. So, therefore, no ghosts, no haunting."

"What do you mean, no ghosts?"

"Everyone knows a ghost can only inhabit the location where it dies," Winnie said.

"Why do you say that?"

"It's common knowledge."

"But how do you explain all the weird things that have happened?" Judy asked.

"All the weird things that only you have seen?"

Judy balked for a moment. "Then what about the séance?"

"What about the séance?" Winnie asked.

"Well, you were there. It's like we had it, then we didn't have it, then we had it again."

Winnie was looking at Judy like she was falling to pieces right before her eyes, and maybe she was. Judy sighed and reached for her coffee.

"I don't know what you're talking about. All I know is that you ruined a perfectly good séance by being silly." Winnie shrugged. "Not that it would've mattered, because nothing would've happened. Bobby's booze is the only spirit in this house."

That night, Judy had the strangest, most frightening dream she had ever experienced. She dreamed she was floating, as if her mind, her spirit, had detached itself from her body. She floated through her bedroom, and there was someone else asleep in her room, but it wasn't her bed. She drifted into the bathroom, and there was a stranger on the toilet, but he hadn't noticed her. She floated into the living room and there were children—children she did not know—watching Saturday morning cartoons, and in her kitchen, some strange women fried bacon and scrambled eggs. And none of these strangers noticed her.

Then there was a noise, as if something striking another object. She glided out the patio door—or rather *through* the door—and into the backyard. There was a man with a shovel, dressed in a dirty white tank top and red ball cap. Empty beer cans lay strewn about the hole he was digging. Judy couldn't see his face, but she could tell by his clothes and actions that it was Bobby. *What was he doing? Burying garbage?* A large plastic bag sat to his right, and when he picked up the bag, it made no noise as of clanking aluminum cans. Bobby approached the hole and let go of the bag. It landed at the bottom with a solid thud.

"I think I figured out what the ghost is," Judy said.

Winnie sighed. "I told you there is no ghost in this house."

"And you're right," Judy said. "Not yet."

"What do you mean, not yet? There can't be a ghost in this house because no one has died in this house."

"No," Judy said. "Not yet."

"I don't follow you," Winnie said, her face etched with concern. "I'm worried about you, Judy. The stress Bobby's putting on you. I think it's taking its toll on you, making you nuts. He's dragging you down. If he doesn't kill you outright, he'll worry you to death."

"He *will* kill me," Judy said bluntly.

Winnie was a bit taken aback by her sister's response. She expected the usual arguments of "he loves me," "he's never really hurt me," or "he pays all the bills." She hadn't expected Judy to just fold her hands in her lap and agree with her. "What do you mean?" Winnie asked.

"Everything I've seen and heard in this house," she said. "It's not a ghost yet. It's a future ghost."

"A future ghost?"

"It's me, Winnie. The ghost is me. I think Bobby is going to kill me, and then my ghost will haunt this house," Judy said.

"Oh, Judy, stop it," Winnie said. Judy's behavior was frightening her. She had never seen her sister act this way.

"What's wrong? You've always said that Bobby will kill me one day," Judy said.

"Yeah, but...you can't be serious. This just doesn't make any sense. How can there be a ghost here if there is no ghost?"

"It has to do with time. Time is being screwed up somehow. Unbalanced. Every strange thing that's happened here has something to do with time. You remember when I told you I heard Bobby coming home, but then he showed up fifteen minutes later? And the séance? I think that whenever the ghost appears, it messes up the way time moves somehow. It either reverses time, or makes it move forward, and that's how the ghost becomes present now. Its actions are here, but it's not."

"That's insane. Why would you do things to get yourself in trouble?"

"I don't know," she answered. "It doesn't know any better, I suppose. Maybe I can't tell myself from any other person who will ever live in this house. Maybe it's trying to scare me away, to force me to leave."

"Are you saying it's trying to warn you?" Winnie asked.

Judy shrugged. "Possibly. But if the ghost is me, that means I *do* die in this house. If that's the case, there's nothing that can be done."

"Yes, there is," Winnie argued. "I think the idea of you becoming a ghost is silly, but I do think you're in danger. I think you should get out now."

"I can't. It's already too late."

"You're scaring me, Judy," Winnie said, tears forming in her eyes.

"Sometimes...sometimes, I scare myself."

The doorbell rang. Judy looked up from her crossword puzzle. She had absentmindedly traced the letter in one of the boxes so many times she had nearly blacked in the entire square. Through the screen door, Winnie stood on the front porch.

"I think I've figured out what the ghost is," Judy said.

"It seems like an awfully low price for a house on so much acreage," the stranger said. "Is it haunted or something?"

The strange woman in the golden jacket laughed nervously and offered to show the couple the kitchen. Judy didn't know what these intruders were doing in her home, but she would politely ask them to leave.

She didn't have to say anything. Before she could even introduce herself, the woman screamed and collapsed into her young husband's arms. The man grabbed the unconscious woman in his arms and hastily left the house. The woman in the golden jacket just sighed and went after them.

It's my house, Judy thought. *What were those people doing in here? And where's all my furniture?*

◆

Bobby's footsteps crunched gravel as he made his way to the front door. It was Monday. Mondays were the worst. Bobby was always in an extremely bad mood, what with the weekend being over and the idea of work a reality again.

"Hi, honey," Judy greeted him as he entered. "How was your day?"

"For shit, that's how my day was," he mumbled. There was already alcohol on his breath. "What's for dinner?"

"Fried chicken," she said. "It'll be ready in fifteen minutes."

"Goddamnit!" Bobby shouted. "Why can't you have a fucking meal ready when I walk in the door? God knows you don't do shit all day. Don't you have enough time to get it ready?"

"I'm sorry, honey."

"*I'm sorry, honey. I'm sorry, honey*," he mocked. "You're always sorry."

Bobby's big, calloused hand swung forward and caught Judy across the face and nose. There was a slap of his palm against her skin, as the cartilage in her nose crushed and the warm flow of blood spilled over her lips.

"I've had enough of your shit!" her husband shouted.

Bobby grabbed Judy by the hair and drove a fist into her belly, forcing the wind from her lungs. She doubled over and fell to the floor gasping for air. She could find none as Bobby's huge hands closed around her throat and began to choke the life from her.

◆

Mondays were the worst. Judy stood at the front door staring out at the horizon, watching for the tell-tale sign of a cloud of dust up the road that would signal Bobby's arrival. When there was nothing, she turned and floated off into the air, pausing to switch off the living room light. There were more strangers in her kitchen, and they looked up and exchanged nervous glances when the light went out.

Don't worry, Judy tried to tell them. That used to happen to me all the time, too.

The Porosity of Souls

Maria gazed up at the finely crafted piece of statuary standing among the many tombstones that dotted the rolling hills of Mount Zion Cemetery. She had never seen anything quite like it. The statue depicted a young boy of perhaps ten years of age collapsed across the stone that bore the information of one person's all-but-forgotten existence on earth. The artistry was exquisite, from the torture and pain in the boy's eyes and the total exhaustion portrayed by his slumping posture, to the beautiful pink hue of the material from which it was fashioned.

Maria could not tell if the piece had been molded, or carved, but the obvious beauty of the stone and the intricate detail led her to believe that it was a one-of-a-kind sculpture, and not a replica cast, and mass produced. Maria stepped back to further drink in the statue's beauty, pausing to pull her coat tighter to her body to shut out the chilly winter winds, and made up her mind. She wanted something like this for her grandmother's grave.

The purpose of visiting her grandmother Natalie's grave was what had brought Maria to Mount Zion in the first place. Natalie Salboni had passed away six years earlier, and until today, Maria had not visited her gravesite. She had attended her grandmother's funeral, but at the time, Maria could not bear to see her laid to rest in the cold, hard earth.

Maria knelt at the base of the statue. The words on the stone were worn, but she could see that the occupant of the grave had died in 1889. She rose and inspected the statue front and back, hoping to find the artist's signature. If it had been there, it had worn off long ago. It did not matter. The sculptor would certainly be dead by now.

The sound of a car door closing drew Maria's attention away from the tombstone. Toward the front of the cemetery, a man was entering the grounds office. Perhaps the man would know more about the artist who created the statue. It was such a beautiful piece of work, surely visitors had inquired about it on more than one occasion.

Maria took a final look at the magnificent sculpture and turned, crunching piles of brilliantly colored leaves under her feet as she made her way toward the office.

The man in the office had been very helpful. Evidently, the creator of the statue that had initially caught Maria's eye had passed his talent and expertise on to his son. According to the cemetery director, statues such as the one at Mount Zion were still being crafted by a man who resided in upstate New York, not far at all from Mount Zion.

Maria steered her Mitsubishi Eclipse into the parking lot and stopped under a sign that read *Rose Hill Cemetery*. There was more of the family's works of art here.

Maria stepped from the car, inhaling the fresh aroma of fallen autumn leaves, and peered through the cemetery's wrought-iron fence. Several of the pink-hued creations stuck up among the many moss-covered, nondescript markers. Excitedly, Maria pushed open the rusted gate and walked quickly to the nearest statue.

It almost made her weep. The statue depicted a sleeping infant curled up in a blanket atop a bed of roses. She could not see the eyes, but the overall visage as it did in the piece at Mount Zion, seemed incredibly lifelike. The child interred in the grave had died in 1976. This piece was evidently the work of the original artist's offspring, but the style and attention to detail was as evident here as it had been in the other statue. Either the original sculptor was an excellent teacher, or his child an apt pupil. Nothing had been lost in the transference of knowledge and talent.

Maria inspected the other statues in the cemetery. It was easy to spot them. They all had the same pink coloring. There was a total of six statues in the graveyard, each one as breathtakingly unique as the one before.

Maria thought of her grandmother's small, square marker, blending in with all the other nameless, faceless tombstones at Mount Zion, with nothing to set it apart, nothing to show that she was remembered. Maria wiped tears from her cheeks. Whatever the cost, her grandmother would have one of these beautiful works of art on her grave.

Maria nervously picked up the telephone and looked down once again at the business card the man at Mount Zion Cemetery had given her. The card bore the artist's name, Letharius, the words *Cemetery Art and Monuments*, and an address and phone number.

Maria glanced at the clock above her dining room table. Her errands had taken longer than she had anticipated. At eleven o'clock, it was likely this man was already in bed. But she had had no luck in attempting to reach him earlier in the day, and her many attempts at contacting him during the past week had gone unrewarded as well.

Maria had checked her financial situation and figured that she could afford whatever the statue would cost. With the obvious effort and sheer blood, sweat, and tears that went into this man's creations, she was expecting the price to hover around the five grand mark. She assumed the payment would be half up front, the rest on completion and acceptance of the final product.

Maria glanced at the clock once again and dialed. She was surprised the other end picked up on the second ring.

"Hello?" a deep, groggy-sounding voice answered.

Stunned at the quick response, Maria was momentarily silenced.

"Hello?" the voice repeated.

"Hello, hi," Maria finally answered. "I hope I didn't wake you."

"No, I was working," Letharius said.

"Working? At this hour?"

The man chuckled, a deep, throaty laugh that seemed to rattle the receiver. "I always work at night. And you are?"

"Oh, I beg your pardon. My name is Maria. I picked up one of your business cards at a cemetery about twenty miles from where I live. I saw some of your work and was very impressed."

"Thank you. That's very nice."

"Well, you do excellent work. In fact, I'd like to commission you to create a piece for my grandmother's grave."

There was a pause. "Are you certain?" Letharius asked.

"Yes. Well, at least I'm certain I want to check on it. You know, prices and all."

"My prices vary greatly, depending on the size and subject matter. What were you envisioning?"

"Well, I was thinking a girl about my age. Mid-twenties, or so."

"Okay, that gives me an idea. But I'm not sure I can create a piece at the moment."

"What do you mean?"

"The materials I use can be difficult to obtain. I must make certain they are available."

"I understand," Maria said.

"I tell you what, Miss...?"

"Balroni. Maria Balroni, call me Maria."

"Maria, where is your grandmother resting?"

"At Mount Zion, just outside of Black River," Maria said.

"Yes, I know where that is. Meet me there two days from now around midnight—"

"Midnight?" Maria interrupted. "You mean, in the dark? In a graveyard?"

"I always work at night."

Maria sighed. "Can't I meet you at your studio, or a coffee shop maybe? Anywhere but a graveyard."

He laughed again. "It's all right, Maria. I just want to see your grandmother's grave so I can get an idea of what will be needed."

Maria sighed. "Okay, I'll meet you there."

She hung up the phone and stared at it for a long moment. *A midnight rendezvous with a total stranger in a graveyard.* What in the hell was she thinking?

Maria pulled into the Mount Zion Cemetery and parked her car next to a black Jeep Cherokee. She assumed the vehicle belonged to the sculptor. *No, it belongs to graverobbers, and you're going to stumble across them and they're going to throw you in an empty grave and bury you alive. Stop it*, she told herself. Maria opened the car door and stepped into the frigid night air. It was very cold, but at least the wind was still. Maria closed the door and peered into the dark cemetery.

"You're a damned fool," she whispered to herself.

Not only were there carjackings, gang warfare, and whatever else New York had to offer, but there was a report on the radio of a young woman being abducted a few days earlier.

But this guy was okay. Letharius was an artist, and Maria had dated enough artists in her day to know they could be an idiosyncratic lot. They each had their own unique personality, their weird little ways of doing things, and this guy just liked to conduct business in a cemetery. That wasn't so odd, considering the type of art he did. It was his choice of working hours that was strange.

Maria paused to push open the swinging gate, noticing the unclasped padlock hanging from a chain. The light emanating from the offices faded as she moved further into the cemetery, and Maria switched on her small flashlight. The beam illuminated the frame of a man standing in front of the statue of the little boy. Maria approached him.

It was evident that this artist was a third-generation talent, for he was young, not much older than her. Maria shined the light across his face as he turned to greet her. He was tall and thin, and the combination of the weak light and his black attire made him appear extremely pale. His hair was long, black and shiny. A crucifix earring dangled from his left lobe. And his eyes—was it a trick of the light?—were pale violet. Maria had never seen anything like them. *Hypnotic*, she mused.

"Maria Balroni?" he asked in his deep voice.

Maria extended her hand. "You must be Letharius."

He took her hand, and Maria was surprised at how cold his fingers were. He must've been waiting for a while.

"You have a key to the front gate," she said.

"I have a key to all the cemeteries that contain my work. I insist they be locked up at night. I don't want my creations vandalized."

Letharius turned and redirected his attention to the statue.

"It's a beautiful piece of work," she said.

"Yes, I'd almost forgotten it. One of my finest weepers."

"You mean your grandfather's," she corrected.

He looked at her momentarily, then turned back to the statue. "Yes, my grandfather." His voice was distant, detached.

"Do you want to see my grandmother's grave?" she asked.

"Yes, of course. That's why we're here."

Maria turned and led the artist toward her grandmother's final resting spot. Letharius seemed nice enough. A bit distracted, a little morbid perhaps, but that was to be expected in his line of work. He was certainly nothing to be feared, and was even attractive in a tragic, Gothic sort of way. What did they call those kids obsessed by death? Deathers?

Maria stopped in front of the woefully small marker at her grandmother's grave. "Well, this is it. Not much to look at, is it?"

"Every tombstone is special in its own way. Everyone is marked by great sadness. Stone is porous, much like the human soul."

"You're speaking metaphorically, right?"

"A sponge is lifeless, yet it absorbs that which it contacts. The soul absorbs emotions in much the same way. But unlike a sponge, it cannot be wrung out, it cannot be cleansed of the dirt and filth it acquires. It keeps it forever. A tombstone absorbs the sadness that it witnesses, the tragedy that surrounds it, and holds it for all eternity. It's sad for me to remove an original, even for the sake of my work." His eyes scanned the cemetery, following the flashlight beam that sliced through the black night. "There is much history in a tombstone."

"It doesn't do much for me," Maria said. "That's why I want you to make a better one."

"A young woman, you said. Correct?" Letharius asked.

"Yeah, about my age."

"A weeper?"

"Yes, very sad. I want it to move people."

"Okay, I believe I have the correct materials at hand. I can start tomorrow. How does that sound?"

"Sounds great," Maria said. "I'm sure you'll do a wonderful job."

"Indeed." He turned to face her. His eyes still shone brightly even in the cloaking darkness. It was as if there was light behind them. "But Maria, I must ask you. Is this really what you want? Do you really want to disturb your grandmother's surroundings? To take away from the unique originality of her grave?"

"You're not much of a salesman, are you? If I didn't know any better, I'd think you were trying to talk me out of it."

"No," Letharius said. He looked back at the statue of the little boy. "I must create again. I need to create. It's just that sometimes, it troubles me so. I just want you to be sure."

"Yeah," Maria said. She wasn't sure what he meant by that, but she didn't really care to attempt to understand an artist's mind. "Yeah, I'm sure."

◆

Maria pulled her scarf closer to her chin and returned her hands to her coat pockets. Sour dirt, an acrid odor of decay, and earth long denied the light of day, found her senses. A new grave had been dug since her last visit. Perhaps tomorrow, the tombstones of Mount Zion would have a new round of emotions to absorb. Maria turned her attention from the freshly dug grave to the glorious work of art that now graced her grandmother's grave. Letharius had done a wonderful job. The piece had turned out greater than she expected.

The young woman, clad in a long, flowing gown, leaned across the new tombstone with her head turned skyward, one hand resting on the marker, the other on her forehead. Her hair fell across part of the tombstone, skillfully done in a type of bas-relief so that it appeared her hair blew in the wind, the strands cleverly dissecting the dates carved into the pink stone. It was so real, so disturbingly lifelike. As with the boy's statue, there was great suffering portrayed in the eyes. It was as if the woman felt the very sadness Maria had experienced when her grandmother passed away, that she was *still* feeling the pain and sorrow. Letharius had captured that essence, the despair of that day, perfectly. The thought saddened Maria. It was an incredibly powerful piece.

Now, when people visited Mount Zion Cemetery to pay a brief visit to deceased loved ones, they would not pass over the grave of Natalie Salboni. They would stop, they would know the woman existed, they would know she was loved, and they would be moved by the artistry of a man named Letharius.

❖

Maria knocked on the door of Letharius' studio. Winter moths swarmed around her head, drawn to the light hanging to the side. Maria listened as the sound of heavy boots on hardwood flooring drifted to her ears. Tumblers clicked loudly in the silence, and the door swung open.

It was only the second time Maria met Letharius, and the first time under adequate lighting. He stood before her, streaks of drying, reddish mud gracing his bare, hairless chest. His long hair fell across his shoulders, and once again, Maria was taken aback by his violet eyes.

"Maria, what a surprise," Letharius said. "Come in, please."

"Thank you," Maria said, stepping into the warmth of his studio apartment. The pleasing aroma of wet clay greeted her, and she paused to remove her coat. Letharius took it and draped the garment over a hardback chair near the door.

"You saw my creation?" he asked.

"Yes," Maria answered. "Earlier today."

"And?"

"What can I say? It was perfect. Incredibly beautiful. Even more so than I imagined."

"I'm pleased you liked it."

"I never doubted that I would. I've come to pay my balance."

"Ah, a prompt payer of debts," Letharius said. "I like that." It was the closest thing to a sense of humor he had yet to display. "Can I get you a drink?"

"Please, anything warm," Maria said, her body still numbed by the northeast winter.

"Coffee?"

Maria nodded as Letharius moved with the grace of a cat across the floor of the one room apartment. A refrigerator, stove, and sink in one corner served as a kitchen. There was a large addition built outward from the kitchen, which Maria assumed housed the massive kiln needed to fire Letharius' creations. A bed and one bookcase graced another corner. The rest of the spacious area was devoted to his craft. A large, splattered canvas covered what was apparently a work in progress.

Maria slowly made her way closer to the work area as Letharius busied himself preparing their drinks. He had given her a brief explanation of how he molded his creations. He used a large armature constructed of a flexible metal wire around which he molded a fire clay mixed with fine sands and certain local earths. He worked the wet clay around the armature with his delicate fingers and various detailing tools, and when the sculpture was complete, he fired it in a large kiln. The entire process fascinated Maria to no end. She was always drawn to the artistic types and their creations, though she had no skills in the area herself.

Maria stopped before the large canvas tarp. Haphazard splatters of wet clay and dark splotches stained the hardwood floor around the area. A big container of wet mud sat near the covered statue, a smaller bucket of clear water next to it. She longed to see what lay beneath the tarp. Appreciating the finished product was one thing, but to view the work in progress, to see how it was created step by step would be a joy to behold.

Maria breathed in the brewing coffee, listened to the jangle of cups from across the apartment, and glanced toward the sound. Letharius' back was still turned to her. She looked back at the tarp, then again at Letharius. A fold of loose canvas hung halfway between the top of the statue and the floor. She could lift it briefly, take a quick peek. Letharius would never know.

Her hand shaking, one eye watching the sculptor, Maria gripped the canvas and lifted it. What was beneath baffled her. There was a smooth, finely detailed foot at the base of the sculpture, but the clay line began just above the ankle. There was a marked difference in the color and texture of the two materials utilized. If Letharius used wire armament, then she should be seeing some sort of metal below the ankle rather than a completed foot. Perhaps he molded the work in wax, or plastic first, then built up the fire clay mixture around this mold.

The creative process intrigued Maria. She had to see more. She didn't know how Letharius would react to someone viewing an unfinished work, but if he was like most artists she had met, he would not be pleased. Maria couldn't help herself. She lifted the canvas a little more, but pulled too hard.

There was a quiet moan as the canvas became heavy in her hand, and the tarp slid to the floor.

"What are you doing?!" Letharius shouted.

Maria screamed and stumbled backwards, knocking over a table covered with rags and small tools. The work of art in progress was not a statue, but a young girl of about twelve partially covered in clay. The girl's head did not move, but her blue eyes let a tear roll down the girl's cheek, mixing with a streak of dried clay and turning it into pink mud.

"Maria, what have you done?" Letharius moved up behind her. "You are not to view a work in progress."

Maria could hardly breathe. She gulped dust-filled air in an attempt to regain her senses. She tried to speak, but only gasps escaped her lips. Finally, she managed to sputter, "You...you...they're not statues...little girl."

"Maria." Letharius took her arms. "Let me explain."

Maria looked into his violet eyes and for a moment, was lost in their tragic depths. "No!" she screamed, jerking away. "Get away from me!"

She turned back to face Letharius. "How could you? Is this how you create all your works? My God, is this what's on my grandmother's grave now? Did you kill someone to make my grandmother's statue?"

"Maria, please," Letharius begged. "You must let me explain. I killed no one. Not really. You...you just don't understand. I merely offer them a choice."

"No!" Maria shouted. "I don't want to hear this! There can be no explanation for this. There can be no art in this. There is nothing beautiful, or creative or artistic that ends with a little girl suffocating to death!" Maria turned and headed quickly for the front door. She grabbed her coat, reached into the pocket for the check she had written for the balance, and ripped it to shreds.

"Maria, she's not suffocating. You weren't meant to see this. But now that you have, you must let me explain."

"There's nothing to explain," Maria gripped the doorknob. She expected it to be locked, but found it wasn't. "Good-bye, Letharius."

◆

Maria stood before the statue that now graced her grandmother Natalie's grave, a statue that had once inspired her with its grace, beauty, and tragedy. In Maria's hand was an aluminum baseball bat she carried in her car for defensive purposes if needed. Now, it would be used on the offensive.

She would not go to the police. Too many questions, too much time involved. But if she destroyed the clay surrounding the dead girl that was obviously encased inside, the groundskeeper would find what lay beneath the next morning, and then the police would certainly become involved.

Maria brought the bat over her head and wept. How had all this happened in such a short time? She had only wanted something unique and beautiful to grace her grandmother's grave, but she had succeeded only in desecrating her final resting spot.

Maria closed her eyes and swung the bat hard, connecting with the left shoulder of the weeping girl. The clay cracked, sending tiny crevices shooting across the surface of the statue like a tiny earthquake on an alien world. She brought the bat down again, and again, until bits of the pink hardened clay flew through the air. Finally, the bat hit something soft, and something slumped to the ground.

Maria could not bear to open her eyes and witness the gruesome sight that certainly lay before her. The girl would've been missing for several weeks now.

Maria moved, her eyes still closed, toward what she thought would be the cemetery entrance. That's when she noticed something shuffling behind her.

Maria turned to the nude woman crouched over her grandmother's grave, the moon shining alabaster across her bare back, her feet crunching broken bits of clay. The girl's head turned upward, looking at Maria with an intense gaze.

No, that's impossible, Maria's frightened mind rationalized. *She's been in there at least two weeks. It can't be.*

Her gaze locked into the girl's violet eyes, just as vivid as Letharius', and the freed woman's lips curled into a grinning sneer, revealing white, sharpened fangs. The girl hissed loudly once, and before Maria could even realize what was happening, pounced on her.

The woman's strength was unbelievable. Maria pounded at her cold body, but the attack was relentless. The girl's nails dug into her flesh, clawing and scratching. She tried to push away but was no match for her assailant. There was a cold wetness on Maria's neck a second before the terrible fangs ripped into her throat.

Maria awakened to find Letharius staring down at her. Her vision blurred around the sculptor a few moments before clearing. She was weak, very cold, and noticed there was a warm stickiness on her neck. Her numb fingers went to the spot and came back bloody. It was then that Maria remembered the night's events.

Letharius took Maria's ravaged body in his arms. "Maria, dear sweet child. Why did you have to do it? Why didn't you let me explain?"

Maria looked up at him, and in the frigid cold of the night air, realized something about Letharius that she should've noticed on their first meeting. His breath created no steam in the chilly air.

"What are you?" she asked weakly.

Letharius held her gently in his arms. "I am a vampire."

"B-b-but, the girl," Maria stuttered.

"A vampire as well," he said. "One of my victims."

Maria coughed and spat. There was a hint of copper in her mouth. "I...I don't understand."

"I did murder the girl, Maria. This girl, the one in my apartment, the boy many years ago. I am a vampire, an immortal, an undead."

"I don't enjoy killing innocent people, Maria, but I must if I am to exist. I must drink the blood of my victims, or die."

Maria looked up into Letharius' violet eyes, so full of sadness and tragedy. She reached out and touched his pale cheek.

"I live with what I do every day. It's a curse. But do you know what's worse than the killing?" Maria slowly shook her head. "It's having to live with the fact that with each victim I take, I create another such as myself. I force the tragedy that is being a vampire upon others. If they were to just die and cease to exist, then perhaps over the centuries, one could grow accustomed to the bloodshed. But no, I must turn them into me. I must make them hunt, make them take human lives, make them feel the guilt of murder, and the guilt of creating others such as themselves. It's a never-ending cycle."

"But...the statues," Marie choked.

"That's what I wanted to tell you in my studio. The offer I make toward my victims. The statues, all of them, were created by me, throughout centuries. Encasing their souls in a mixture of fire clay, sand, and their own native soil, combined with their blood, puts them in a state of suspended animation, where they remain alive and undead, but incapable of murder, for all of eternity."

He looked down at Maria, stroking her dark hair in his porcelain-smooth fingers. "You are dying, Maria. Angela chose to be contained in her own soil. I always thought my victims could feel no pain, no emotions, but Angela still hungered, I suppose. I don't know, maybe the pain is worse that way. She is the only one who has been freed after being suspended. Perhaps the confinement, the anguish of the hunger consumed her. When you freed her, she attacked."

"Don't you see, Maria? I'm not really an artist. I'm a judge, jury, and executioner. I'm also the criminal, but most of all, I try to be a savior. I try to help as best I can in a terrible situation. It may be wrong, but it must be one way, or the other. Either way, I lose."

"What will happen to me after I die?" Maria asked, her voice weakening.

"In a week, you will rise," he said. "And then, you will have a choice to make."

Dark storm clouds rolled overhead. A few flurries began to waft in and out of the bare branches of the graveyard trees. Brittle leaves chased one another in the cold wind, crashing into and bouncing off tombstones. The air grew colder, the snow fell harder.

Maria looked out across the cemetery, with her view limited only to what was directly in front of her. Tombstones, scraggly trees, a barren landscape. *Sadness*. Letharius was wrong. She *could* feel. She *could* hurt. Her eyes cried, but no tears fell forth. She hungered for sustenance, but her pangs went unanswered. Passing in front of Maria's vision, an elderly man shuffled toward his car through the light dusting of snow. Perhaps if the weather was not so frightful, he would stay longer. Perhaps, he would pass by her. Perhaps, he would revel in her beauty, and the exquisite craftsmanship evident in her creation, and maybe he would inquire as to where he could commission such a stunning piece of art to adorn his loved one's final resting place.

Perhaps, if the weather wasn't so terrible.

But it was, and the elderly gentlemen started his car's engine and drove away, leaving Maria alone in the barren land of death and sadness.

She was in pain. She was hungry. She was filled with anguish

And in a state of porosity, unmatched by even the most absorbent sponge, a tiny crack formed in her soul, and the sadness, the loneliness, and the terrible, bitter cold began to seep in.

The Chill of an Early Fall

The rickety old bait stand looms over the pier like a trusted sentinel, its clapboard siding grayed a shade darker by another season of summer rains and salt spray blown in from the Atlantic, its windows boarded up for another seven long months. Hanging from its rafters, creaking and swaying in the late afternoon breeze, a sign announces the sale of fishing licenses and bait shrimp by the quart. Beyond the tired old shack, the empty pier sits languidly in the threshold of the shallow surf, the shadows of the posts and ropes stretching almost endlessly across the wooden planks. The golden sunset spits a warm, lush glow across the beachfront scene, but despite the cozy colors that engulf the perpetual landmarks, the approaching chill in the gentle winds cannot be denied. From deep across the horizon, steel gray storm clouds stretch ever closer to the tiny island resort, signaling the end of another season and the onset of winter.

She stands at the bridge that had carried hundreds of tourists to the pier, her bare toes cool in the shifting sands. A smattering of many gulls blends with the steady drone of the wind and the lazy splash of the waves lapping against the pier supports, and if she closes her eyes, she can almost imagine summer still surrounds her.

She turns her head northward, brushing wisps of golden hair from her pale face, and peers up the coastline. The winter mists are already beginning to engulf the island. She can barely make out the outer edges of the coast of Massachusetts. All the tourists are gone now. The lifeblood of the land has ebbed back to the mainland, leaving the desolate island to sleep its winter slumber.

During the summer, the island is a thriving tourist attraction. The warm waters, sandy beaches, and the rolling, floral hillsides attract the throngs in masses. Families, fishermen, artists, and writers. The little island teams with laughter, color, and merriment from April through September. Fishing boats are chartered for hour-long bouts with sailfish, tuna, and the occasional shark. Families picnic along miles and miles of white sandy beach. Artists and their easels dot the island from the coastline to the forests and up into the hills. The activities extend from the early morning hours into the late night. The island is a pleasant place to be, filled with the sounds of people enjoying life.

A gust of wind blows ocean mist into her face, and she has to hold her dress down in the brisk breeze. She shudders. Every gust of wind seems to lower the temperature a few more degrees. The island is empty now, save for the remote few, the locals who somehow manage to blunder their way through the drab, gray months of winter. As the warmth of the summer sun departs, life seems to leave the island. Similarly, the icy winds of chill are the harbingers of death.

The island itself becomes lifeless and gray upon the arrival of winter. The aquamarine waves roll and churn to a monochromatic taupe. The once-bright skies are transformed to a monotonous ashen shade. The trees are all stripped bare. The lush green hills, now devoid of chlorophyll, turn a drab brown. Winter brings with it a sheer, plastic sheeting, gray in color, and drapes it over the land.

She steps over the chain railing along the sidewalk and begins to make her way up the coastline. Hundreds of fallen leaves, colored a familiar earth tone, bounce and dance down the asphalt toward the ocean, sounding like the legs of thousands of tiny lobsters stampeding to the sea. The trees stretch their naked, scrawny arms toward the dismal sky. A single leaf, struggling valiantly to cling to its mother branch, loses its battle and tumbles to the clammy ground in pursuit of its siblings. She wants to cry, but cannot.

She continues down the sidewalk past the inn, the white-washed building that had held so many happy tourists during the previous months. Now, the only sign of life inside the colonial structure is a lamp glowing in the window of the sitting room. She moves past the inn, through the heart of the town, pausing solemnly to inspect each boarded window. Through knotholes she peers, inspecting the insides of the deserted shops, the winter dust already settling on the once-cheery interiors.

Past the outskirts of town, the lay of the land begins to take on a slight incline, but she does not notice. She strays from the sidewalk, cutting through the brown weeds, the blades of faded grass feeling cold and lifeless to her bare feet. She labors slightly as she descends the grassy hill, trudging past the sight where so many painters had set up their easels to create their oil and acrylic renditions of birch trees, Devil's paintbrushes, and colorful wildflowers. Now, the hill is as barren and lifeless as the paintings that were created. She wants to cry but cannot.

At last, the brown covering of grass gives way to the pale sands of the beach, and she continues in her circle of the island. Hundreds of gulls strut and hop along the shoreline, conducting their final cleaning of summer scraps left behind by the tourists. She wants to smile at their hapless guffawing, but she can't find it in her being to show happiness in the face of the lifeless winter.

Out on the ocean, a lone scalloper makes its way back toward the pier, the sole occupant of a vast stretch of water that so recently had been filled with countless multi-colored sails. Now, only the scalloper remains, and soon, it too, is gone. The only evidence that distinguishes the ocean's surface from an expanse of gray carpet is the constant parade of rolling whitecaps. She wants to cry but cannot.

She lowers her head, momentarily enthralled by how the fine granules tumble down the slopes of her feet when her weight presses into the sand. She lets the whine of the winds, the roar of the ocean, and the shrill cries of the seabirds' meld together until they are but one dull cacophony of winter noises.

She stops at the ramshackle bait stand. Her trip has come full cycle. It is time to go home, just as the tourists, and indeed, the thrill of life has gone. She shuffles past the bait stand toward the water's edge.

Yes, for the season, life has left the tiny island. As robustly as life embraced the island in summer, so terribly does the essence of death grip it in winter. No outsider could know the island as it is in winter. No one knows how bitter is the night, how fiercely blows the wind, how dreary are the skies, how dark grows the mind.

The island is not without tourists in the winter, but they are certainly visitors of a different sort. Ask any family of mother, father, and two, or three kids who visited the island in June, and they could not recall any of the eight suicides that occurred on the island during the previous winter season. Question any chartered fishing boat hauling its jubilant catch of bluefin, and no one aboard could tell of the locals who must scrape out their living, of the weathered fishermen who must brave the fierce winter sea for a meager bounty of lobster during the cold winter months, after the happy tourists have returned to their gay mainland lives. Ask any budding Rembrandt splashing bright swatches of pastels across a pre-stretched canvas, and he would know nothing of his winter counterpart who spends long bone-chilling months uninspired in front of a blank canvas gripping a single tube each of black and white paint, endlessly mixing various shades of gray on his palette, forever searching for, but never finding, color. None of them would know what happens on this happy little island when the season of death engulfs it.

Just as the sun and its warmth bring the carefree masses of people to life, so the dark icy grip of winter brings the dead to the island. The dead come to revel in the cold, bone-chilling winds, to circle the empty shell of an island, and to ponder their lonely existence, the only existence they know, in the netherworld.

She turns to glance once more at the weathered bait stand, the sound of the rusted bait sign still audible even from this distance. She strains her ears, and for a moment, she can almost hear them. The cries of the children, the laughter of the adults, the bustle of life. *Summer sounds.* But it's only the wind. Only the wind.

She turns back to the gray ocean, its murky depths beckoning her back to her home. The tide assails the beach with more ferocity than even moments earlier, claiming any lingering evidence of summer and carrying it back to its frigid lair. Death grips the island in the cold of winter. Death owns all in the gray void.

She wants to cry, but cannot.

Only the living can cry.

Tears on a Pillow of Down

Detective Lloyd Treber surveyed the scene with the same hardened, aloof face he always wore, a byproduct of viewing similar scenes hundreds of times over. The names changed, but the characters stayed the same, becoming almost stereotypical in their predictability. The frightened child, the cowering mother, the drunken, belligerent father. And many times, the individual scenes repeated themselves, as with this one. This wasn't the first time he had answered a child endangerment call at this address. Sometimes, the never-ending cycle just didn't seem worth it, but this case would soon prove different. When Detective Johnny Sloan called him over to look at the dead cat, Treber knew this child abuse case would be unlike any he had ever worked before.

Treber had been talking to the mother, getting the usual bullshit load of "he pays the bills," or "he only does this when he's drinking," even the dreaded "but I love him." Treber excused himself from the woman and reentered the little girl's bedroom.

"What do you got?"

"I'm not sure, Lloyd," Sloan said. "Take a look."

A uniformed policeman knelt and removed the garbage bag from the cat's corpse.

It looked like a cat in form only. That's where the similarities ceased. The cat was pure white and hairless. In its side was a large hole courtesy of the father's .32., but there was no blood. Only a mound of a fluffy white substance, somewhat resembling dried cottage cheese. The cat's eyes, round and black, reminded Treber of a doll, or a stuffed animal, and he fought the urge to attempt closing them. Somehow, he didn't think they were *capable* of closing. The thought chilled him.

Treber looked up from the cat, his eyes scanning from the uniformed cop to Sloan. "What the hell is this? Is it real?"

"It seems to be something that was alive," the cop said. "It's like a cat, only...only it's not."

"And that's not all, Lloyd. It's sexless. Yeah," Sloan continued when he noticed the confused look on his partner's face. "Raise the tail. No genitals."

Treber donned a pair of surgical gloves and carefully lifted the cat's hairless tail. Nothing broke the smoothness of the cat's underbelly. He lowered the tail and reached for the mound of white substance, taking a pinch between his thumb and middle finger. Even through the latex, Treber noted the texture of it. The substance reminded him of powdered graphite, or down, and it made Treber cringe.

"Neutered?" Treber offered.

"They don't cut the pecker off," the cop said.

"No, I guess not. Do we have a coroner here?" Treber asked.

"Lloyd, it's a cat," Sloan said.

"I know it's a cat, but it's unlike any cat we've ever seen."

"Another thing," Sloan said. "The mother says they don't own a cat."

"Then where the hell did it come from? A stray?"

Just then, the little girl shrieked loudly from the living room area where she and her mother were being questioned. Treber hastily threw the bag over the strange corpse and headed that way.

"He killed Angel!" the little girl cried as Treber and Sloan approached. "Daddy killed my Angel!"

"What did she say?" Treber asked.

"She said her daddy killed her Angel," Sloan answered. "Guess that was the cat's name."

"But you said they didn't own a cat."

Sloan shrugged. "That's what they said. The father doesn't remember getting the gun, or so he says. Doesn't even remember seeing a cat, but he has scratches on his face and arms."

"What do you think? Could it be from the kid?"

"Don't think so," Sloan said. "Evidence says the father should remember the cat, 'cause the cat fucked his face up pretty good."

"Good for the cat," Treber grumbled. "Make sure they bag that cat up tight. We're gonna need it for evidence." Treber pulled out a cigar and lit it as he exited through the front door.

"Lloyd?" Sloan called after him. His face appeared around the door frame. "Lloyd, you alright?"

"Yeah, I'm fine, Johnny. Just get your evidence. Secure the scene."

"Okay," Sloan said, sounding confused, and turned to reenter the house.

Treber took a long drag from the foul-smelling cigar, exhaled, and stared across the street as evening shadows crept closer to the house. It wasn't until he flicked the cigar stub away that Treber realized he was still wearing the rubber gloves.

Detective Treber didn't expect to be back at the same house so soon. The fact that he was investigating a murder now instead of simple child abuse did little to soothe his anger.

Treber pulled his car against the curb and stepped out onto the rain-slick street. Yellow police tape graced the bushes along the house like festive holiday decorations. Treber sighed and started for the front door.

"There was no one left to watch over her!" the old man cried.

Treber jumped back. He had not noticed the man standing next to the bushes.

"It was gone! She had no one to protect her, no one to watch over her!"

"Get lost, buddy," Treber growled. "This is a crime scene."

"He killed Angel!" the man shouted frantically. "There's no one to watch over the precious darling!"

"What?" Treber asked, turning around to face the old man. "What did you say?"

The old man took a frightened glance over his shoulder and bounded down the sidewalk.

"Hey!" Treber shouted after him. "Come back here!"

Treber gazed at the old man fleeing, until he was a mere speck on the distant sidewalk. He turned back to the house, to the matter at hand, and braced himself to undertake his grisly task.

"Goddamned son of a bitch," he mumbled under his breath.

Detective Treber moved quickly to the back entrance of the animal hospital. Detective Sloan's call had sounded urgent.

The "cat" had been dropped off at a local animal hospital the previous night, where it awaited examination. Chief Barnes had ordered Sloan to check on it the next morning. It was to be a random questioning in order to tie up any loose ends and complete the paperwork on the case. That's what it was *supposed* to be.

Treber pounded on the heavy steel door. Seconds later, a pretty vet's assistant, looking visibly shaken, answered the door. She led Detective Treber into a room where Sloan and a man in a long, white coat stood before a commercial refrigerator.

"Johnny, what is it? You sounded scared shitless."

"Are you ready for this, Lloyd?"

Treber half shrugged, and the veterinarian opened the refrigerator and removed a package of white butcher paper. The vet laid the paper on a stainless-steel table and opened the package. The crinkling of the stiff paper was deafening in the tension-filled room. The vet smoothed the edges of the bundle and stepped back. Treber leaned forward and looked.

"Powder," he said.

"That's all that's left of our cat," Sloan said.

Treber touched a finger to the white powder and brought it to his nose. It was odorless, and it had that same slick texture. He had no intention of tasting it.

"Were you able to perform any tests?" Treber asked the vet.

"No," the man said. "It was dropped off here late last night. I was going to study it this morning, but this is what I found."

"Did you look at it at all last night?"

"I looked at it, yeah," the vet said.

"And?"

The veterinarian shrugged. "What can I say? I was stumped. It was evidently a living, breathing creature. Yet, it had no...no working parts."

"Have you gotten a sample to take to the lab?" Treber asked Sloan.

"Yeah, I got a sample, but you know what I think, Lloyd?" Sloan asked. "I don't think we need a chemical analyst. I don't think we need a vet. I think we need a goddamned ghost hunter."

The test results came back from the analysis lab later that evening. Mostly normal organic animal compounds. Some vegetable. A little mineral.

Dust. Ordinary simple dust.

The cat had disintegrated into dust.

It was later that same night that the first humanoid corpse was found. Two patrolmen found it while answering a report of gunfire on the lower east side, a part of the city known for its gang activities.

Treber and Sloan arrived on the scene within minutes of the initial report. A crowd of uniformed police hovered around the body. This time, a coroner was present, and from the looks of it, a couple of guys from the press were there as well. *Damn,* Treber thought. *It doesn't take them long to sniff out a hot story.*

The corpse looked very similar to the cat, except for its obvious human figure. Its skin was smooth, white, and hairless. Like the cat, it was devoid of any sexual organs. Obvious cause of death—if it could be called that—was a single gunshot wound to the head, evidently from some sort of high-powered automatic weapon. The choice weapon of the best-equipped gang member on the streets.

This thing appeared to be the victim of a gang hit.

The coroner and his assistant were busy scraping the cottage cheese-looking spray pattern from the brick wall against which the body lay crumpled.

"Have they been briefed?" Treber asked the commanding officer on the scene.

"About what happened with the cat?" the office asked, then nodded.

"What do you think, Doc?"

The coroner looked particularly gray-faced tonight. He carefully removed a chunk of the white gore from the brick with a pair of tweezers and placed it into a jar.

"We want to preserve any bit we can," the coroner said. "We're going to try different things. Freeze some of it. Place some in formaldehyde. Hopefully, we can keep enough of the specimens intact to run proper tests."

"Yeah, that's all fine and dandy on a logical end," Treber said. "But what do you *think*, Dr. Wilson?"

"I'm trying not to think about the logical, Detective Treber, because this defies all logic. This thing has no internal organs. It has no way to think, to communicate, to even move."

"And we don't even know if it can do those things," Sloan said. "We haven't seen one alive."

"Why a cat and then a human?" Treber asked.

"Detective, there's no point in asking any questions because, at this point, I don't have any answers. We're going to have to call in all types of professionals for this. It'll be months before we know anything, if even then."

"You know what it looks like," a young beat cop said, staring down at the crater in the thing's head. The others turned to meet his gaze. "It looks like a goddamned alien. Like those things that people who've been abducted are always describing. That's what it looks like to me."

Treber looked down at the dead thing on the ground. *Aliens*, he thought with a stifled chuckle. *Close encounters of the fourth fuckin' kind.*

Treber and Sloan turned their heads in the direction of a commotion farther down the alley. A patrolman had found the body of a young Hispanic kid. His brains decorated the inside of a dumpster.

◆

Dust. Every piece the medical examiner collected had turned to white powder before the next day's light. The frozen pieces had become hardened blocks of dust. The pieces supposedly preserved in formaldehyde settled to the bottom of the jars in flakes.

Fruitless tests on the dust revealed the exact same composition as that of the cat.

Experts were prepared to act quickly if given the chance to examine another of these creatures.

Detective Treber figured they wouldn't have to wait long.

◆

Treber stood at the window near the water cooler, watching the summer rain fall on the grimy city streets below. When he had first joined the Child Welfare department of Precinct 101 twelve years ago (after three years as a beat cop for the same precinct), Treber had been oh, so gung-ho. With his college minor in child psychology, it seemed like a logical decision. Single-handedly he would solve the problems of the children of the world. The plight of children held a dear place in his heart. Treber had grown up in an abusive household. His father was a hopeless alcoholic, and his mother was only a mistress and maid to his father, never a mother to him. His only brother had been killed in an accident while in the Army. His entire childhood had been a fiasco, and Treber was determined to not allow the cycle to repeat itself. He would do what he could.

Two more creatures had been found the previous night in a shantytown populated by homeless people. Leaders in major biology and medical fields were busy preparing the remains for testing, but Treber had a feeling they wouldn't be in time.

Word of the strange, murdered creatures had leaked to the press, and every television station and newspaper in the country had speculative versions of what was taking place. Alien invasions succumbing to Earth's violent ways, mutated humans, signs of Judgement Day were only a few of the latest headlines.

Reports were coming in of similar incidents in various parts of the world. Corpses were found on the Gaza Strip after a bus carrying Israeli schoolchildren exploded. Dead creatures littered the streets of Bosnia, near a playground in a so-called "safe" zone that had been shelled. This new phenomena Treber had discovered was quickly becoming a global event.

Treber sighed and slam-dunked a Dixie cup into the nearest trash receptacle.

"Hey, Lloyd. What's eating you?" Sloan asked.

Treber continued to eye the falling rain. "Rain. It won't stop raining."

"Come on. I know you better than that."

Treber frowned. "Are we really making a difference, Johnny? Do we ever *really* make a difference? I mean, we work backbreaking hours. We take bad guys off the streets. We try to protect the kids, but does it do any good?"

"What do you mean?"

"Don't you ever feel like we're fighting a losing battle, a battle that can't even be won? Parents keep hurting their kids. Molesters don't spend any time in jail. Kids keep killing each other."

Sloan sighed. "Yeah, well, we do what we can, Lloyd. That's all anyone can ask of us."

"Yeah, but is it enough? And now we've got this other thing happening, too."

"What do you make of it, Lloyd?" Sloan asked. He, too, seemed enthralled by the rainfall. Perhaps a bit of normalcy was what they both needed.

"I don't know, Johnny. I just don't know."

"Why now? Why all of a sudden?"

Treber shook his head slowly. "Kids," he said softly.

"What?"

"Kids," he repeated. "It always involves kids. Kids and violence. Death. There's something symbolic about all this."

"Symbolic?"

"That day the little girl with the cat was killed by her father," Treber began. "When I arrived on the scene, there was this old man. Looked like a street person. Ragged clothes, dirty as hell."

He paused. "I blew it off. I didn't pay any attention. I just thought he was a nut."

"What do you mean?" Sloan asked.

"He said angel," Treber continued. He shook his head again as if he was struggling with an inner demon. "No way he could've known that the cat was named Angel."

"Did you get a name?"

"No, no. He just rabbled something about no one watching the girl, and then he ran like hell. Like I said, I just blew it off."

"Hmmph," Sloan grunted. "Yeah, you're probably right. He was just a nut."

"Yeah, but maybe..."

"What?"

"Nothing."

Treber turned his attention back to the rain. It continued to fall on the grimy streets below in nature's efforts to cleanse the filthy streets.

Nature was losing.

The doors of St. Francis of Assisi Catholic Church were always standing wide open during the spring and summer months as Treber passed the huge archaic structure on his way to the station every morning. Many furtive glances had offered a glimpse inside the main sanctuary, at the rows and rows of richly stained pews, at the large altar, the silver chalice, and the beautiful stained-glass windows that towered above them all. In fifteen years at Precinct 101, he had never stopped. Today was different. Today, it just felt right.

Treber dashed the ten feet to the door through the warm steady rain that had fallen continuously the last several days, pausing at the entrance to shake the excess water from his shoes.

He entered the church quietly, letting his eyes adjust to the dark surroundings.

Several people were seated near the altar, heads bowed in prayer. An obese woman emerged from a confessional booth that looked somehow too small for her girth. A priest stood before the altar, busily filling a censer with incense. Treber started down the center aisle toward the confessional, the sound of dripping rainwater diminishing with each step. A woman rose from the benches, crossed herself, and headed for the doors.

Treber sighed, parted the small curtain and stepped into the confessional. The seat was small, the padding worn. Treber hitched his slacks up a little and sat down. "Bless me Father for I have sinned," he began.

"When was your last confession, my son?" the voice asked from beyond the screen.

Treber started to speak, then cleared his throat. "Years, I guess. I'm not sure." Treber had been raised Catholic, though his family rarely attended services. He vaguely remembered his mother taking him to confession when he was about eleven, though he couldn't remember why.

"What sin do you wish to confess?"

"I'm not sure it is a sin, Father. You see, I work in a job where I help kids. Or that would be the idea, anyway. It seems that, often times, no matter what we do, it's not enough."

"These are troubled times," the priest answered. "Children have many temptations with which they must deal. It is not easy growing up in today's society."

"I know," Treber said. "I realize that. But...it's just that it seems...so pointless sometimes. I feel like I should just give up, but then, I think, if not me...then who? If I don't do what small part that I manage to contribute, will it make things that much worse?"

"Each child was created by the Lord for a purpose. Each child, if it is the Lord's, will, *will* fulfill that purpose."

"But we lose so many," Treber said. "Why does God allow so many children to be created, if He's going to just make them live in a hell, then take them away? It just doesn't make any sense."

"We are not ones to question God's judgement," the priest said.

Treber thought he could detect a bit of annoyance in his voice.

"Of course, Father. But it...it just seems so unfair-"

"Doubt," the priest interrupted, "is the Devil's emotion."

Treber decided to change the course of the conversation and get to the real reason he was here. "Father, may I ask one other question, on a completely different subject?" Treber looked up at the ceiling of the small booth. "What can you tell me about angels?"

"Angels?" the father repeated. "Well, basically, they're the Lord's messengers, according to scripture. At one point, the Lord stopped appearing to His prophets. He sent angels in His place."

"Uh-huh," Treber said. "Do angels ever appear on Earth?"

"Well, I suppose that's up to the individual. Throughout time, there have been many eyewitness accounts of angels. Many of those are explained away by science. Hallucinations during times of stress, wanting a miracle so bad that the mind makes up one. That sort of thing. In biblical times, angels appeared often. Now there are those who believe UFOs are angels, appearing in a form more appropriate for our advanced technology."

"Appearing in a form?" Treber asked.

"Oh, yes. Angels can take any form they so desire, any shape to help those they appear to understand them better."

"Like an animal, maybe?"

"Animals. People. Deceased loved ones. Male or female," the priest continued.

Treber's head snapped to attention. "What do you mean by that?"

"Angels have no gender. They can be male, or female. Whatever best fits the situation."

Treber thought of the sexless cat they had discovered the night this all began, and of the disappearing alien-like creatures.

"Father, do little children have guardian angels? You know, someone in Heaven that watches over them?"

"According to the Bible, Matthew 18:10, each human being has a celestial patron. Everyone has a guardian angel, my son. Everyone."

Treber began to mull the priest's statement over after thanking him for his time. He exited the confessional and headed back down the aisle. The light from the cloud-choked sun strained through the tall window's-stained glass, throwing multi-colored reflections along the walk. Treber had just reached the front door, bracing himself to run through the torrential rains, when the voice spoke.

"Everyone has a guardian angel, Detective. Everyone."

Treber turned to his right. At the far end of the nearest bench, hidden in the shadows, sat the old man he had encountered while investigating the little girl's murder. Treber scooted sideways between the benches to reach the old man.

"You come looking for angels. You think you're in the right place, eh?"

Treber leaned against the next bench and folded his arms over his chest. "Who are you?"

"Name's Duncan," the man said. "But you won't find any angels here."

"How did you know that little girl had a cat named Angel?"

The old man coughed, a phlegmy street-infested hack that made Treber cringe. He spat into a brown and yellow cloth and shoved it into his coat pocket. "Didn't have a cat. Wasn't no one's cat."

"How did you know about angel?" Treber pressed.

"When he took the angel, there was no one left to watch over her. No one to protect her."

"What do you mean?"

"Well, I think you had it right when you were talking to the priest," the old man said.

"Guardian angels?" Treber asked, then smirked.

"Now you sound as if you don't believe. Everyone has a guardian angel, Detective. Even you."

"What I got is a bunch of funny looking corpses that turn to dust before anyone can look at them. That's what I got," Treber said.

"How many times you skin your knee as a kid? How many times you fall off a bicycle? How many times you come this close to falling out of a tree, only to grab that saving branch at the last second? What might've happened if she wasn't there?"

"They're sexless," Treber said.

"I figure you'd be the female angel type. Of course, I could be wrong."

"I'm a *no angel* type."

"Then why come here?"

Treber sighed and looked up at the cavernous ceiling.

"You see little kids dying everywhere nowadays. Little tiny children. Somalia, Bosnia, even in our own backyards. Ain't that a shame, Detective. Ain't that just a crying shame? We're supposed to hold and protect and love our children, but we're not doing that anymore, are we? We let sex offenders back on the streets, we return children to battered homes, knowing that they'll get more of the same. Hasn't that been driving you insane of late? Isn't that why you came here today in the first place?"

"What does that have to do with angels?" Treber asked, growing annoyed.

"Oh, it has everything to do with angels. What happens to the children of the world if there are no more guardian angels? Who protects them? Their parents? The government? Society? No, no one does. Hope is fading fast. The love is dying. God turns His back on a dying world. He turns His back on the very beings He sent to protect us. Even angels grow upset when children die needlessly. Even angels want to do what they can. Even if it means going against the Lord's will."

"Yeah, the world's a real shithole," Treber said, then, remembering he was in a church, glanced around to see if the Monsignor had heard.

"It is. It's in decay. The angels are here to protect us, but if God turns away, who protects our angels?"

"Have you seen your guardian angel?" Treber asked sarcastically. He was suddenly a little ashamed for asking such a cruel question of an old man who had obviously been down on his luck for a long time.

Duncan the street person shook his head slowly, then said, distantly, almost too quiet to hear, "No. Not in a long, long time."

Treber gave him an apologetic smile then, feeling embarrassed, trotted out into the rain to his car.

◈

The lower east side was usually quiet on weeknights. Most of the action went down on Friday and Saturday nights. But now and then, when all seemed peaceful, all hell might break loose at any given time.

The rain had stopped falling earlier, but the cool, damp air served as a reminder of the shower's intensity. Treber kicked around in the alley where the first humanoid body, and the Hispanic kid, were found. He didn't know what he was looking for, but something had drawn him here. And he had a feeling that it had little to do with concern for children's safety.

Treber had been thinking a lot about his earlier conversation with Duncan the homeless man at the church. The old guy had brought up a lot of things that he couldn't have possibly known unless he had listened to Treber's confession.

But who was this strange man? If he was the one pulling on Treber's subconscious, then why here? Why not the church, or the little girl's house—places where Treber had encountered the man?

It didn't make sense, but then, little of the past few days' events did.

First the cat. Hairless, genderless, lifeless, seemingly even before death. Then the humanoid corpse. Similar physical appearance. Then more corpses, always found practically side by side with a dead kid. Then worldwide, always where children are suffering the most.

Where did it lead? What was happening with the world? What did the old man mean when he said love and hope were dying? Mankind's hope? Or was he talking on a grander scale? Was God abandoning hope? Could anyone blame Him?

Tires screeched at the front of the alley a few seconds before doors began opening. More vehicles screeched to a halt, and more doors opened. Then footsteps, voices. Hushed tones. More cars. Louder voices. Shouts.

Something was going down. A normally placid weeknight was about to become the Saturday night from hell.

Treber slipped quietly forward, ducking behind the dumpster where the Mexican kid had lain down for his final night's sleep. He peeked around the corner, keeping his head out of sight.

There were at least twenty kids standing around the cars, and from Treber's vantage point, he could tell that they wore different colors. The Boneheads and the Jax.

Treber had to get back to his car. He would need a lot of backup, and he was going to need it quick, before all chaos broke loose. He began to devise a plan. Crawl in through this broken window, through the empty warehouse, and come out farther down the street behind his car.

It would've worked, too, if the first shot hadn't rung out just as Treber had gotten one foot in the window. The shot echoed long and loud down the narrow alley, and its repercussions were still bouncing between the walls of the dilapidated buildings when more shots rang out, faster and with more fury. Treber looked around the dumpster. There were already several dead kids lying in the street. He couldn't see the rest, but tell-tale flashes of gunfire told him where they were. Several of the kids ran down the dead-end alley. Angered voices followed and then more shots.

Something cold and wet hit his face seconds before the sound of something hitting the pavement echoed before him. He wiped his hand across his face and held it before his eyes.

The substance looked like wet cottage cheese. Treber did not want to look down, but he did.

The creature lay on its face at Treber's feet. The huge hole in its back seemed to smoke, or steam, and the creamy white substance leaked onto the asphalt. Cautiously, Treber knelt and turned the creature over. Its dark round eyes stared up at the sky. It was still alive. Its breathing came in small, whiny gasps.

Treber laid his hand on the being's chest. It lolled its head toward the touch, and though Treber couldn't be sure because of its unusual eyes, he got the sensation that it was looking at him. Sounds escaped its mouth, but they were nothing Treber could understand.

Then there was another moan. The gangbangers that had fled down the alley lay dying in pools of thick, dark blood. And, as he expected, there was another dead creature.

Treber looked back down the alley. Some of the cars were gone. The vehicles of the losing gang remained where they had stopped, engines still idling. Even from where he stood, it was clear that there were more dead kids around the car and more creatures. Treber dropped to his knees.

"Oh, God, why?" he cried, clutching his face in his hands. "Why must this go on?"

Treber cried for what seemed like hours. The kids were all dead. Their rival gang members had made sure of that. Treber walked heavy-footed back to his car and radioed for assistance. "Call the FBI. Bring whatever it is they bring to study these things, and lots of it. And lots of body bags."

Treber leaned against his car and rubbed his eyes. He wanted a smoke. He wanted a drink. He wanted a new life.

"Still looking for angels, Detective?"

Treber looked up, startled by the sudden voice. Duncan the homeless man stood before him, clad in his omnipresent wardrobe of torn, grubby handouts.

"Well, you came to the right place this time," the old man said.

"What do you know about this?" Treber asked, his voice weak and cracking.

The old man smiled, revealing blackened nubs that passed for teeth. "I may not have been clear when we spoke at the church. God still cares, I suppose. But...sometimes, we don't always agree with His decisions."

"W-w-what?" Treber choked. "What do you mean? Please tell me."

"You're not the only one who's tired of the suffering, Detective, but what can you do? You watch over the kids. You see that they're safe, but the world just keeps rotting and stinking, a little more each day, and no matter what you do, there's something ready to snatch them away. It's always passed off as God's will. Detective, how many times have you zipped up a dead kid, or maybe, worked a traffic accident where a carload of promising young kids have combined to paint the car a different color? And what do relatives say? It was God's will. They say that to help them deal with the pain of their loss, and some of them might even believe it, and it is true. It is God's will, but that don't make it right."

"I don't understand," Treber said.

"Well, understand this then. You're doing your part, Detective. It may not seem like it at times. It may seem like the whole system is against you, but I'm here to tell you that you do make a difference. It may be a small difference. Hell, it may even be invisible, but it is a difference. And that's all anyone can ask of you."

"So, I'm here to tell you, Detective. Don't do what you've been thinking of. Don't do it. The kids need you. If not you, then who?"

Treber looked down at his feet. He noticed a chunk of brain from one of the dead kids clinging to the broken curb. He started to speak when the wind began to grow fierce. Papers and wrappers began to spin through the air. Dust from the streets peppered Treber's face like tiny needles.

"No!" the old man shouted. "Leave him be! He has a job to do!"

Treber shielded his eyes and stared at the old man. He seemed to be shouting into the air at nothing. The streetlight suddenly exploded, showering the two men with tiny shards of glass. The street grew very dark.

"No! No! Goddamn you all! You can't have him!" the old man screamed defiantly. "You can't take him! Not now! Not after so long!"

Treber peered into the blackness, trying to let his eyes adjust, when he noticed the blackness was moving. It drifted up and into the air above them like a giant black curtain, billowing and floating on the powerful gusts of wind. Treber looked up in sheer terror as the mass of darkness floated just above them. He noticed two circles of dark mass, even blacker than the surrounding surface, and he realized he was looking into this thing's eyes.

Treber's soul suddenly screamed out. In the creature's eyes, Treber could see every child he had ever lost, every dead kid he had ever collected, every precious young soul he had failed to save. Inside the black beast's soul lay every failure Treber had ever endured.

Duncan stood tall against the force of the wind, still screaming into the gale. The wind was so strong and loud that Treber could no longer comprehend the old man's words. Suddenly, Duncan's feet left the sidewalk, and he was carried up toward the black creature. Treber stared up into the black as the old man's shape grew smaller and smaller. Then a light appeared in the center of the dark creature's mass, so vivid and bright in the surrounding blackness that it temporarily blinded Treber. The old man screamed, and beams of light shot forth in all directions. Droplets of cold liquid bounced on his arms and neck. He fought to move forward against the wind, flailing his arms about in an effort to reach Duncan.

Then, just as suddenly as it had appeared, the gale died. The gigantic black creature was gone.

The only thing that remained was a strange, hairless white creature lying on the sidewalk where Duncan had stood before being swept away by the wind. Treber bolted forward and knelt at the creature's side, carefully lifting its head onto his lap.

White steam floated from the creature's ruined chest, and a white milky liquid dribbled from its tiny "O" of a mouth. The dark eyes shifted to look at Treber, and it coughed, spewing a white mist.

"Did you ever think you'd really find the angels, little Lloyd?" the creature said.

"Don't talk," Treber said. "We'll get help."

"No, no. There is no help for me, but there is for you. Remember what I said earlier. Don't give up on the kids. You must do your part."

"I'll try," Treber said. "I'll try."

The creature's mouth turned into a sideways oval, and Treber thought that it was trying to smile. "I did all right with you, didn't I, little Lloyd? You turned out okay. That time you went over the handlebars on your bike. I caught you. You only got a broken wrist out of that one. And when you wrecked your dad's truck doing donuts on the ice. You barely missed that tree." The creature coughed up more cottage cheese. "And three years ago, when that bullet barely caught your bullet-proof vest. You gotta promise me, Lloyd. You gotta be extra careful now. Now that the angels are gone."

"Are...are you my guardian angel?" Treber asked.

The oval grew narrower. "That I am, child."

"But...but how, for so long. These others...they're dying as kids."

"Times were simpler when you grew up. You got into your share of trouble, kept me running in circles, that's for sure, but it's nothing like today. Kids have too much to fight these days. We tried to compensate by protecting them, but it was against the Lord's word. So many kids are dying so young. We feel it shouldn't be that way. We did our best to protect them."

"What was that black thing?" Treber asked.

"Dark..." The guardian angel coughed. "A dark...angel. God sends them when we protect our children, too much. If we prevent the Lord's word from occurring, He relieves us of duty. Like it, or not. If it's the Lord's will to take a child, then He won't allow us to stand in the way."

"But...but that means..."

"Watch the kids, little Lloyd. They don't have anyone to watch over them anymore."

Treber's guardian angel spewed one more blast of white gore and lay still. His round black eyes still stared up at the night sky. Treber leaned forward to hug the strange, but wonderful, creature. When he lifted his head, his hands held only white powder.

◈

It's a losing battle, Treber admitted to himself. No matter what anyone says, even his very own guardian angel, there's no way they could win.

Sirens blared in the distance, growing closer and louder with each passing second. Treber looked around at the multitude of dead children lying in their blood on the grimy city streets. The creatures were all gone, their mounds of dust blown to wherever on the soft night breeze.

Treber chambered one round in his service revolver.

It's a losing battle.

Treber had made a promise to himself, a promise to the kids, a promise to someone that had helped him in his quest to grow tall and strong.

Maybe not now, maybe not tonight, but somewhere down the road, days, weeks, months, years from now, when it all got to be too much for him, could he be faulted if he broke that promise?

After all, there was no one left to watch over *him* now.

Harvest Moon

Had I been thinking with my head and not my dick like I should've been, I'd have seen right away that the girl on the bicycle was a werewolf. She had dark, bushy eyebrows that met above her nose, and I'd always read that was a classic sign. She was young—twenty-one at the most. She wore cutoff jeans that hung low on her hips, and one of those little baby T-shirts that rode high on her tits, and there was a lot of bare belly in between. She was pale, rail-thin, and her tits were small. Call it the waif-look, the little boy look, whatever. It was a look that worked for me. I fell for her, and I fell hard.

I was working somewhere in the "hill country" of southeast Texas doing highway repair when I met her. Our crew was patching holes on Highway 69. The road hadn't been repaired in years, and it was in bad shape. It was steady summer work, but it was hotter than blazes on that asphalt.

I was working alone that day. It was late September, and the work was about to end for the season. Jose, my partner in our two-man crews, had had enough earlier that morning and had taken off down 69 toward the first bus station he could find. I was doing the work of two men, hauling the steaming black tar shit down the road from the main truck and patting it into the holes.

That's when Anna came riding up on her bicycle. She rode by me once, turned and circled around me a few times. The summer sun kept me bronzed and the hard work kept me pumped, so I knew she was checking me out. Our glaring age difference kept me from saying anything to her, but no one was watching, so I said hell with it.

"What are you doing?"

"Riding."

"In circles?"

She shrugged. "You know, I'm getting that black shit all over my tires."

I laughed. "Don't you want the road fixed? Makes for a smoother ride."

She shrugged again. "The shoulder's not so bad."

She stopped the bike in front of me and stared me down for a moment. "You don't live around here."

"No, I live in Dallas. They put me up in a cheap motel every night."

"What's your name?"

"Johnny," I told her.

"You want to come to a party tonight, Johnny?" she asked. She was a bold little vixen.

"Maybe."

"FM 44," she said, pointing back in the direction from which she had come. "Big barn about fifty yards off the road. It'll be fun."

"Will there be beer?" I asked.

"Of course," she said, and smiled.

Like I said, I fell hard. Eyebrows and all.

Anna met me coming up the road to the big old barn. She was smiling wide, and had a cold beer waiting for me. She wore a short little summer dress, and she looked so damned good.

She took my hand and led me toward the barn. There were many voices and loud grunge music pumping from the barn's open doors. The dilapidated building seemed to swell with the beat of the music. The sun was setting in the west, and there was a pale-yellow halo of moon in the distant sky. *Full moon.* I didn't pay any attention to that, either.

Anna took me into the barn and introduced me to her friends. There were over two hundred people in the big old barn, and they were all a lot younger than me. I started to feel a little silly. Me, thirty-one years old, partying with a bunch of kids. But soon, the combination of beer, the music, and Anna's smiles melted away my apprehension.

I spent most of the time just talking to Anna. She was so sweet and so cool. Anna told me all kinds of things as we sat there listening to the music and downing cold ones. I was really falling in love.

The party went on pretty much as any normal party would, until about one in the morning, when the moon was high in the sky.

That's when everyone started getting naked.

Now, mind you, I'm no babe in the woods. I've had my share, done my number of wild things, and I know kids are having sex all the time. I watch the talk shows.

But this was a full-fledged orgy.

They all piled in the middle of the hay, couples on top of others, intertwined in all positions, engaged in all kinds of sex. This was just a little rural barn filled with a bunch of horny young people, but there were some serious shenanigans going on. Even I started to get a little embarrassed.

I tried to find Anna, but she was nowhere in sight. My best guess was that she was somewhere at the bottom of that pile. The thought kind of made me sick, but it turned me on a little, too.

Hell, I'd had a few free beers. It was time to head back to the motel.

That's when the howling started.

I thought it was dogs at first, way off in the distance, or maybe coyotes. I had seen a few coyotes splattered along the highway. The howl was low and soft, like a faraway siren. Then it started getting a little louder, a little shriller. Soon, the old barn was vibrating with the sound of howling.

The light from all the Coleman lanterns was growing dimmer as the night wore on, making it harder for me to understand what was happening. A dog had wandered into the barn. Big one, too. Then there was another one, right in the middle of the big sex scene.

It was then that I noticed one of the dogs had a human body. Another one had a human head.

It was too dark to see, and I was too drunk to make rational observations. I kept telling myself these things.

But they were there. The kids were turning into wolves, right before my eyes. Some of them had changed completely into wolves. Some of them had just gotten hairy. Some had mixed parts. It was like they were only changing what they wanted to change, and all this time, they were still having sex. They were moving from partner to partner, and I wasn't even sure the couples were of opposite sexes anymore. I know dogs don't care. The musky aroma of spent sex, semen, and pussy juice, mixing with the pungent odor of wet dog filled my senses. It made me want to puke, but at the same time, I found it kind of exciting.

I continued to observe until most of the sex was over. The huge pile of hairy bodies slowly began to dissipate. I thought the party would end soon when I noticed something being lowered by a rope from the barn's rafters.

It was Jose. He was naked, tied at the wrists, and he'd had the shit beaten out of him. His face was black and purple. Fresh blood dribbled down his chest.

THE POROSITY OF SOULS

A big wolf standing on two legs walked over to Jose. Its eyes were even with Jose's, and the massive wolfen head dwarfed my former partner's. Jose seemed too tired to care, but when the wolf looked into his eyes, Jose started screaming. He never could speak much English, so I couldn't understand what he was saying, but I imagine it was something along the lines of "Help!"

The other kids had gathered in a circle around the hanging Mexican, eagerly awaiting what was about to happen. They sat patiently, a low, rumbling growl emanating from their throats. The collective sound was like the buzzing of faulty speakers. Their wolfen eyes sparkled. Tails wagged expectantly.

The big wolf raked a single claw from Jose's breastbone to his crotch, and everything from Jose's rib cage to his dick spilled out onto the hay with a sickening wet plop. The odor hit me immediately, and I lost it. The wolves pounced upon the pile of entrails, snapping up the glistening organs like they were pre-packaged doggy treats, slicing them in two, playing tug of war with an unwound coil of intestine. I think Jose lived for a few seconds while they feasted on his organs. He screamed a little while longer anyway.

When the guts were gone, the big wolf sliced the rope clean through, and the insatiable wolf-kids pounced on what was left of Jose. The guts were bad enough, but when they crunched through his legs and snapped the thick bones in their powerful jaws, I lost it again.

I regained control of myself quickly when I noticed Anna setting the baby down on the blood-drenched hay. Chunks of gore and pieces of splintered bone still littered the area under the severed rope. Anna knelt before the baby and the kids gathered in a circle once again.

"*Noo!*" I screamed, finally breaking my silence and charging from the loft where I had been sitting.

I bolted forward, shoving one bitch werewolf out of my way, and lunged for the baby. I grabbed the kid in my arms and held him protectively. "You can't do this! Not a child! Not a little baby!"

The guy with the big wolf head started toward me, but Anna stepped between us. She took the child in her hands, and when her eyes met mine, I released my grip on the baby. She set the baby back down on the bloody hay.

"We're not going to kill the baby," Anna said. "He's one of us. He's ours."

I stood there breathing heavily. "B-b-b-but..." I stammered, "what...what are you doing?"

"It's the harvest moon," Anna said. "It's time to wean the child."

That's when I noticed the baby was growling at me. Anna reached down and retrieved something that had fallen from Jose's ravaged body. She held the slippery piece of meat to the child, gently rubbing it against the baby's lips. His mouth parted, and Anna slipped the bloody chunk inside.

The wolves started howling again.

The baby crawled around in the hay, retrieving pieces of Jose by himself, and popping them into his tiny mouth.

Anna took my hand and led me back to the loft, though it was a while before I could tear my eyes from the feeding child. She sat me down and made me look at her.

"Every full moon of the autumn months is the harvest moon," she began. "Our children are born in the late summer so that they can be weaned during the next year's harvest moons. The feeding initiates the process."

"You see, I'm not as young as I appear to be, Johnny. I'm much older than you would believe, but we don't age, Johnny. As long as we do what you witnessed tonight, during every harvest moon, we will never age, or die of natural causes. We must change and eat human flesh every harvest moon, or we will age as every mortal does."

"But how do you grow to this age?" I asked.

"Our children grow like normal humans until they reach puberty. Then we help them to change. They never physically age. We stay young and beautiful forever. The feeding of human flesh as young children starts the process of lycanthropy."

I shook my head. It was all too difficult for me to comprehend. "But why did you bring me here? Why did you make me witness this?"

Anna sighed and looked away for a moment. "Honestly?" I nodded. "I invited you here with every intention of doing to you the same thing that was done to that other man, but when I talked to you and got to know you, I grew to care for you. You aren't like the others."

"But how can you do this?" I asked. "How can you kill people and not get discovered?" "They're drifters. Illegal aliens. People that will never be missed. Do you understand now?"

No, I didn't understand any of it. My mind was just a seething swarm of emotions, bouncing off the walls of my brain, until the strongest emotion, the only one I could truly trust, fought its way to the forefront of my thoughts, and I blurted out, "I love you, Anna."

"I know," she said, "but you mustn't."

"Why not?"

She pressed a finger to my lips and shushed me. "I can only give you this."

Anna leaned forward, her bare breasts pressing against my chest, and I closed my eyes. There was something warm and wet against my lips. I thought she was kissing me until a coppery tang found my tongue.

"I can only give you a taste of what we're like," she said softly. "Only a taste."

Her fingers parted my lips, and the wet thing slid into my mouth and down my throat like a raw oyster. It was bitter, and it seemed spicy. I was suddenly aware of the way Jose smelled when we all piled into the truck after sweating in the sun all day. The feeling suddenly aroused me as the piece of Jose worked its way into my stomach, and my dick started getting hard.

I opened my eyes, and Anna was there. "Can't I be with you, with all of you, all the time?" She shook her head. "Can't you bite me, or something and turn me into a werewolf?"

"It doesn't work like that, Johnny. You don't become a werewolf. You're born a werewolf. I can't make you into one."

"I can't stay, can I?" I asked.

She shook her head again, and I followed her green eyes as they moved from side to side. "You could be in danger here, being an outsider. You'll have to leave now. We'll all be going home soon."

She stood to leave.

"Anna, I love you," I said.

"Maybe I love you a little, too."

I smiled weakly at her. That suited me just fine. A little was all I asked.

Every fall, when the trees grow bare and the air turns cool, I head to the hill country. I go to the barn during every harvest moon and just observe. I can't be with Anna, can't be with any of them, but I stare through a sliver in the boards, and I watch the festival under the bright harvest moon.

I know I can't be a part of them, but I do my share. During the summer months, a lot of drifters come down Highway 69 toward Padre Island. I strike up a conversation, tell them there's a party if they want to come. It's usually easy.

The werewolves know I bring them food. They know I'm always outside, too, I think, but they don't seem to mind. They never come outside. Anna never comes to see me.

Sometimes though, during the party, someone will throw a bone out to me. If I'm lucky, there's still a little meat on it. My jaw isn't nearly as powerful as those of the werewolves, and I have trouble chewing the bones, but I think I'll get the hang of it eventually. My digestive system isn't used to the ground-up bone either. It hurts like hell when I shit, but it's getting easier and easier. And when the party ends and all the werewolves go home, I sneak into the old barn and rummage through the hay. Sometimes, they miss a morsel here and there. At times, the hay is still wet, and I just sit and suck from the straws, imagining what it would be like to be a part of Anna's unique world, to be in the middle of the wonderful ritual I experienced on that cool, autumn night under the harvest moon.

I appreciate the little bits of their lives that the werewolves let me experience. In my mind, each bit seems to bring me just a little closer to Anna.

And a little's all I ask.

Second Chances

Joseph Chaney stood at the kitchen window of his dirty, little one-bedroom apartment, peering forlornly down into the dismal streets of New York City. The pristine whiteness of winter snow drifted down onto the filthy, decaying sidewalks, the pure mingling with the diseased. From somewhere below, the joyful refrains of "Winter Wonderland" wafted up to Joe's ears, and he took a long, slow drink from his bottle. Looking at the container of little white pills in his other hand, his eyes fixed on the words "Fifty Count," and a grim parody of a Paul Simon tune rang through his head.

Fifty ways to end your miserable life.

It was Christmas Eve...again. Kids always seemed to wish Christmas would last forever, but Joe wished the holidays would never come. *The holidays*, he thought, and chuckled. Sounds so goddamn cheery, but not for him. Not for Joseph Chaney. It was always the same. Every year, the same questions came crashing down on him. Why are you here? What are you doing with your life? What's the point of going on? Who would miss you? Who would give a shit if you were found face down in an alley somewhere, reeking of cheap wine, your vomit frozen to your face?

Joe opened the window, the frigid air chasing a wave of snowflakes into his kitchen. He leaned out of the window and stared down into the empty streets below. There was no one out tonight. *That's because they're all with someone*, he told himself. They all have families and friends who care about them. They all have lives. They all have things to look forward to, reasons to live.

He knew that wasn't necessarily true though. His graveyard shifts at the morgue on the lower east side confirmed that. Christmas Eve boasted the highest suicide rate of any day of the year, and Joe experienced it every season. After midnight, they would start rolling in, one after the other. That had always made his struggle to join them that much more difficult. So far, he had been able to resist the almost uncontrollable urge, but did that make him better? Or were they the lucky ones? Was he a failure, even when he tried to take the easy way out?

Joe pulled himself back inside and shut the window. The little snowflakes wilted and melted until they were mere puddles on the windowsill. Coming from above him on one of the higher floors, there was laughter, the sounds of happy people having a happy time. Joe looked at the clock above the refrigerator. It was eleven o'clock. He had to be at the morgue in an hour.

Joe took another swill of whiskey and pulled the bottle of pills from his pocket. He stared at it for an eternity, a myriad of melancholy thoughts racing through his muddled brain, and Paul Simon began to sing again.

Joe made his way through the newly fallen snow toward his workplace, the fine powder and the brisk wind chilling his spirits even more. The empty streets seemed to emphasize his loneliness, like a ghostly spotlight singling out his desolation. Except for the occasional police cruiser passing on the streets, there was nothing. Joe passed an empty Salvation Army post, the bellringer long since departed for a festive evening with family and friends. The snow began to fall a little harder, and the cheerful sounds of "Oh, Come All Ye Faithful" drifting from an apartment above were drowned out by the lonely wail of an ambulance racing to claim another victim of the holiday season.

At last, Joe reached his destination and ascended the steps up to the front doors of the City Morgue. He took out his keys and unlocked the doors. Stepping inside, he stamped the snow from his boots, looked down the long hallway to his office, and sighed. Joe didn't know if he could cope with the death that he would witness tonight. This Christmas Eve was the worst yet. He seemed to be more depressed than ever.

Joe started down the long walk to his office, pausing at the entrance to the refrigeration room. He put his ear to the door. The steady drone of the compressor was the only sound emanating from the room. *For now*, Joe thought. It would soon be alive with the hustle and bustle of incoming death.

Joe turned from the room and entered his office. Frankie Valdoni, who worked the shift before Joe's, sat at the desk, watching Frosty the Snowman on the television.

"Hey, Joey!" Frankie said, excitedly. "How are you?" He jumped to his feet and shook Joe's hand enthusiastically.

"Great," Joe said, putting on a happy face for Frankie's sake. "Just fine."

Joe knew that Frankie would be leaving the morgue to spend Christmas Eve with his wife Angela and their little boy, Tony. He didn't want to do anything to spoil Frankie's jovial mood.

"You okay, Joey?" Frankie asked. Frankie always called him Joey.

"Yeah," Joe said reassuringly. "Yeah, I'm fine. Just have a little cold. That's all." Joe sniffled and pretended to wipe his nose.

"Minestrone with chicken, and lots and lots of oregano," Frankie said. "Best thing in the world for a cold. That's what Momma always gave us kids when we were little."

"I'll remember that," Joe said. "Been busy?"

Frankie sighed. "Yeah. Yeah. Couple of murders. Heart attacks. And, of course, the suicides. Eight suicides, and the night ain't half over. Can you believe it?" Frankie turned to face Joe. "Why do they do it, Joey? Why do people kill themselves? Especially on Christmas Eve?"

"I don't know, Frankie," Joe said. "I guess some people just get...lonely."

"Yeah, I guess so."

"Hey, you'd better be going. Tony's probably giving Angela fits by now."

"Yeah, he gets to open one present tonight and the rest in the morning, but not the bike. That's what he wanted the most." Frankie winked at Joe. "That's what Santa's bringing him."

Joe smiled and handed Frankie his coat, and they walked slowly down the long hall to the front door. "You be careful walking home, Frankie. And say hi to the family for me."

"I will, and I will." Frankie turned in the doorway. "And Joey. Merry Christmas."

Joe smiled, and his eyes glazed over. "Merry Christmas, Frankie."

Frankie closed the door behind him, and Joe's eyes followed him through the small window. Frankie's head bobbed as he bounced down the stairs until it finally disappeared in a wind-blown flurry of flakes.

Joe stared out the window for a long moment before returning to the office. He reached slowly inside his coat for the whiskey bottle, the stubby neck somehow feeling reassuring to him, like the touch of a mother tucking her child into bed on a snowy Christmas Eve. Joe took a long drink from the bottle. In his other pocket rested the sleeping pills.

Joe sat behind the desk and leaned back with the bottle of pills clutched tightly in his hands. He reached for the whiskey again, and shook the pills, rattling the tiny saviors around in their cell to the tune of "Jingle Bells."

THE POROSITY OF SOULS

◆

Joe awoke abruptly to a noise that seemed to come from the refrigeration room. His heart leapt up into his throat at his sudden arousal. *Must be another arrival*, he thought.

Joe walked around the desk and peered out into the dimly lit hallway. Nothing but silence.

"Hello?" he asked cautiously. "Anyone there?"

There was no answer. Curious, Joe moved toward the refrigeration room. He put his ear to the door and there was nothing but the compressor. Then laughter.

Joe stepped back from the door, shocked. These ambulance drivers must be having a damn good time to be laughing it up inside a morgue. Joe unlocked the door and shoved it open.

There were no ambulance drivers in the refrigeration room. There were seven people, each dressed in a white gown. There was a blonde-haired girl dancing with a young man. Standing on top of a table was another young man, singing and laughing. Sitting on the edge of the table were two middle-aged men, apparently involved in conversation, and standing to the side, watching the young couple dance, were two men—one elderly and one a slightly younger Black man. None of them seemed to notice Joe's entrance.

Joe stood wide-eyed, staring in disbelief at the strange group of people. He had no idea who they were, or how they had managed to get in through the locked doors. Something wasn't right. It was only then that Joe noticed the seven open drawers, all of them empty.

"Who the hell are you people?" Joe shouted.

They all stopped and turned to look at Joe. The way they stared at him made Joe think he was the intruder.

"Look, everyone!" the man on the table cried. "It's Santa Claus!" They all laughed. "What'd you bring us, Santa? What'd you bring us?"

"How did you people get in here?" Joe asked, ignoring the empty drawers.

"Never mind that, young man," the elderly man spoke up. "How do we get out?"

Joe scratched his head and approached the group. He looked at his watch. It was two-thirty. He looked at the young couple, still embracing. "How did you get in here?" Joe asked, sternly.

"Come on, man. It's Christmas Eve. Don't talk that way. There's love and happiness in the air," the dancer said, pirouetting like a ballerina.

The man on the table snickered. "Bogus."

"How did you all get in here?" Joe repeated.

"How do you think we got in here, bogus?" the joker asked.

"Come on, it's Christmas Eve," the young man said.

"Yeah, lighten up," the girl said.

"Yeah, where's your holiday spirit?" they all chimed in.

Joe put his hands to his ears to silence the cacophony of sour voices directed at him. "Shut up!" he yelled. "All of you just shut up!"

"Wow, you sure are a grouch. What are you? The grinch who stole Christmas?" the funny man said. He acted just like a nightclub comedian reject.

They all chuckled at the comedian's remark. Joe took a deep breath. "I'm going to ask you one more time. How did you get in here?"

One of the middle-aged men approached Joe. "We got in here the same way anyone gets in here," he said, looking Joe straight in the eyes. "On our backs, lying on a cold steel table with a sheet thrown over our faces."

Joe looked over at the open drawers, and back at the strange people. He shook his head and laughed quietly. "All right. Joke's over. Everyone out. This has gone on long enough."

"Finally," the girl said. "That's what we wanted all along. Just for someone to come and let us out."

"Well, you're going out now," Joe said. "Just tell me what you did with my bodies, and I'll let you out."

"Bodies?"

Joe laughed. "That's good. That's funny. Well, you couldn't have hidden them that good, so where are they?"

"You are bogus, aren't you?"

"Yeah, I'm bogus. So where are they?"

"It's Christmas Eve," the girl reminded.

"I know what day it is, sister," Joe said, "and that just makes you people even weirder, so hand over my bodies."

"You don't get it, do you?" the girl's boyfriend said.

"Get what?"

They all shook their heads. "That's a shame. It really is. If only you knew."

Joe looked them each in the eye, attempting to study each one's feelings and thoughts. He really knew the answer, deep down, but his sanity refused to let him accept the truth. Maybe he was dreaming. Maybe he was still asleep in his office, and all this madness was just an extremely vivid liquor-induced nightmare.

"It's Christmas Eve," the dancer said. "We just want to go home now, that's all. We just want to go home."

"We made a mistake," the girl joined in. "We're sorry you can't find...your stuff. But...we just made a mistake, that's all."

"What are you talking about?" Joe asked, his voice shaking slightly.

"What we did was so stupid, so incredibly stupid," one of the middle-aged men said. "It's not the answer. It's not. God, we're so very fortunate tonight."

"It's Christmas Eve," the girl said, a tear rolling down her soft cheek. "We want to go home."

"This town is so big, so cruel, so intimidating," her boyfriend said. "Sometimes, you feel so alone, it just gets the best of you, you know?"

"I don't understand," Joe said.

"All the times I cried for someone to love, all the heartaches I endured, all the sad times I lived through," the man said. "And Michelle was out there the whole time, and I just didn't know it." He hugged the girl tightly. "I quit before I should've. My answer was out there, but I gave up the battle too soon."

"I'm just as guilty as you are, Donald. I gave up, too. But we found each other now, and that's all that matters."

"Oh, isn't that sweet? I think I'm going to cry," the joker said, pretending to wipe tears from his eyes with an imaginary tissue.

The others gathered around the couple, applauding and hugging them. Joe stepped back, as if he were a spectator outside the screen, watching the show.

One of the middle-aged men spoke up. "I'm Evan Howard, accountant. My business just had the worst fiscal year in its history. I was at a loss. Christmas time, and I couldn't afford gifts for my family. Do you have any idea what it's like to have to tell your son you can't get him a Christmas present? All he asked for was a goddamn baseball glove, and I couldn't even afford that. I couldn't face my family knowing I was a failure. I...took the coward's way out."

The other man spoke. "I'm Vernon Blake. I lost everything I had in a business venture. Like an idiot, I listened to some people that I had no business listening to, and we all lost our asses. I suppose my associates dealt with the losses better than I did."

Evan put his arm around Vernon and comforted him. Michelle and Donald did the same. Joe backed against the table, shaking his head in denial.

The old man cleared his throat and began to speak. "I'm Howard Dow III. I had everything. Yessir, I had everything money could buy. Everything I tried was a complete success. Got to the point where I was sick of it all. Life posed no challenge anymore. I was bored, and when I get bored, I get depressed. How can a man who has so much, have so little? No kids, no family, just material things."

"I'm Jackson Warrington," the Black man said. "I never did have anything. I've lived on the streets as long as I can remember. Never havin' nothing to eat. Always cold. Always scared. Guess I decided I couldn't take it no more."

Joe buried his face in his hands and sobbed quietly. *This must be it*, he thought. *I've finally lost my mind. After all the years of struggling with thoughts of suicide, my brain finally snapped. I've gone off the deep end. I'm imagining all this. That must be the answer.*

The comedian on the table cackled hysterically. "This is good stuff! Damn, why didn't I think of this before! This is so rich!" He fell to the floor, holding his stomach, laughing uncontrollably.

Joe dropped to his knees, rolling himself up into a defenseless ball, and wept for his lost sanity. Seemingly unaware of Joe's actions, the strange group laughed joyously, and the girl began to sing "We Wish You a Merry Christmas." They all joined in as the joker jumped back on the table and began to dance from one end to the other. Michelle and Donald waltzed across the stark white floor. Howard, the millionaire, danced with Jackson, the street person, laughing and singing aloud. Evan, the accountant, did the Twist with Vernon, the ruined man, stepping around Joe's crumpled form.

"It's Christmas Eve!" the comedian screamed. "And all is right with the world!"

Joe sat up on the floor and wiped tears from his bloodshot eyes. "Shut up," he mumbled quietly. No one heard him over the happy banter. "Shut up," Joe said a little louder. The happiness continued. Joe jumped to his feet. "Shut up! Do you hear me? Shut up! Shut up! Shut up!"

They did. They all stared, wide-eyed and amazed, at Joe. Joe stood in their midst, sweat pouring from his forehead, panting like a spent dog. There was silence, save for Joe's heavy breathing.

"You people are dead! Do you hear me? Dead! You can't just get up and go on with your lives just because it's Christmas Eve and you feel sorry for yourselves! You committed suicide, each and every one of you, and now, you think you've changed your minds! Well, I've got news for you people, it doesn't work that way! You're dead, and dead people can't do this! Now shut up and get back in your drawers!" Joe yelled, gesturing toward the drawers.

Howard looked up at the comedian. "What was that word you used? Bogus?" The joker nodded and giggled. Howard turned back to Joe. "You really are bogus, aren't you?"

Joe began to shove the old man back toward his drawer. "No, I'm not bogus. I'm insane. That's all. A simple case of insanity."

Michelle reached out and grabbed Joe's arm. "No, you don't understand. You said we can't come back from death just because it's Christmas Eve, but maybe that's exactly why we can come back. I can't explain it any better than you can, but it's true. We were all dead, but now we're alive. I don't know why. I don't know how, but we're alive, and you've got to believe us."

"I know why," Evan said. "We each found something tonight. We found something in death that we couldn't find in life. We found that little something, whatever it is, that was missing in our lives. You see, I can help Vernon and his business associates file for bankruptcy. He gets on his feet again, and my company gets new business, new leads, new hope."

"Yeah," Jackson said. "And Howard is gonna give me and my homeless friends jobs and places to live, and he can see what the other half lives like. We help each other."

"I never gave a thought to helping others before, but now, I intend to make up for all those lost years. I finally have a purpose in life. Jackson will be my right-hand man. Together, we'll abolish the term 'homeless'," Howard said.

Donald grabbed Michelle and kissed her. "And we found each other."

Joe started to say something, but couldn't think of anything that made sense. Nothing did.

"So, how do we get out of here?" Donald asked Joe.

Joe sighed and pointed to the door leading to the hallway. "Out the door, take a left." He took out his keys, removing the one that fit the front door, and handed it to Donald.

"Gotcha." Donald shook Joe's hand and smiled. "Don't be so bogus, man. You've got some serious problems in your life. If you don't take the time to get them straightened out, you're going to end up like us. Only you may not be so lucky."

Joe nodded as the others left through the refrigerator room door. Only he and the comedian remained.

"Why didn't I see this before?" the comedian asked. "It's so painfully obvious. There I was, all depressed because all of my acts sucked so bad, and the funniest damn routine was under my nose the whole time."

"What's that?" Joe asked quietly.

"Life, man," the comedian said. "There's nothing more utterly ridiculous than life. Nothing more stupid and ironic than just being on this old earth." He smiled. "So that's it. Life. That's my whole act now. Just observe life. All the material I need is right at my feet. And to think, it took death to make me see life."

Joe shrugged as the comedian hopped off the table. "Well, bogus. I'm outta here. The name's Dan, catch my act sometime if you get a chance." He headed for the door. "Damn, these gowns are drafty," he said, clenching the garment tighter against his bare legs.

Joe laughed to himself as the last of the strange group left the building. He stood in the center of the room for a long moment, collecting and sorting his own private thoughts. His eye finally caught a glimpse of a clipboard with the word *suicide* written across the top of the page. Joe moved slowly over to the drawer and studied the paper more closely. The last suicide victim in the room. Joe sighed and pulled the drawer open.

The man in the drawer was middle-aged. Despite the peaceful look of death, the dead man's face seemed in torment, and that saddened Joe. He leaned over and propped himself up with his elbow, positioning his face just above the deceased.

"So, what's your story, buddy?" Joe asked. "Why didn't you join the others?"

"He can't," said a voice from behind. Joe jumped up and wheeled about to meet the owner of the voice.

It was a hearse driver. He was a tall, pale, thin man, and he wore a red and white Santa Claus hat. He was pushing a stretcher along in front of him.

"What do you mean he can't?" Joe asked.

The ambulance driver, smacking on a wad of gum, raised his eyebrows and smiled. "Weird night, huh?"

"What do you mean he can't?" Joe repeated.

The driver shrugged. "Maybe it's not the first time."

"What do you mean the first time?" Joe persisted. "The first time for what? Suicide? Do you mean suicide?"

"I've said enough already," the driver said. "Help me lift him onto the stretcher, would you?"

"Are you saying people get a second chance when they commit suicide?" Joe asked, grunting as they lifted the body and placed it gently onto the waiting stretcher.

The driver laughed. "I'm not saying anything, buddy."

"But why?" Joe asked. "I mean, suicide is supposed to be the ultimate sin. Why would anyone be given a second chance?"

The driver pulled the sheet over the man's head and sighed. "Consider it a Christmas present, alright?"

The driver turned to wheel the corpse away in the direction from which he had come. Joe rubbed his chin. *A Christmas present?* he thought. *Is that why they all came back?*

The driver turned around before exiting the door. "Oh, by the way," he said. "Merry Christmas."

Joe raised his hand and waved. "Merry Christmas," he said, not aware he was saying it.

So that's it, Joe thought. *All those people tonight thought they had nothing to live for, so they committed suicide. Then, in death, they all found that key ingredient that had been missing from their lives. They all found a reason to live, and that reason was so strong, so powerful, that they were able to defy death and walk away.*

Joe sniffed back a tear. "God bless," he said quietly. "God bless you all."

Joe thought back to the earlier struggles with himself, and knew what he had to do. He closed all the empty drawers and went back into the office.

Never again would he entertain thoughts of suicide. Not on Christmas Eve, not on any day of the year.

Joe reached blindly for the whiskey bottle, and it almost flew from his hand as he lifted it. It was lighter than he had anticipated. Much lighter. His quivering hand reached for the pill bottle, but his mind was already telling him what he would find.

Joe had every intention of going into the office and emptying the whiskey and the pills into the nearest sink he could find.

But the bottles were already empty.

Oh, by the way, Merry Christmas.

Joe turned and rested against the edge of the desk. His knees were not supporting him properly. He stared up the long hallway, to the front door, through the little window.

Tiny snowflakes bounced against the glass, and the happy sound of carolers drifted up the hall from the snowbound streets.

Friday Night in the Gun Cabinet

Burt Collier stumbled out of his trailer home, already half-way into his usual Friday night drunk, and climbed into his beat-up Ford pickup. He lit a Marlboro, coughed, and hacked like a man with only forty percent of his lungs remaining, then rolled down the window, and spit. Taking a big swill of Wild Turkey, Burt started the ramshackle old truck and headed for the pool hall on the outskirts of town. It wasn't until the trailer was perfectly quiet, the dust had settled, and the choking and spewing of the old Ford's engine had faded away in the distance, that the guns in Burt Collier's gun cabinet began to speak.

"I hate belonging to that man," said Frank, Burt's twelve-year old Winchester 30/06 Bolt-Action Deer Rifle. Frank leaned back casually against the rack, his smokey-blue barrel cool in the pale light, his rich tung oiled stock, hand-buffed to a soft luster with #0000 steel wool, gleaming in the reflection in the glass. "He scares me."

"Yeah," agreed Smitty, the Daisy Red Ryder BB gun that belonged to Burt's kid, Danny. Smitty was slightly out of Frank's league as far as power, but they had always been good friends. Smitty leaned back smoothly against the notches in the maple cabinet, trying his best to imitate his idol. "He's an asshole, too."

"Same thing every Friday night," Frank added. "The sorry bastard sends Danny to his grandma's, and he goes off and ties one on."

Smitty nodded, and Frank looked about the rest of the gun cabinet. Shorty, Burt's Smith & Wesson .38 snub-nose, sat quietly in the upper storage area between boxes of .22 long rifle cartridges and shotgun shells, peering through the glass at the window on the other side of the room. Ace, the Marlin .22 rifle that had replaced Smitty as Danny's gun several years earlier, leaned against the storage box, saying nothing. Frank cast his gaze to the floor of the cabinet. He looked at the butt of Buck, a Remington 12-gauge magnum shotgun. Buck was Burt's favorite. Frank smirked to himself. If ever a man and a gun were made for each other, it was Burt and Buck. They went almost everywhere together. Frank's gaze moved up the dark finish of Buck's stock, past the magazine, all the way up his sleek, solid barrel. Buck shot him a mean glare, and Frank looked away and sighed.

"I'm telling you, Smitty," Frank whispered. "I don't like it here. I want out."

"What can you do about it, Frank? I mean, you're stuck here," Smitty said matter-of-factly. "I don't want to sound negative, but you're Burt Collier's gun. Signed, sealed, and delivered."

"I know, Smitty. I know," he said, looking down at the butt of his stock, "but haven't you ever wished you were somewhere else? Don't you wish you belonged to a housewife somewhere, where all you had to do was protect your owner whenever you were needed, like it should be?"

"Well, Frank," Smitty said, "we're kind of stuck between a rock and a hard place here. A BB gun isn't much protection from anything, and a 30/06 deer rifle...well, let's just say I don't think you'd be the first choice for a housewife, either."

Frank looked away and frowned. "I know. I just get tired of the killing, that's all."

Smitty knew what Frank meant. Deer season opened last weekend, and Burt Collier was one of the first ones in town to bag a deer. Every November for the last ten years, Burt had hauled Frank off to Bowie County along the Sulphur River, or Bossier County in Louisiana, and each year had brought home a trophy worthy of any hunter's envy. None of Burt's hunting buddies knew if it was because Burt Collier was such a good hunter, or because Frank was such a damned fine piece of equipment. If it were the latter, such a distinction didn't make Frank very proud.

"Last weekend was pretty rough, huh?"

Frank sighed. "Yeah," he said, looking across the room at the newest of Burt's trophies mounted on the wall. A twelve-point whitetail that field dressed one hundred and forty-eight pounds and scored 121 on the Boone-Crockett scale. It hung there on the wall, staring back at him with its lifeless marble eyes, the same dead look that had gazed up at Frank when he and Burt had approached it. To the left of it was the nine-pointer Burt had shot last year, the eight-point mule deer he had bagged near El Paso three years ago, and the rest of Burt's shameful collection of trophies. All compliments of Frank and his damned pin-point accuracy. "I remember staring into the deer's eyes. I could see them through the scope," Frank said, shuddering from the memory. "He looked so innocent, so peaceful...so unaware of any danger. We were a hundred yards away, down-wind." Frank shook his head. "Poor thing never knew what hit him."

Smitty cleared his throat. "Yeah, I know what you mean. I remember Danny using me to shoot at sparrows and crows. It's on a much smaller scale, mind you, but you never get over the sadness, the shame," he said. "You'd think a kid that small wouldn't have a good aim, but he got his share."

"Takes after his old man," Frank said. "It's in their blood."

"Now Danny's graduated to rabbits," Ace said, entering the conversation. "Rabbits, mice, rats, raccoons, stray dogs, whatever he sees. Drags me all over the pastures, the woods. Kid shoots at anything that moves. Doesn't even seem to consider life or death. Just does it."

"I can't imagine why people want to shoot things for the sake of killing them, much less introducing their children to guns at such an early age," Smitty said. "Danny was four when Burt bought me for him, and seven when he bought Ace. The kid'll probably have a .410 by the time he's eleven, be hunting game animals by fifteen."

Frank chuckled, but it was woefully void of any humor.

"What?" Smitty asked.

"The euphemisms they use. *Wildlife. Sport.* Big *game.* That's all it is to them—a big game."

"What about you, Shorty? You've been pretty quiet. What's Burt use you for? What's your dubious distinction? Your proudest moment?" Ace asked, moving over to the storage area.

Shorty looked up from the glass door. He was the youngest of Burt's guns. Burt had bought him brand-new at the local Wal-Mart a year earlier. "You remember Smokey, the dog that Danny used to have? Well, you remember when he got mange? Burt was too cheap to take him to the vet, so he took me out back where Smokey was chained up. He held me down, straight at Smokey's head, and I could look right into the poor dog's eyes. He just looked up at me with those sad brown eyes, like he was just pleading for help."

Shorty choked back a tear. "Burt lowered me to the dog's head. I couldn't look, but I did. I wanted to look away. Smokey jumped, and the bullet went into his throat instead. He fell over and just laid there on the ground...crying and kicking. Burt cussed at him for moving, then he shot Smokey in the head. He didn't kick anymore." Shorty's voice quivered, and he paused for a moment. "That was the first time I'd ever been fired."

"Welcome to Burt's world," Ace said.

"I remember that," Frank said. "I remember hearing the shots, and you coming back here. Your barrel was warm, but the rest of you was cold—stone cold."

"I felt cold," Shorty said. "It was horrible. I don't think I'll ever get over that."

"You didn't do it, Shorty," Ace said. "You have to remember that. Burt pulled the trigger, not you."

"Burt pulls all our triggers," Frank said. "We can't kill anything without Burt pulling the trigger."

Shorty was about to speak when a giant shadow fell over his stubby barrel, blocking the light from the dim bulb on the living room ceiling. Shorty stared in fright past the long rifle barrels. It was Buck. He loomed behind the rifles, glaring at them all like a schoolyard bully. "What a bunch of damned pussies!" Buck roared.

The others stepped back, moving away from the larger shotgun. Buck ambled slowly towards them, his thick barrel twisting down at them angrily. "I can't believe what I'm hearin' from you. Burt pulled the trigger. We can't kill unless Burt pulls the trigger," Buck whined mockingly. *"Bullshit!"*

"Stay out of this, Buck," Frank said, standing up to the menacing shotgun. He was smaller than Buck, but he wasn't about to back down from him. "This is none of your business."

"It is so my business," Buck said. "I have to share a cabinet with you freaks, and I don't want to hear any more of this talk. We're guns, dammit! We're weapons of destruction! We were made to kill! That's our job! That's what we're here for!"

"No, it isn't!" Ace shouted. "People made us into what we are. We weren't born this way. We were forged from the earth—metals and wood that are just as natural as part of God's world as man. Man is the one that formed us into the shapes of guns. He made us into this."

"What a crock!" Buck snarled. "Yer a killin' machine the minute yer conceived, you little bastard! You can't go actin' like some goddamned pacifist. Yer a *gun*, for Chris'sake!"

"We're not like you, Buck. We don't enjoy killing. We don't like to watch things squirm and scream and die right in front of our eyes. It makes us sick. It's wrong, and we're tired of it. We can't live with it anymore," Ace said.

"Blame it on the bullets then, if yer that freaked out over it," Buck argued. "They're the ones that do the actual damage. We just kinda help 'em along."

"No," Frank said. "No, that's wrong. We go hand in hand, bullets and guns. One is useless without the other."

"It doesn't have to be this way," Shorty said. "It wasn't meant to be like this in the beginning. Man made us for protection, and to help provide sustenance for his survival. Now he uses us to kill innocent animals for sport."

"And to kill other men," Smitty added.

"Yeah," Frank said. "What do you say to that, Buck?"

"We do what man wants us to do."

"Right. We're simply a means to do his destruction," Frank said.

"We were made to *kill*!" Buck growled.

"We can't kill unless man wills it."

"Why you son of a bitch," Buck grimaced, his barrel twisting into an evil snarl. "If Burt were here to hoist me up..."

"Exactly," Frank interrupted. "If Burt were here. You can't do it without him."

"Oh, I'm tired of arguin' with you morons," Buck said, turning away.

"If there was only some way we could shut ourselves down," Shorty said. "Some way we could make ourselves malfunction. Guns across the entire world refusing to do their owners' wills."

"And how the hell are you gonna do that?" Buck asked, rejoining the argument. "You think semi-automatic rifles in the

Middle East are just gonna lay down and die? You think the terrorists' weapons are just gonna quit? Just like that? No way, man. Those guys have been killin' people for a long time. Believe me, buddy. They *enjoy* it."

"It's a start," Ace said. "As long as there's a start, there's a chance for a finish."

"Oh, man," Buck said, a look of utter disgust etched across his barrel. "You're livin' in a *dreamworld*. Some goddamned warped utopia."

"Perhaps we could shut down, somehow damage our firing mechanisms," Frank pondered.

"It's *suicide*," Buck said. "Mechanical suicide. You can screw yourself up, buddy, but count me out of it." He moved right up against Frank. "You know why Burt likes me best? 'Cause I make big holes in things. I'm a messy blood-splattering gun. Burt likes that, and I like that."

"You're sick," Frank said, staring Buck down.

Buck turned and huffed away to the opposite corner of the gun cabinet. The others relaxed a little and released little sighs of relief. No one said anything for a few minutes, as they attempted to sort out the evening's events.

"Do you think we could do it?" Shorty finally asked Frank. "Shut ourselves down, I mean? Would it be right?"

"I don't know, Shorty. There are a lot of guns in the world, and I've got a sick feeling most of them are like Burt, but like Ace said, it's a start. It's a start."

At that moment, headlight beams flashed across the living room wall, illuminating Burt's horrid trophy wall in all its shameful glory. The guns froze as the old pickup screeched to a halt just outside the front door.

The door suddenly crashed inward, and Burt Collier staggered in, in worse condition than when he had left. He belched and wiped his sweating forehead. Cursing loudly, Burt approached the gun cabinet with Mack, his .357, gripped tightly in his hands. The weapons inside the cabinet stood still, breathless as he opened the door. Still shouting obscenities into the air, Burt grabbed a handful of slugs and shoved one into each chamber of Mack's cylinder.

The guns moved quickly to the front of the cabinet, the tall rifles peering from the rack as Buck stood pouting in the corner. Even from a distance, Burt reeked of alcohol, but there was another undeniable odor present as well. The scent of gunpowder.

"Mack, your barrel is steaming hot," Shorty said, his voice panicked. "What happened?"

"Please tell us that Burt took you out to the city dump to shoot at rats. Please tell us that's all it is."

Before Mack could respond, he was shoved into Burt's grimy trousers. Mack's muffled voice hummed, but another sound began to rise in the distance. Frank strained to listen, until the sudden recognition of the intensifying noise sent a wave of cold shivers dancing down his barrel.

Sirens.

Buck, sensing the tension in the air, stood straight and moved slowly over to the others, the sinister grin returning to his dark barrel.

Burt took a final gulp of whiskey and smashed the empty bottle against the trophy wall. The impact knocked loose the prize whitetail, and the mount bounced on the floor once before rolling to a stop, staring up at the cabinet. Burt turned back to the storage rack, reassuringly feeling the handle of the .357 jutting from his pants.

The wail of the siren was deafening now. The sound of screeching tires and popping gravel was just outside of the trailer. Suddenly, the sirens ceased, and the swirl of red and blue lights danced across the wall, reflecting in the eyes of Burt's trophies, momentarily returning a hint of life to the dead orbs.

The guns backed away from Burt, huddling together for comfort against the uncertainty of the situation. Their drunken owner stood before them for what seemed like hours, teetering back and forth until it seemed he would collapse to the floor. Shorty was crying, and Ace pushed him deeper into the cabinet. Frank closed his eyes and turned away.

"Me, me, me, me," Buck whispered excitedly, moving closer to the cabinet's open doors.

Car doors slammed and dozens of feet shuffled across the gravel parking lot. Excited voices drifted through the trailer's thin walls, and the amplified din of a bullhorn rattled the windows. Burt lingered indecisively in front of the cabinet, finally reaching for the rack, in Buck's direction. The powerful shotgun shouted joyously, but then Burt's hand suddenly stopped.

"Me, me, me," Buck pleaded.

Burt mumbled something about "distance" and "accuracy," and his hand moved away from the shotgun.

"No!" Buck shouted. "Take me! Take me!"

Burt's hot and sweaty hand curled around the base of his stock. The feeling was sickening. Frank sensed himself being lifted from the cabinet, and Burt reached for the cartridges as he swung Frank around.

Ace reached for Frank, but there was nothing the smaller gun could do. Frank stared back frightfully at his comrades, the cabinet growing smaller and smaller as Burt walked away from his arsenal. Out of the corner of his eye, Frank noticed Mack squirming around just below Burt's belt line.

One by one, the cold, unforgiving cartridges were slammed into Frank's sleek, accommodating magazine, until he was gorged. Burt moved over to the living room window. The pretty red and blue lights, many of them, flashed brightly against the panes. Burt's clammy fingers pulled back on the bolt, and the sleek projectile slid smoothly into Frank's chamber. Burt coughed, spit on the worn carpet, and leveled the 30/06 deer rifle. Frank closed his eyes as he was swung upward. The curtains tickled the tip of his barrel.

Mack's voice drifted up from below Frank. It was muffled and weak, but the message was clear. "The *real* killing started tonight."

Frank's scope peered out into the crowded, brightly lit driveway, surveying its domain, swaying from side to side like a cobra ready to strike. Frank slowly opened his eyes and braced himself. Forget the sparrows in the back yard. Forget the rats at the dump. Forget the mule deer from El Paso. Forget the whitetail from Bossier County.

The real killing started tonight.

The crosshairs of the scope wavered unsteadily a moment before stabilizing and centering on the blue suit, just to the left of the shiny, silver badge.

Frank prayed that he would miss, but he knew that he wouldn't.

Burt was too good of a shot.

And Frank was just too damned fine a piece of equipment.

Monkeyspeak

Dr. Deacon Madison peered into the enclosed case that held the ancient, yellowed pieces of parchment, pressing his nose against the glass like a kid at a toy store window during the Christmas blitz. The manuscript held some kind of fascination for him, even at first glance. He supposed that it could be the feeling of antiquity that often overwhelmed him when viewing an artifact for the first time, but at two-hundred forty years, the manuscript was a virtual babe, archaeologically. He had seen older things. It was more than likely the fact that Dr. Alex Black, his friend and colleague from the university, had been chasing clues revealed by the manuscript when he ventured into the South American jungles and seemingly blinked out of existence.

"Can we open the case?" Dr. Madison asked, turning to face the curator of the library.

"I'll open the case, but try to touch it as little as possible," the man answered. "It's extremely fragile."

The pleasant scent of old books lingered in the library air, but the pungent odor of the decaying parchment wafting to Dr. Madison's nostrils quickly obliterated other smells. Slowly, carefully, Deacon reached for the sheets. Without removing the manuscript from its protective case, he began turning the pages, one by one. The sheets were badly yellowed, extremely brittle, and had been gnawed in many places by the gnawing of the *copim* insect. Deacon turned the pages back to their original position. Scrawled in a cryptic pattern in Portuguese across the top of the first page was the following passage: *Relaçao historica de huma occulta, e grande povoaçoe antiguissima sem moradores, que se descubrio no anno de 1753.*

He didn't decipher the entire paragraph at once, but he knew *povoaçoe* was the Portuguese word for "city." That wasn't what worried him.

"*Sem moradores,*" he whispered.

Sem moradores meant "without inhabitants." That's what frightened him. The last fax the university had received from Dr. Black had clearly stated the city *was* inhabited. By whom, Dr. Madison could only guess.

Suddenly there was a shrill, electronic beep to his right. Mark Fenner, one of his students from Quanaghua University in west Texas, stood clutching a small black object in his hand. It looked like a calculator.

"Damn," Mark whispered. "Wait. Let me try it again."

The little box chirped rapidly several times in succession, and Mark held it up to Dr. Madison, beaming proudly. "There," he said. "Without inhabitants. That's what it says. They found an uninhabited city."

"I know what it says, Mark. I can read Portuguese fairly well."

"Oh." Looking dejected, Mark quietly returned the electronic translator to his pocket.

Deacon turned back to the curator. "This was penned in 1753?"

"If you go by the date, and I assume we must, yes."

"How long ago was it that Dr. Black inspected this piece?"

Mr. Ruez put a hand to his chin and rubbed. "I would say a month ago. He spent a week here translating the manuscript, as we cannot allow it to leave the library. You understand?"

"Yes, of course," Dr. Madison said. "Mr. Ruez, you've been most cooperative, and I appreciate it. One other thing before we leave. This book mentioned in the manuscript, the one the expedition found. Has it ever been seen?"

"Only by that one group," Mr. Ruez said. "As you have probably heard, the expedition was not conducted in the name of science. The men were merely searching for lost silver mines. There was apparently a bout of some sort between the members of the expedition and the author left the site ahead of the rest of the group. We probably would not have this testimony had he not."

"Why is that?" Dr. Madison asked, only half-interested.

"The rest of the men were never heard from again."

Deacon's eyes snapped back to the curator. "Hmm," he mused. "Interesting." More than interesting. The similarities were downright uncanny.

Dr. Madison looked down from the soaring helicopter at the sprawling canopy of green below him. As far as the eye could see, the treetops stretched relentlessly onward. He had taken similar trips by air across the Amazonian jungles before, but never while faced with the prospect of finding a missing comrade. The area had never seemed so vast before. Dr. Madison sighed, took another long look at the ceaseless landscape. *Dr. Black could be anywhere down there.*

The university had not heard from Dr. Alex Black in two weeks. A month earlier, Dr. Black had left the school for the depths of the Brazilian jungles, in search of the dead city of Tiahuanacu. At his insistence, he had gone alone, save for the local guides who had helped him find the city. He had reported twice via a satellite-link fax machine transmission and hadn't been heard from since. The university feared the worst.

Deacon feared more than that.

A formerly uninhabited city had suddenly grown a population.

Something had happened to Alex, that much was certain. Deacon was pretty sure that it involved natives. As far as anyone knew, Dr. Alex Black was the first civilized man to set foot in Tiahuanacu in many years. If an uncivilized tribe of aborigines claimed the areas as theirs, there could've been trouble.

Deacon had had many dealings with local tribes along the Great Amazon during previous archaeological expeditions. The Parrarys, the Abederys, and the Kataushys had all proved harmless. Deacon's knowledge and familiarity with some of the older tribes, and his ability to speak some of the more ancient tribal languages, was the reason the university had wanted Dr. Madison to join the search for Alex Black.

"What is it exactly that Black was doing out here?" Dr. Wesley Keylon, expert on American pyramids and consultant to the university asked. "Still trying to prove that civilization began in South America?"

Deacon smiled. He was well aware Alex and Keylon disputed one another's beliefs. "I'm not sure," he said. "The obvious answer would be that he's researching the pyramids, but I think there's more to it. The buildings themselves have been studied before, as you know. There's nothing more to learn from them, I think. I assume he thought he was on to something he learned from the manuscript."

"Such as this mysterious book?"

"Possibly," Deacon replied.

"Oh, c'mon, Dr. Madison. You know as well as I that book doesn't exist, if it ever *did* exist."

"You don't know that, Dr. Keylon. You've never even visited this site—"

"Because there's nothing there to visit," Keylon interrupted. "I'm only coming along to help find the fool. These pyramids were a dead subject even in the thirties. Why try to revive them now?"

"The discovery of the manuscript," Deacon said, turning to face Keylon, "and the possible existence of this book seems to me incentive enough to reexamine the subject. If this book is found, it could shed some light on the builders of the pyramids, or even the gods they were built to honor."

"The Nahui-Quiahuitl?" Keylon asked. "Another dead subject. There's never been any solid evidence of that cult actually existing."

"No, but the idea is incredibly ancient, and the local tribes still mention the Nahui-Quiahuitl to this day, so it had to have existed. That's why Alex wanted to locate the book. In my opinion anyway."

Dr. Keylon only shrugged at Deacon's comment. The two men turned their attention to the windows. The helicopter was descending.

◆

The first sight of the pyramids, faint and obscure through the low-hanging clouds that drifted through the mountains, nearly took Deacon's breath away. He'd seen many American pyramids, but never in this setting. The structures were situated on an immense high plateau seemingly carved into the surface of the mountain range. Only when the helicopters dropped past the cloud cover could Deacon fully appreciate the accomplishment of the pyramids' enigmatic builders. The entire flat expanse of land, centered high in the cordillera, was incredible to behold.

It was difficult to estimate how close to the ground the chopper was. Judging by the cloud of dust being kicked up by the rotors, he assumed they were about to touch down. Through the dust, Dr. Madison could barely make out the shape of a giant stone carving next to one of the smaller pyramids. The sight got Deacon's archeological blood to flowing. He started to turn to the pilot when a flash of movement caught his eye. It had appeared briefly at the top of the carving before the dust had swallowed it up. Deacon squinted in the direction of the statue, but could see nothing. The helicopter touched the ground, and the thought left Dr. Madison

◈

It took some time for the air to clear after the land of the three helicopters. The guides and a few helpful students busied themselves unloading the cargo chopper. Drs. Madison and Keylon began investigating the site.

The plateau was divided into several layers, with crude stone steps carved into the mountain leading to each new rise. Tall, thick trees with huge leaves surrounded the courtyard of the pyramids. The atmosphere was cool and damp. Low-hanging clouds darkened the site. A cobbled road extended approximately twenty feet ahead where it stopped at the foot of another staircase. Beyond that, the first great pyramid rose to the heavens. Smaller pyramids, along with various square structures, all covered with thin patches of green moss and apparently damp, sat at diverse positions to either side of the great pyramid. Stone statues lined the sides of the stairs and the path leading to the buildings. Some of the statues were life-sized replicas of humanoid figures. Others were huge human faces, like the Moai on Easter Island.

"My God," Deacon whispered. "I've never seen anything like it."

"The size of this entire plateau is incredible," Mark said.

"Let's go on," Deacon suggested, motioning to the native guides.

"Feel how still everything is up here," Mark said. "It's eerie how quiet it is."

"Miles away from civilization, young man," Dr. Keylon said. "And, perhaps, standing where it all began."

Dr. Madison didn't know if Keylon's comment was meant to ridicule Dr. Black's beliefs, or if his companion, stricken with the awe of the site, had decided to believe their missing comrade.

A swift movement caught his attention, a flash of light that barely entered his consciousness. "What was that?"

"I didn't see anything."

"Something moved," Deacon said. "Something quick. I barely noticed it."

"I didn't—"

They all saw it that time. It was incredibly swift, a blur, and it was gone.

"Natives?" Keylon asked.

"I don't like this," Mark said nervously.

"Take it easy, Mark. It's probably nothing."

A flash of movement appeared to the right before disappearing. The sound of a stone bouncing on solid rock pulled their attention in the other direction. A movement to the right, a rustling of leaves, an unexplained noise behind them. The group instinctively moved closer together in a defensive circle.

Then, there was the first one. It scurried up the base of a statue, peeked around it, then settled on the top of the stone head. Another appeared on the roof of one of the smaller buildings, and another crawled from behind the ear of one of the facial reliefs.

"Jesus Christ," Deacon whispered. "Monkeys."

The monkeys, hundreds of them, began appearing from all directions, and then they froze. They rested on the tops of statues, along the roofs of the pyramids, on the steps of the stairs. Movement ceased completely. The air grew silent.

"This is what Alex must've meant when he said this place was inhabited," Dr. Madison said. "He was talking about the monkeys."

"Goddamn, this is spooky," Mark said. "Look at them, just sitting there, watching us, not making a sound."

The men, still gathered in their protective circle, stared at the unmoving sentinels. The monkeys were small, only about two feet high, and tailless. They were covered in smooth, snow-white fur, and their faces were bright red. The innocent, inquisitive look normally seen on a monkey's face was absent and, instead, the monkeys seemed serious, studious.

"Anteel," Dr. Madison whispered to his guide. "What are these? What kind of monkeys?"

"*Nao sei*," the guide answered. "I have not seen these ever."

"Well, they can't be dangerous," Dr. Madison said, "as small as they are."

Brave words, but no one moved forward to investigate.

"Maybe they're not dangerous, but this is *goddamned weird*," Dr. Keylon said. "A huge plateau in the middle of this mountain, this ghost town, monkeys out of thin air."

Anteel began to move slowly forward, toward the large pyramid in the center. The monkeys' heads moved slowly, in unison, following Anteel's every move. They did not move, or make a sound otherwise.

"Incredible," Madison mumbled.

Convinced that the monkeys were passive, the group moved cautiously up the remaining stairs. The monkeys ahead stood their ground, but looking back, Dr. Madison noticed that the ones they had passed were leaping up and moving swiftly along the ground on all fours, establishing new perches ahead of the intruders. *The monkeys were following them.*

The faint whistle of the wind was picking up again, a slow, steady, almost mesmerizing drone, an unaltered melody. Deacon found himself thinking of Dr. Black, of his disappearance.

The area around him grew darker from the increasing cloud cover. A gentle breeze began to blow in, the cool wind lapping at his face. The elements combined to produce a very soothing effect.

"Listen to that wind," one of the students said. "It's almost like music, like a pipe organ."

"I've never heard anything like this," Dr. Keylon marveled. "Just listen to that wind whipping through the branches. Must have something to do with the size of those leaves."

"It's not the wind," Deacon suddenly realized. "Look."

He pointed to one of the monkeys squatting atop the nearest statue. Its mouth was open, its teeth bared, almost as if the monkey was grinning. Dr. Madison looked behind him at another monkey, then turned to the closest building to study another group. All the monkeys' faces were fixed in identical expressions.

"I don't believe this," Keylon said. "It's the monkeys."

The sounds were indeed coming from the monkeys. They were humming in unison, harmonizing in a steady, unwavering tone. The tone continued at the same level, never changing, until the group's ears seemed to buzz.

"God," Dr. Keylon said, putting his hands to his ears, "that's unnerving."

"It's like the Sirens," a student said. "It's almost hypnotic. It's beautiful."

"What are they doing, Anteel?" Dr. Madison asked.

"I do not know," the guide said. "Perhaps it is a song."

"*Hey, hey we're the Monkees*," one of the students quipped.

The joke was obvious, but the remark gave them an opportunity to release a bit of nervous laughter.

"Let's just try to ignore it," Dr. Madison said.

As they neared the great pyramid, the pitch of the singing monkeys seemed to increase. Their song did not cease, and they never took their eyes off the intruders.

During the next few days, the howling of the monkeys was virtually ceaseless, pausing only for short spells. Drs. Madison and Keylon explored many of the pyramids and buildings, but could find no trace of Dr. Black, nor his equipment. It was as if he had never been there.

Deacon grew more worried by the hour. The entire plateau seemed an aboriginal ghost town, eerily quiet except for the singing monkeys. Deacon could not help but wonder if the monkeys had inhabited there all along. Perhaps earlier explorers had simply ignored them as part of the mountains' natural flora and fauna. Alex hadn't mentioned them specifically himself.

Deacon sighed and cupped his hands around his lighter, shielding it from the breeze, and lit his pipe. He snapped the cover on the lighter and walked toward the base of the steps.

He was aware of the stares of hundreds of monkeys. From some of the students busy taking notes on one of the statues along the smaller pyramids, Deacon caught the words *statue*, *pyramid*, *stone*, *black*. Something about the black clouds.

After two days, Deacon had grown accustomed to the buzzing of the monkeys to the point that it had become mere background noise. Now and then, there was a different sound from the monkeys. A quick high-pitched chirp, perhaps a warning, or alarm. The words from the students kept drifting into Deacon's field of perception, but he wasn't really listening to them. There was a group of students, mixed with some of the natives, behind him to his left. He could hear them better, and there was some Portuguese mixed in with the English.

The monkeys began chirping loudly again.

Black. Black.

Why were the students worried about the weather? The clouds didn't look terribly ominous.

Chirp. Chirp. Chirp.

The monkey was close to him now, chirping frantically.
Black. Black. Black.
What were the students talking about? Was it Portuguese or English?
Black. Black.
Dr. Madison looked over his right shoulder at the group of students, but that side of the plateau was deserted.

Except for monkeys.
Chirp. Chirp. Chirp.
The monkey was sitting on the bridge of the nose of one of the full facial depictions. Its beady, black eyes appeared sunken against the fierce red of its face, and they fixed motionless on Dr. Madison's eyes. The monkey's fur was shocking white, making the others' hair seem the color of old parchment.

I wasn't hearing English, or Portuguese, Deacon thought. *But I was hearing the word "black."*

Dr. Madison looked back to where he had seen the first group of students. They had moved on. He was alone now. Deacon looked back at the monkey.

Its eyes burned into his.
Chirp. Chirp. Black. Black.
The pipe fell from Deacon's lips. It struck his foot, then bounced down the stairs. The pipe stopped a few steps down, and Deacon's eyes focused on it.
Black. Black.
Deacon recognized the word. It was from the language of the Papayul, an Amazonian tribe from the late 1600s. He had been hearing the word "black."
Black. Black.
The monkey wasn't chirping. The monkey wasn't humming, and the monkey wasn't buzzing.

The monkey was speaking.

The voice was high-pitched, whiny, and distorted, but the Papayul Indian word for "black" was definitely emanating from the monkey's mouth.

Black. Black.

Dr. Madison was so accustomed to the language of the Papayul, he had subconsciously translated the word to English without even realizing the word's origin. Or its speaker.

Dr. Madison sat, glued to his spot, too terrified and amazed to move. He stared at the monkey. It did not move. The monkey chattered again, a long string of high screeches. Most of it was indiscernible and, indeed sounded like normal monkey squealing, until Deacon caught another word.

The word was "doctor," but it hadn't been from the Papayul language. The word's origin was from an earlier Amazonian tribe.

The monkey had used the words "doctor" and "black," from two greatly differing languages that had originated hundreds of years apart.

Doctor. Black.

Deacon wiped sweat from his brow. Although the dense clouds were still rolling through the mountain range, and the cool breeze still blew through his hair, he was suddenly very hot and uncomfortable.

◆

"I don't know, Deacon," Dr. Keylon said. "It still just sounds like a monkey chattering to me."

Dr. Keylon and Dr. Madison, along with some of their students, had gathered around the monkey. Deacon had shouted for the others to join him. He didn't want to take his eyes off the monkey for fear of losing it in the crowd.

"You're not familiar with these ancient languages like I am. You're not trained to hear it. It's almost unintelligible and it's ragged, but it's there."

"Okay, let's assume this monkey is speaking to you. How do you suppose it learned these languages, this speech from tribes that died out two hundred years ago?"

"I don't know," Deacon admitted. "Perhaps they've picked up bits of speech through the years. Maybe it's due to evolution."

"Look, Deacon, I'm just as open-minded about evolution as the next guy, and I'm no zoologist, but you know as well as I do that monkeys don't have the vocal capacity for speech."

"I'm not saying that this animal is carrying on a normal conversation with me, Wesley," Deacon argued. "I'm just saying that it's forming words used by Indians that used to inhabit this general region."

"Granted, the languages are extremely primitive, but they're still human languages and not a natural form of animal communication. I've heard words from at least six different primitive tongues from this monkey in no particular order, as if the animal is babbling."

"Like a parrot," Mark added.

"Exactly," Deacon agreed. "It knows the words, but not how to string them together. It doesn't have the ability to place words of a single language together."

"But it's definitely using human words."

The monkey looked up at the group of men gathered in front of its statue. It did not seem frightened by the intruders.

"So, what do you think, Dr. Madison?" Mark asked.

Deacon looked at Mark and pointed to the electronic translator jutting from his jacket. "Mark, do you think you could set up a voice analyzer on a computer system?"

"What do you mean?" the young man asked.

"Okay, for example, say you hooked Anteel up to some kind of analyzer, have him speak Portuguese, and have the computer print out his responses in English."

"Yeah, that can be done with a voice-activated translator unit," Mark said. "That's basically how they made my translator."

"Okay, then, is there a way we can hook this monkey up to the computer, have the computer analyze the monkey's voice and, if any words match a human tongue, have the computer print them on the screen?"

"What are you getting at, Deacon?" Keylon asked. "You already claim to know what the monkey is saying, if anything."

"No, I'm not getting all of it," Deacon said.

"Well sir, you'd have to have these ancient languages you're talking about programmed into the computer, so that the system could search for the words."

"But if I worked up a program covering all the known words from these languages, it could be done?"

"It's feasible," the kid said.

"What are you talking about, Madison?" Keylon said, apparently growing annoyed.

"If we can do that, and I can convey some of the words to the monkey, maybe I can communicate with it."

"But you said it's just spouting random words, if that," Keylon argued.

"But what if it's not?" Deacon persisted. "What if it's trying to communicate with us?"

"Have you flipped?"

"All I'm saying is that the idea of this creature speaking a word, period, is cause enough for immediate research."

"For a zoologist maybe, not an archaeologist," Keylon argued. He stared into his colleague's unyielding eyes for a long moment. "And what about Black? We came here to find Dr. Black, not to do research. How is this going to help bring him back?"

"I don't know," Dr. Madison said. "But I know this. That monkey said the words 'doctor' and 'black.' As crazy as it sounds, I think it knows more about Alex's whereabouts than we do."

The monkey sat inside the wire cage atop Dr. Madison's desk, motionless but for the constant roving of its tiny, round eyes. The lights were low in the lab at Quanaghua University, and the monochrome green of the computer screen cast an eerie glow over the room's furnishings. A pair of thin black wires ran from the translator module to the small microphone connected to the cage just above the monkey's head. Another cord ran from the analyzer to the serial port of the computer. Dr. Madison sat in front of his desk, his fingers resting on the keyboard. He glanced anxiously at Mark.

"Everything's ready to go," he said, his voice cracking against his will. "Let's see what happens."

Dr. Keylon had found nothing significant in four days of searching and researching every structure and pyramid in the dead city of Tiahuanacu. There was nothing new to document and, of course, no trace of Dr. Alex Black. In fact, the only new discovery was the presence of the monkeys. Dr. Keylon began to wonder if Dr. Madison's avenue of research might be the only viable way to go.

Until he found the concealed stairway.

Perseverance, fate, or blind luck led to the unlikely discovery. Dr. Keylon had been admiring the symmetry of the flagstones that made up the floor of the largest pyramid. He thought one of the stones had been chipped on each side, but upon closer inspection found that these imperfections were stone stoppers concealing handholds in the flagstones. When he removed the stoppers and lifted the stone, it pivoted, revealing a debris-filled stairway which led down into darkness.

Dr. Keylon hastily reviewed his notes from previous studies of the pyramids. The staircase, like the monkeys, had never been mentioned.

◆

"Como è o sue nome?" Dr. Madison asked.

"Portuguese?" Mark asked. Deacon nodded.

The monkey did not respond.

"I'm not sure if I ever heard it use Portuguese or not," Dr. Madison explained. "I figured I would start with the easiest language."

"It doesn't seem to respond," Mark observed.

"Let's try this," Deacon said, and hit the F1 key. A list of language programs ran across the screen. "I'll have my question translated onto the screen."

"You're assuming it can read?" Mark asked.

Deacon shrugged. "Hell, I'm game for anything. If it can say it, maybe it can read it."

Dr. Madison leaned closer to his microphone. "Do you have a name?"

A soft, whirring sound issued from the computer, and the screen hesitated. The word "searching" appeared at the cursor, and the computer clicked again. The phrase appeared on the screen translated and written in the language of the Papayul Indian.

Deacon looked at the monkey. The monkey glanced from Dr. Madison to Mark, and then to the wires running to the microphone. Deacon shifted the screen so that the monkey could see it better.

"He's not responding," Mark said.

"Perhaps it only knows bits of each language. Maybe it doesn't know one entire language. Let's try this."

Dr. Madison took the keyboard and quickly typed the word "name" six times on the screen, utilizing each of the six languages he had heard the monkey use. He pointed to the words on the screen, then recited each word slowly and carefully.

Still, the monkey showed no sign of comprehension.

Again, Dr. Madison pointed to the words and repeated each one.

The monkey chirped once.

"Did it say something?" Mark asked, flushed with excitement.

"Yeah," Deacon said. "It said 'black' again, just like it was saying at the site."

◆

Dr. Keylon shone his flashlight down the length of the stairs. The stairwell was dark, musty-smelling, and large pieces of stone littered the steps, making footing hazardous. The light illuminated the steps for about twenty feet before the path faded into darkness. He took one step into the opening. The area was small, and he had to bend slightly to enter.

Excited by the thought of new discovery, Dr. Keylon forgot about the search for Dr. Black. With a nod to his students, he led the small group of explorers on their descent into the belly of the pyramid.

◆

Dr. Madison rubbed his weary eyes and stared at the monkey in the cage. The only word he could get it to say was the Papayul word for "black." The monitor continued to flash the word in English.

Perhaps he had been too zealous. It was possible this monkey could've evolved over the years the ability to pseudo-mouth a word it picked up hereor there. Hell, that was much more likely than for Deacon to carry on a conversation with the animal. The whole idea suddenly seemed very foolish.

The monkey chirped, and the computer went into action.

Searching...

Word Not Found

"Dammit," Mark said.

"I think I know what it said," Deacon said. "It sounded like Tiahuanacu. The city where we came from. It's home."

The monkey screeched again, and the screen began flashing words.

Searching...

Word Not Found

"Well, shit," Deacon muttered. "I don't understand. If it's saying words from one of these six languages, then the analyzer should read it. Unless...unless it's not one of these languages."

"Mark, can it print out the word on the screen in the language that the monkey is using, if it's even a language?"

"I think so," he said. "Let me see."

Mark reached for the keyboard and began tapping keys. The screen hesitated, then a series of characters appeared.

#*&%@nah*#^@ui-#*#%quia$@#*&*hui*@#tl

"What the hell is that?"

#*&%@nah*#^@ui-#*#%quia$@#*&*hui*@#tl

"The computer's trying to figure it out."

"It must be some kind of word that can't be translated to English," Mark surmised.

"Which means it could be just so much monkey gibberish."

THE POROSITY OF SOULS

※

The rank odor of soured earth, long denied the light of the sun, wafted to Dr. Keylon's nostrils as he, his students, and their guides made their way down into the subterranean depths of the pyramid. The powerful flashlight lit the stairwell more than adequately, but the walls were nondescript. No writing, no drawings, no characters. As with the rest of the city of Tiahuanacu, nothing to indicate that humans had ever made it their home.

※

The monkey released an extended series of what seemed like nervous chattering. The computer whirred to life, and the screen flickered with anticipation.

Searching...
Word Not Found
Depressant
Word Not Found
not necessary
Word Not Found
Followed
Word Not Found
willfully

The monkey sat still in the cage, its eyes unwavering from the stares of Dr. Madison and his assistant.

"'Word not found'?" Deacon grumbled. "This is not working out as I'd hoped."

"Wait a minute, Prof'," Mark said. "Read what's there. 'Depressant not necessary, followed willfully.' The...the tranquilizer," Mark stuttered. "It's talking about the tranquilizer dart we used during transport."

"Coincidence?" Dr. Madison asked.

"I don't think so. What else would it mean? And it's highly unlikely that those words, in that arrangement, are just coincidental."

Deacon suddenly found himself skeptical. The thought of his experiment beginning to work frightened him a little. "We had to subdue you for the transport," Deacon said, in answer to the screen's remark.

Searching...
Word Not Found
Caged
Word Not Found
beast

Dr. Keylon and Mark exchanged awed glances. "Like a caged beast."

"This is incredible," Mark said. "It's working, Doc. It's actually working."

The two men leaned forward in their chairs, anticipating a breakthrough in their experiment. "You have continued to repeat the word 'black.' Why?"

The monkey chirped.

Searching...
Word Not Found
Friend
Word Not Found
you

"Yes, he is a friend to me. He is missing. Do you know where he is?"

Searching...
us

"Us," Dr. Madison said, glancing at Mark. "Does he mean Dr. Black is with them, back in Brazil?"

THE POROSITY OF SOULS

Searching...
us
"Is he alive?"
Searching...
yes

"Listen," Scott said. "Do you hear it?"

The others cocked their heads and strained their ears. A low drone was emanating from somewhere around them, in the far distance. In the small confines of the stairs, it was difficult to determine the source of the noise.

"What the hell is that?" Keylon asked.

"I know what it is," said one of the guides. The others looked at him. "It's the monkeys."

"How did you learn the native tongues of these Amazonian tribes?" Dr. Madison asked.

Searching...
many years
Word Not Found
Lived...many words
Word Not Found
learned
"Can all of the monkeys speak?"
Searching...
yes
"How is it that monkeys developed the powers of speech? It is a physical impossibility."
Searching...

Word Not Found
for monkeys
Word Not Found
not for man
"What?" Mark asked.
Dr. Madison shook his head. "What do you mean by that?"
Searching...
wise man doctor
Word Not Found
man sees
Word Not Found
wants to see
Word Not Found
no understand
Word Not Found
can not see
"I'm not following this," Mark said.
Searching...
black searched
Word Not Found
truth found
"Black!" Mark shouted. "He said Black!"
Dr. Madison held up a hand to hush Mark. "Dr. Black found the truth? Truth to what?"
The monkey paused, then chirped.
Searching...
life
"Life?"
Searching...
eternal
"Life eternal," Dr. Madison whispered.
The monkey screeched.
Searching...
book

"Book," Mark said. "The book in the manuscript?"
Deacon nodded. "Dr. Black found a book?"
The monkey looked at the screen, said nothing, and nodded.
"What was in this book?"
Searching...
ancient secrets
"Of?"
The computer beeped, and the screen read:
#*&%@nah*#^@ui-#*#%quia$@#*&*hui*@#tl
"Now it's doing that again," Mark said, disgusted.
"What are those words? Do they mean something?"
Searching...
masters
"Masters?" Mark said.

Deacon nodded. "Of course! Eliminate that garbage, and it spells Nahui-Quiahuitl. The computer can't translate it because it's not one of our languages. But it's printing out anyway. That's strange."

Searching...
language masters
"Language of the masters," Deacon said. "Gods. Religion."
"Monkeys worshipping God? That doesn't make sense," Mark said.
Searching...
not God... The Four Rains

Mark looked at the doctor, his eyes demanding explanation, but Dr. Madison could only shrug.

The monkey screeched.
Searching...
Great Lords of Antiquity
"He's talking religion. How can a monkey have religion?"
Searching...
know religion
Word Not Found

more than you know...built pyramids
Word Not Found
masters
"Who built the city? What tribe?"
Searching...
us

◆

The light from the flashlight fanned out in the darkness before them, and Dr. Keylon and his group found themselves in a room. The odor of mildew and decay was nauseating. The group gathered around the doctor, and he shone the light into the room.

It was empty, except for the small altar in the center of the room.

◆

Searching...
  built temples
  Word Not Found
  same way
  Word Not Found
  learned languages
  "How?" Dr. Madison asked into the microphone.
Searching...
were there
"You were there?" he asked. "You and the rest of the monkeys were there? But that was over five hundred years ago."
Searching...
no monkeys...humans
"I don't understand."

Searching...
neither us
Word Not Found
said earlier
Word Not Found
man sees
Word Not Found
wants to see
Searching...
wanted more...learn more...book
"Book again," Deacon said.
Searching...
Read
Word Not Found
Four Rains
Word Not Found
destroyed all... You Bible...flood

"The world was destroyed by a flood in ancient times," Deacon said. He turned to Mark. "Every ancient religion has a retelling of the flood."

Searching...
high ground...not destroyed...punished
Searching...
we read

"You were punished for reading the book?"

Dr. Keylon didn't notice the compartment under the altar until he was standing directly in front of it. The high beam of the flashlight gleamed across the damp surface of the stone object. The smell of mildew was heavy in the air, but Dr. Keylon could detect another odor.

When he squatted and shone the light into the altar's hidden compartment, he noticed the ancient, dust-covered tome, and realized the odor was parchment.

Searching...
no...punished
Word Not Found
everything destroyed...survivors punished
"Everyone fortunate enough to survive the flood was punished. Your city is on high ground, so you survived," Deacon said. "How were you punished?"

The monkey landed on Dr. Keylon's back just as he reached for the book. Its savage shriek split the damp air, sounding like a screaming locomotive in the cramped underground quarters. His flashlight went sailing, producing a momentary strobe effect as it bounced on the hard, stone floor. Dr. Keylon screamed as the monkey's teeth ripped into the back of his neck.

"Somebody get it off of me!" he cried.

One of the guides had retrieved the flashlight. The powerful beam burned brightly in Dr. Keylon's face. The teeth still digging into his neck, were locked into his flesh like a rabid pit bull terrier. One of the monkey's arms flailed about in front of his eyes. The monkey had brown fur, unlike the others.

One of his students grabbed the monkey by its hind legs and pulled it loose. The crazed monkey immediately leapt at the student's throat, but the young man managed to swat it aside.

The native boy shone the light all around the room, trying frantically to relocate the animal. Another loud screech, and the monkey was on Dr. Keylon again. The doctor's left hand reached behind him, attempting to grab the monkey, while his right hand reached for his belt.

"Everyone stand back!" he shouted madly.

Dr. Keylon pulled the revolver smoothly from his trousers as his left hand clasped the back of the monkey's head. With one deft swoop, he removed the monkey, kicking and screaming, and dropped to the floor, pinning the animal to the stone blocks. He pointed the pistol at the monkey's head. The retort echoed maddeningly throughout the underground lair.

Searching...
  should that not be obvious

Dr. Madison stared through the wire cage at the monkey. Its mouth curled upward in a seeming grin, and its yellowed teeth gleamed green in the computer glow. Dr. Madison could not look away from the monkey's small black eyes. They bored into him, as if reading his thoughts. It was like looking into the eyes of a madman.

"Jesus, listen to the monkeys," Scott said as they exited the long, cramped staircase and stepped back into the main courtyard of the large pyramid. "They're going crazy."

The monkeys were outside the entrance to the pyramid. They were all situated at the entrance, standing on statues, hanging from the doors, looking in the open windows. The monkeys' unison buzzing grew in intensity, the loudest it had been yet.

"Do you think they know that you killed that monkey?"

"I don't know," Dr. Keylon said, clutching the ancient book in his sweaty hands. "I don't know."

Dr. Keylon moved past the large statue of the monkey in the courtyard, past their campground where the humming of the generator was silenced by the call of the monkeys, and stood before the fax machine.

◆

The sudden startling ring of the phone nearly caused Dr. Madison to fall from his chair. With an unsteady hand, he reached for the receiver and held it to his ears.

"Hello?" he said, his voice quivering.

"Deacon, it's Wesley."

"It's Dr. Keylon," Deacon said to Mark. "Wesley, anything happen?"

"Everything has happened. Enough to make me sing a different tune." His voice was weak and static-laden. "We've found proof that humans inhabited this city at last. From the looks of it though, it was a long, long time ago."

"What did you find?"

"The book. Evidently, the one mentioned in the manuscript. It's written in a language I can't make any sense of."

"A...book?" Deacon said. It was as if his voice was detached from the rest of his body.

"Yeah, strangest thing also. There was a monkey in this little room where we found it. All alone, like it was guarding it. It went crazy when we started to take the book. It bit me and one of my students. Hope the little bastard's not diseased."

"My God," Deacon whispered.

"You say something, Deacon?"

"Wes...what did you do with the monkey?"

There was a pause on the other end. "Jesus, will you get this monkey thing out of your—"

"What did you do with the monkey?!" Deacon shouted.

"I had to kill it, Deacon. It wouldn't stop attacking. It was like it was determined to stop us from taking the book. Listen, I'd better hang up now. We're going to pack up and head back to Rio." He paused again for a moment. "Damn, you should hear these monkeys now. They're really going crazy."

"Yeah, I can imagine."

"Oh, what was it about this monkey? You were saying?"

"Never mind," Deacon said, his voice sounding weaker than he wanted. "You wouldn't believe me anyway. I'm trying real damned hard not to believe it myself."

"Okay, if you say so," he answered. "Talk to you later, Deacon."

"Yeah," Dr. Madison said. The line clicked on the other end, and he listened to the pointless static for a few more moments. The sweat poured from his forehead, but he paid it no heed when it ran into his eyes, stinging them. He looked into the cage at the monkey.

Chirp. Chirp. Black. Black.

The screen blinked, flickering in the waning light. The word flashed on the screen.

And the monkey laughed, a stark emotion as old as the beginnings of civilization, a form of communication that needed no twentieth-century technology to be translated.

CHECK OUT THESE OTHER GREAT READS FROM ROWAN PROSE:

When he's not writing, Terry Campbell enjoys e-bike riding, exploring small towns, abandoned places, haunted buildings, and antique wandering. He was a finalist in the inaugural Longhorn Prize from Saddlebag Dispatches Magazine. He resides in Texas.

www.ingramcontent.com/pod-product-compliance
Lightning Source LLC
LaVergne TN
LVHW040137080526
838202LV00042B/2941